a DAUGHTER'S CRY

a DAUGHTER'S CRY

a search for purpose

DORIS CHRISTIAN

TATE PUBLISHING *& Enterprises*

Published by Tate Publishing & Enterprises, LLC
127 E. Trade Center Terrace | Mustang, Oklahoma 73064 USA
1.888.361.9473 | www.tatepublishing.com

Tate Publishing is committed to excellence in the publishing industry. The company reflects the philosophy established by the founders, based on Psalm 68:11,
"The Lord gave the word and great was the company of those who published it."

Book design copyright © 2008 by Tate Publishing, LLC. All rights reserved.
Cover design by Leah LeFlore
Interior design by Steven Jeffrey

Published in the United States of America

ISBN: 978-1-60462-438-0
1. Christian Fiction: Romance/Suspense
08.01.08

IN DEDICATION

To all of those who have been abused, used and
neglected by someone they love. No matter the
trial or heartache, we have a merciful God who will
comfort and sustain us. His love never fails.

CHAPTER ONE

A white cloud of steam hissed from beneath the train as the two women shared one last hug. "Thank you, Aunt Marie, for everything," Ellie said, fighting her tears. "If it weren't for you, this wouldn't be happening and I'd still be in Kansas." Ending the embrace, they looked at each other.

"No one deserves it more, my dear," Marie said, gently tucking a strand of her niece's hair beneath the red tam. "I wish you a happy new life. Be sure to write once you're settled, okay? And don't worry about your mother, I'll look after her."

When hearing that, Ellie felt a new wave of guilt. "I hate leaving Mother out there in the middle of nowhere. If only we could get her to move here with you, Auntie. Crippled or not, she sews beautifully, and I've no doubt she could earn a living with that," Ellie said, remembering the pretty dresses her mother had recently sewn for her.

"You can't live her life, Lizzie," Marie said, using her pet name. "You've suffered enough and now it's time *you* live yours. Remember, if things don't work out, you come back; you'll always have a home with me."

"Thank you, Aunt Marie, but I'll *make* it work...somehow," Ellie vowed. For Eleanor Elizabeth Cooper, named after both her grandmothers, life now promised to hold the adventures she always dreamed of.

As the porter helped with her two suitcases, Ellie climbed the steps and soon found a seat near the window. Only a scattering of other passengers were seen. From the platform, her aunt waved and smiled, yet, Ellie easily noticed eyes welling with tears.

As the train slowly pulled from the station, in La Junta, Colorado, Ellie choked back her own emotion and waved, then blew one final kiss.

When her aunt's face disappeared from view, Ellie suddenly felt alone. *I can't be afraid; I have a new life waiting for me. I'll miss Mother and Aunt Marie terribly, but I'll see them again*, the young woman assured herself.

Despite the unknown, Ellie felt happy to leave behind the flatlands of Kansas. Not only was it the place of her birth, but for eighteen years the unpainted old farmhouse, where she lived with her parents, had been her prison. Yet, unlike penitentiaries run by the state, she had received no time off for good behavior.

As she watched the train disappear, Marie wiped her tears and swallowed the lump in her throat. "Take care, dear Lizzie, and *do* be happy," she whispered, staring after the red caboose.

Slowly, she headed for her car as her mind filled with questions. *Did I do the right thing? Should I have talked Rose into letting her daughter go so far away?* Marie wondered, feeling responsible for whatever might happen to her niece. *She was helpless and abused so I had to rescue her. Rose isn't capable of standing up for herself…let alone her daughter. I had to give Lizzie a chance at life!* Marie thought adamantly.

Climbing in behind the wheel of her five-year-old Studebaker, she, too, had concerns for Ellie's mother, her own younger sister, Rose.

Stricken with polio at age thirteen, Rose was dependant on leg braces. At seventeen, she met Morton Cooper. Although he was a known alcoholic, Rose started dating him and soon fell victim to his charm. Later, despite everyone urging her not to, she accepted his marriage proposal. "There are worse things than being an old maid," Marie muttered out loud, putting her car in gear. *And you know it too, dear sister, after all the misery!*

Tears stung Marie's eyes as memories flooded her mind. She remembered how Rose nearly died giving birth to her only child, and then struggled to take care of her daughter without the slightest help from her husband. *Oh sister, if I hadn't had my own troubles going on, I could have helped you,* Marie thought, remembering the tragic fall her beloved husband had suffered on his job. *Life isn't fair sometimes, but at least we have our dear, sweet Lizzie.*

As she headed for her home on Cimarron Avenue, Marie passed by the park where spring flowers bloomed in abundance. The early morning sun filtered through the trees, casting shadows across the road as she drove.

Just yesterday, Lizzie and I walked through the park and had such a nice talk as we strolled, the woman thought, letting out a deep sigh. *It's been wonderful having her here these past few months; I'm going to miss her terribly,* Marie thought, turning down her street.

When she had reached her driveway, she noticed a small dog lying on her front lawn. Light tan in color, the medium sized animal lifted its head and looked at her. "Who are *you,* little fella?" Marie said, glancing out her window as she eased her car past him. Making no attempt to move, the canine only looked up at her.

"Hello, little guy…where do you live?" Marie asked softly, after she had parked and exited her car. Not wanting to scare the poor thing, she slowly approached. After a few wags of its tail, the animal stretched out on the grass.

"Oh, you're hurt," Marie moaned, seeing blood on its front leg. After a quick assessment and seeing a cut, she lifted the animal off the ground and took him inside. When she brought water, the dog lapped the bowl dry and showed his appreciation by licking Marie's hand. "What a sweet boy you are; I think we'd get along just fine. Would you care to stick around?" she rambled on as she cleaned and wrapped the dog's injury with a sterile white bandage.

Having worked at the Humane Society some years earlier, Marie was well aware that people abandon or drop off dogs and cats in nice neighborhoods, thinking their pets would find a good home. Since the dog wore no license or collar, it seemed likely this terrier mix had been such a victim.

While meeting the dog's needs, Marie realized she no longer felt sad at her niece's departure. "You've come to console my heart, haven't you," she said as she gently petted the animal's head. "You need a name, but what?"

It was obvious, Marie Fuller, a forty-year old widow, had found someone else who needed her love and attention.

_____

The year was nineteen sixty and with Alaska gaining statehood two years earlier, the men of the 'new frontier' sought eligible women to marry. Most would place full page ads in magazines, coaxing young women to the sparsely populated state. With promises of love and adventure, it seemed to be the answer for many, including Ellie Cooper.

From her seat near the window, Ellie sat mesmerized. With a sense of freedom and adventure welling up from inside, her eyes hungrily scanned the view, devouring each new sight. Spring flowers of yellow and gold dotted the hillsides, and it seemed as though the prairie had no end as it stretched on as far as she could see. In the fields cattle grazed on tender new grass that glistened with morning dew.

Soon, lulled by the steady sway and sounds of the train, Ellie's mind was on the future. *What kind of man are you, Mr. Rudy Davis? Will you feel disappointed when you see me? Will you call me plain and ugly like the boys at school?* Sighing, Ellie could only wonder what fate awaited her.

Like so many times in the past two months, she again opened the magazine to Rudy's picture. There, from the page, he smiled at her. With dark hair and eyes, the clean shaven man appeared kind and loving, just as the article boasted. Despite the noticeable scars on his face, Rudy was nice looking and certainly, if his words were true, would meet the expectation of any young woman.

After closing the magazine, Ellie retrieved the letter of introduction he had written her weeks before. As she unfolded the white piece of paper, she remembered the excitement she felt at receiving an answer to her enquiry.

Dear Miss Cooper,

I am pleased to hear of your interest in coming to Alaska. I am a hard worker and have my own cabin, suitable for two. It has a good stove and a comfortable bed. I will be happy to buy whatever else you need.

Please send me a picture and tell me your qualifications for becoming my wife. I expect good meals and clean clothes. When I receive your let-

ter, I will send money for your traveling expenses.
Thank you.

Sincerely,

Rudy Davis.

Again, Ellie found her excitement hard to contain. Due to her lack of education and no money to pursue training, she felt this was her chance for a new life. With each passing mile she felt less shackled to her dismal past.

From the train, Ellie saw farming communities; cantaloupe and watermelon farms where melons, fresh and tasty, would later grow in abundance. Next, for the first time, she saw mountains looming in the distance. With snow-capped peaks, their majestic beauty brought a gasp of surprise. "Oh! They're even more beautiful than what the magazine showed," she muttered in awe.

A few hours later, the train slowed and black smoke boiled from the exhaust port as the diesel engines worked hard to pull the steep grade. As they inched their way upward, Ellie became fascinated with the fast moving streams as they tumbled along their banks. Now turbulent from the melting mountain snow, the white water reminded Ellie of frothy milk. For a moment she thought about the farm, and all the chores that had been her responsibility.

I won't be milking cows or butchering chickens, she vowed, remembering the worst jobs of all.

"Good day, miss, isn't it a lovely time of year?" a man asked, surprising Ellie. Looking up, she

noticed a well-dressed man wearing a strange looking hat that he quickly removed and now held in
his hand.

"Yes, it certainly is. I *love* springtime," she replied,
returning his smile.

"I noticed you sitting here. Are you traveling
alone?" he then asked.

"Yes, but I'm enjoying it very much. It's all so
beautiful!"

"Indeed it is. Would you mind if I sat for a
while?" the man asked, nodding at the empty seat
facing Ellie. "I find these trips quite long and bor-
ing without someone to talk to," he added.

When hearing the man's comments, Ellie decided
it *would* be nice to share conversation with an obvious traveler. "Yes, of course, you may sit here."

As the man seated himself, Ellie noticed a sweet,
somewhat spicy smell. Although she was eighteen
years old, she'd had little opportunity to be around
well-dressed males with polite manners. Yet, she
was aware that such gentlemen did wear cologne.

"Are *you* traveling alone?" she asked curiously.

"Unfortunately I travel alone most of the time,"
he answered. "By the way, my name is Craig
McGuire. And you are…?"

"Eleanor Cooper," she replied, offering her
hand.

"Well, Miss Cooper, it's very nice to make your
acquaintance," he said, smiling as he gently took
her hand. "May I ask your destination?"

"Alaska, where I'm getting married," Ellie
boasted, feeling quite pleased to tell this stranger

her happy news. Seemingly stunned, the man said nothing as he looked back at her.

"*Married...* well, my congratulations, Miss Cooper. I must admit I'm surprised your future husband is letting you travel such a distance without him," the man remarked, frowning.

"He's meeting me there, but I'll be just fine," Ellie replied confidently. Soon, the two were engaged in conversation regarding the changing countryside outside their window. Then, as the man talked about his job for the government regarding oil exploration, Ellie sat in awe as she listened.

It seemed no time at all until the conductor was announcing dinner being served in the dining car. "Would you allow me the pleasure of escorting you to dinner, Miss Cooper?" the man asked sometime later. "Then I promise I'll let you get back to your solitude."

"Thank you, but no, Mr. McGuire. My aunt, Marie, packed a lunch for me and I wouldn't want it to be wasted," Ellie told the man.

"I quite understand, but perhaps I can persuade you to accept my offer tomorrow, before I reach my destination," he replied. "Until then, I bid you goodnight." With that, Craig McGuire nodded and walked away.

Despite the man's kind and friendly manner, Ellie had to wonder why such a handsome stranger would spend time with her. *I'm plain looking and uneducated; certainly nothing like he's use to,* she thought, reaching for the bag containing her sandwiches.

By the time Ellie had finished her sandwiches and drank the thermos full of hot tea, the sun was setting. Then, from one of her bags, she removed the quilt Aunt Marie had made for her. Already the air felt cool and she looked forward to cuddling beneath its soft flannel.

The train's occupants had dwindled even further. At each stop some had gotten off, but few had embarked, leaving most of the seats vacant.

Deciding to find the ladies room before she settled in for the night, Ellie retrieved a few items she needed and left her seat. Finally, after getting directions from the porter, she found the lavatory two cars away.

When she'd finished brushing her teeth and using the toilet, Ellie headed back. Dim lights hung from the wall of the train, and as twilight lingered, she hurried toward her own coach.

By now, most passengers were reclined in their seats with their eyes closed, or softly conversing with their neighbor. At the end of each car, a door opened onto a small platform where nothing stood between that person and certain death, except a small accordion-type gate stretched across the steps.

The cold wind blasted Ellie each time she opened the door, and the sound of the train moving over the rails was louder than expected. Just as she opened the last door before entering her own car, she was surprised to see a man standing on the platform. With his back to her, he seemed unaware that she needed to get by.

"Excuse me, please," Ellie said, touching the man's shoulder. In the next instant, the man turned and grabbed her, pinning her against the door. With brute force he held her as he started to kiss her. Moving her head from side to side to avoid contact, Ellie was suddenly in the Kansas farmhouse where she'd grown up, fighting similar advances.

Now, after freeing herself of those vile attacks, Ellie refused to let anyone degrade her again in such a manner. With every ounce of strength she fought to get free. No longer a helpless child, she was now a determined woman filled with rage against such violations.

Again, the smell of a barnyard filled her senses. Was it real or was it her mind playing tricks? She smelled the same rancid nicotine breath as he pressed his face next to hers. *No! Not again!* Ellie vowed.

When unable to free her arms, she suddenly remembered what Aunt Marie had told her. *The knees and elbows are powerful weapons.* With those words echoing through her mind, Ellie drove her knee into the man's crotch. With a moan he let go of her as he crouched in pain. With her hands shaking she reached for the door.

"No you don't!" he growled, lunging for her. Suddenly, all the pent up rage Ellie felt exploded inside her, causing her to land a mighty kick square in her assailant's chest. In shock, she could only watch as the man fell back against the flimsy gate which gave way under his weight.

In the dim light she saw the look of fear in his eyes. It appeared to be slow motion as the man's arms flailed to reach for something to stop the inevitable, but found nothing. He could only scream in horror as he tumbled backwards, disappearing in the dark.

Ellie couldn't move. Her feet seemed welded in place as she stared at the black opening. Somehow she expected to wake from this sudden nightmare. *He's dead; you killed him! You killed a man and you don't even know his name,* her thoughts wailed as she suddenly felt sick.

Although in shock, Ellie somehow managed to open the door to her car and step through it. As it banged shut behind her, she found the nearest seat and sat down. *What should I do? Who do I tell? Will they believe me?*

It was several minutes before Ellie trusted her legs to hold her. Finally, she left the seat and headed toward the other end of the car. By the time she reached her place, her body shook uncontrollably. With great effort she unfolded the quilt and covered herself. Pulling it over her head, Ellie curled up on the seat trying to escape reality. With memories bombarding her mind, she wondered if she'd ever be free of abuse.

CHAPTER TWO

For most of the night Ellie huddled on her seat. No longer did the sway and sound of the train bring a feeling of freedom, instead, it was a reminder of yet another attack on her innocence. When she closed her eyes, the stranger's face would appear. Over and over her mind echoed his scream.

What am I going to do? Keep quiet and pretend nothing happened? Should I tell the truth and take my chances? Although she weighed each possibility, Ellie found no answer. *If only Aunt Marie was here, she'd know what to do!*

Weeks earlier, due to her excitement, she had memorized her itinerary. But now, she fought hard just to remember the arrival time in California. *Another whole day!* Ellie moaned, when finally realizing her schedule. *At least I can change trains when I get there. Now, I just have to figure out how to get through the next eighteen hours.*

Although the tinge of pink announced the sunrise, Ellie's usual excitement at seeing such splendor had vanished. Instead, she knew daylight would soon follow and, if the man's body was discovered somewhere along the tracks, an investigation would ensue.

She imagined men interrogating her like Joe Friday did on *Dragnet*, her aunt's favorite television show. Although the program no longer aired, Ellie had vivid memories of the lawbreakers being questioned.

I have to tell someone, she decided, letting out a deep sigh. As the sun peeked over the horizon and bathed the landscape in its morning glow, the weary traveler retrieved a comb from her purse. Slowly, Ellie began removing the tangles from her hair.

Long and thick, her brown mane hung straight, framing her oval face. No matter how much coaxing she had received from her aunt, Ellie refused to cut her hair. Somehow, hiding beneath its bulk made her feel inconspicuous. For that same reason she had chosen over-sized frames for her new glasses.

Because of her hard work on the farm, Ellie was strong. At five-feet-nine, she often worried she would grow to her dad's height of six-one. Well proportioned, she carried no excess weight, and beneath her loose-fitting clothes, there was a shapely young woman.

The sun was well up by the time Ellie noticed the

conductor heading her way. Her insides quivered and her hands felt clammy. As the man approached, his eyes rested on her, causing Ellie to wonder if he already knew.

"Good morning, miss. Did you get any sleep?" he asked, stopping beside her. Taking a deep breath, Ellie prepared herself for the inevitable.

"No, sir...I didn't," she told him. "I had a *horrible* night. Do you mind sitting here while I tell you what happened?"

Glancing at his watch, the kind-looking man let out a deep sigh before answering. "I'm afraid not, miss. I have my morning routine to finish before my shift ends. I *am* sorry you had a bad night, perhaps tonight will be better."

"Of course...thank you," Ellie replied, wondering what to do next. Before she could say anything further, the man walked away. *So much for that idea; now what?*

Needing to use the restroom, Ellie prepared to leave her seat. Suddenly, she realized the case holding her toothbrush was missing. *I must have dropped it last night. I know I had it in my hand,* she thought, deciding it had to be on the platform.

After folding the quilt, Ellie left her seat and headed down the aisle. With some passengers still snuggled under blankets, and others busy with their luggage, they paid only the slightest attention to Ellie as she passed by. *What would they think if they knew what happened while they slept? Would they be surprised I pushed someone to his death? Where is*

Mr. McGuire? Do I dare tell him what happened? Ellie wondered, remembering his kindness.

When she opened the first door and stepped onto the platform, she quickly scanned the floor for the small blue case. It wasn't there. Then she saw the gate. *How can this be? It was barely hanging on its hinge last night, but now it looks new!* Sure enough, the small gate had no signs of damage; no hint that anyone had fallen through it.

"Good morning, Miss Cooper," Craig McGuire said, startling her as he stepped onto the platform. "Is anything wrong? You look a bit puzzled."

"Good morning, Mr. McGuire," Ellie responded, feeling unsure of how much to say at the moment. "I'm just on my way to the ladies room."

"Well, I don't want to keep you then, but would you care to have breakfast with me this morning?" he asked. "I have something I'd like to discuss with you."

When hearing the man's remark, Ellie's heart started pounding. *Does he already know what happened? But how could he?* "Yes, that would be very nice, thank you," she replied. "I can meet you in the dining car if you'd like."

"No, I'll come by your coach and we can go together," he told her. "Let's say in about an hour?" he added, glancing at his watch.

"That would be fine," Ellie said, trying to calm the quivering in her voice.

With that, she slipped past the man and hurried on her way. Without looking back, Ellie somehow sensed Craig McGuire's eyes were on her.

Just over an hour later, Ellie and Mr. McGuire were being seated in the dining car by the hostess. For now, she'd forget about the tragedy of last night; for these brief moments she only wanted to feel special.

How beautiful! Ellie thought, when seeing a small vase of flowers on each table. Here, with a handsome and distinguished looking man, seeing a dozen or so tables covered with white linen tablecloths, holding perfectly matched china dishes and shiny silverware, she could almost forget where she came from. Yet, memories suddenly flooded her mind.

In that moment, she was in her mother's kitchen, washing the chipped and unmatched dishes and the old bent kettles with missing handles. She saw the once sturdy chrome kitchen table and chairs that now sat wobbly and marred, due to its fall from the back of her dad's pickup. Her memory echoed Morton's vile curses aimed at her mother for complaining about his careless driving that had caused the furniture's condition. *The neighbors gave us that set, yet he couldn't bring it safely to our house six miles away!* Ellie fumed inside.

"Are you all right, Miss Cooper?" she heard someone say, bringing her back to the present. "You look upset," Mr. McGuire remarked, laying his hand on hers. "Is there something you care to talk about? I'm a good listener."

"I *am* sorry," Ellie replied, trying to smile. "I

have a lot on my mind and I guess I get a little bogged down now and then. As a matter of fact, I *do* have something to tell you, but I'm not sure how to begin."

Just then a young waiter arrived at their table. "What may I get you?" he asked, looking at them. "Coffee … hot tea … water?"

"May I order for you, Miss Cooper?" her companion kindly offered.

"Yes, thank you," Ellie replied, feeling grateful due her limited experience of eating in restaurants.

"Very well, we'll start off with coffee and water to drink. For the entrée we'll each have a broccoli quiche and a serving of fresh fruit *and* whole wheat toast," Mr. McGuire told the waiter. "Would you care to add anything to that?"

"Oh, not at all; that all sounds perfectly fine," Ellie replied, although she had no idea what a *quiche* was.

"Thank you. I'll bring your drinks right away," the waiter told them as he hurried away.

"Now, Miss Cooper, you were saying?" Mr. McGuire stated, looking at her.

"Please call me Ellie, after all, you *are* buying me breakfast," she said, studying the man's face. "Yes, I was saying: I have something to tell you. But it's very hard to talk about, especially while we're enjoying all this," she added softly as her eyes swept the rather elegant surroundings.

"Very well then, we can wait until after we've eaten," Mr. McGuire told her. "I wouldn't want to spoil your meal."

Nodding her head, Ellie turned her attention to the countryside drenched in morning sunlight as it paraded by her window. "It's so beautiful. I love the mornings," she remarked. "I've always gotten up early to do chores. Rain or shine, they *had* to be done," Ellie said, somewhat under her breath.

"May I ask where your home is?" Mr. McGuire then questioned, surprising her.

"Near Syracuse, Kansas; I lived on a farm with my parents. That is, until recently," Ellie replied, realizing her answer might increase his curiosity.

"Have you no siblings?" he asked as the waiter arrived with their drinks. While the young man served their coffee and water, Ellie unfolded her napkin and laid it across her lap, feeling indebted to her aunt for teaching her basic etiquette. At the same time she searched for a way to change the subject. After all, she had no desire to talk about her childhood, to anyone.

"No, I'm an only child, but one day I hope to have several children of my own," she quickly replied. "I'd like that. Are you married, Mr. McGuire?"

At her remark, Ellie noticed a slight grin on the man's face as he poured cream in his coffee. Then, after sitting the small glass pitcher back on the table, he answered. "No, I'm *not* married. I'm afraid all my traveling would be quite unfair to a wife and family. Perhaps one day that will change, but for now I feel I must remain single," he said.

"I agree, that *would* be hard," Ellie replied, spooning sugar in her coffee. "I want *my* husband home every evening after work where I'll have a nice hot meal waiting for him. You wanted to discuss something with me?" she then asked, feeling grateful for a new area of conversation.

"Yes, Ellie, about this man you're planning to marry. Are you *quite* determined to carry on with those plans?" he asked, again surprising her.

"I'm *very* determined, after all, he's paying my expenses so I *can't* back out," she quickly answered. "Besides, I have nowhere else to go."

"What if I paid him back? I'd be happy to send him *more* than he has invested, to appease his disappointment," Mr. McGuire offered.

Thankfully their breakfast arrived just at that moment, allowing her time to digest what she'd just heard. *I can't change my plans, not without discussing them first with Aunt Marie,* Ellie hastily decided.

When seeing her breakfast, Ellie knew she had never seen such a pretty plate of food. "I declare, I never *dreamed* traveling could be so fine!" she cheered rather loudly.

Across the table, Mr. McGuire only looked at her and smiled.

As the two began eating, Craig McGuire searched for the right words to say to his breakfast companion. *She's innocent but certainly not helpless. No doubt a hard worker, and her youth would be an asset to my sister's business,* he thought, studying Ellie from across the table. *I'd lay odds she's a fine looking filly under all that hair and those sack clothes she's wearing!*

"Well, it's my experience, Ellie, that *everyone* has

a price. I don't mean to say they fold under bribery, but rather, most people will find, given enough monetary compensation, plans *can* change. Don't you agree?" he asked Ellie.

From the look he saw, Craig wondered if she understood his remark.

"Are you saying that if you pay Rudy Davis enough money, he'll forget about wanting to marry me? And then I'll be free to do what *you* want me to do?" Ellie fired back, surprising him.

When hearing the young woman's rather loud remark, those dining nearby gave hurried glances, and then resumed eating amid low whispers.

"I'm sorry, Ellie, perhaps we should save this until later also," Craig said softly, trying to defuse her obvious anger. "Are you finding your breakfast quite satisfactory?"

"Yes, it's *quite* delicious!" she snapped, keeping her eyes on her plate. For the remainder of the meal, neither one spoke except for a polite word of thanks to the waiter who was very good at keeping their coffee cups filled.

By the time she finished her breakfast, Ellie's nerves were a mess. *What's gotten into me? I'm unappreciative and rude! I must tell someone about last night! I'll go crazy if I don't,* she thought, wondering if Craig would be the best place to start.

"Thank you for allowing me the pleasure of your company," Craig said when he had finished the last of his coffee. "It's much nicer than dining alone."

"I enjoyed it also," she simply answered.

When they left the dining car, neither she nor Craig mentioned their beforehand subjects of conversation. "Thank you for breakfast. I should be getting back to my seat," Ellie told him as they reached the door of her car.

"Miss Cooper…Ellie, please let me explain what I said earlier," Craig remarked, taking hold of her arm. "I didn't mean that I intended to buy off this man Rudy, but rather, I meant if *you* were better paid, perhaps *you* might reconsider your plans. I do apologize for not making myself clear."

After hearing the man's explanation, Ellie felt embarrassed. Not only had she misjudged his statement, but she looked childish and inconsiderate. "I *am* sorry. I hope you'll forgive my outburst," she told him. "I *do* have something to tell you. Would this be a good time?"

"Of course, would you care to talk in the observation car?" Craig asked. "And we'll have a wonderful view from there. I promise."

"That sounds very nice," Ellie replied, wondering why she hadn't heard of the observation car before now. "Please lead the way."

With a nod, Craig headed down the aisle of the train, passing by Ellie's seat and into the next two cars forward. As they arrived at the observation car, Craig led the way up a small flight of stairs to an upper level.

"Oh, *my!*" Ellie blurted as her hand flew to her mouth. When scanning her surroundings, she was shocked to see solid windows. From floor to ceiling and curved overhead, there was nothing but clear glass. Individual seats faced the wall of windows and small tables sat sporadically throughout the car. Nothing blocked the view that passed by outside.

A lone couple sat at the far end. "Would this be all right?" Craig asked, motioning toward two seats a short distance from the door they just entered.

"Oh yes, this is perfect," Ellie said, gazing at the view. On one side she saw only the side of a mountain as it passed by in a blur, but on the other was a view that sent chills of excitement up her spine.

Far below she saw a rushing river, flanked by trees newly dressed in various shades of green. Bushes and vegetation of all kinds were sprouting new life after the long, cold winter. Beyond the river, Ellie saw baby calves and newborn lambs romping in the morning sun. For an instant, she thought about the many farm animals she had loved, only to be brokenhearted when they had to be sold or used for her family's winter meat.

"I never tire of seeing all this," Craig commented, letting out a long sigh.

"Every season brings its own special beauty."

"Oh, yes, but I *especially* love springtime," Ellie replied. "I hate winter."

"Then I'm surprised you're going to Alaska. Their winters are much longer *and* colder, I might add," Craig told her. "What I have in mind would promise you no more cold weather."

When hearing his remark, Ellie felt curious. Still, there was no way she could change her plans.

"Perhaps one day I'll leave Alaska, but for now, I must stay on course," she told him.

"As you wish. Now, would you care to tell me your news?" Craig asked.

For a moment, when seeing evidence of new life from her window, Ellie had to wonder about the life snuffed out last night. *Was he married; did he have a family who awaits his arrival?*

Taking a deep breath, Ellie knew she must tell her shocking news. Yet, somehow she wasn't sure if Craig McGuire was the right person to tell.

"Yes, I do have something to tell you," she began, looking straight ahead. "It's terribly sad, and I don't know what to do. I tried—"

"Good morning, folks. I'm sorry to disturb you," someone said from the doorway, interrupting Ellie. "It seems we have an emergency and we're asking everyone to return to their seats. We apologize for any inconvenience, but I'm sure this won't take long."

When hearing the announcement, Ellie's heart began pounding. *This is it! They found the man's body and now they'll start asking questions. Why didn't I tell someone before now?* Ellie lamented, feeling sure no one would believe her after all this time. *Besides, someone had to see the damaged gate!*

"Well, my dear, it looks as though we may not get the chance to finish our conversation after all. I'm due to disembark in less than two hours," Craig told Ellie, glancing at his watch. "I guess we should do as the man says."

Without a reply Ellie got to her feet. Her legs felt

weak and her insides quivered. *I must tell the truth! Auntie says lies only get bigger and lead to a greater mess. But I tried to tell someone. The conductor will surely remember what I said,* Ellie thought confidently. *No he won't! His shift was nearly over and I'm sure he's gone by now,* she reminded herself, feeling even more afraid.

As they headed toward her own coach, Ellie saw passengers huddled in small groups, talking. Most looked puzzled.

When they arrived at her seat, Ellie felt relieved to sit down. In her mind she had visions of a naked light bulb hanging overhead as mean looking men scowled down at her, demanding the truth. Never before had she felt so scared and unsure of what to do. Her throat was dry and fear gripped her, making it hard to breathe.

"Everything will be all right, Ellie. Don't worry," Craig said assuredly from the seat facing her.

Just then, a barrel-chested man came through the door of Ellie's car. His face was solemn as he drew near and stopped just feet away. At first his attention was further down the aisle, but then he looked at her, unsmiling.

"I'm Deputy Rosen...an investigator for this railroad and I need your attention," he began. "Early this morning a man's body was found along the tracks, and in his pocket was a ticket scheduled for this train. Since he was an obvious passenger, we're asking if anyone might know this man by his description. He was approximately six-feet tall, between one hundred eighty-to two hundred pounds. He had dark hair and eyes and was clean shaven. When his body was found, he was wearing dark colored shirt and trousers," Mr. Rosen told those listening. "The name on the ticket was Harvey Combs. If any of you know who he was, I need you to come forward," the man urged.

I must tell what happened; I can't live with myself any longer! Ellie thought, knowing the weight of her secret would only get heavier. "Sir, may I please speak to you?" she asked the investigator who had remained nearby.

"Of course, do you know something?" he asked, stepping up beside Ellie.

"Yes, I mean, I didn't know his name…but—"

"What she's trying to say is: we had occasion to talk to the man," Craig interrupted, smiling at Ellie. "In the observation car yesterday, we chatted for a brief moment. I believe he mentioned his name was Harvey, and he *does* fit your description. Don't you remember, my dear?" he asked, looking at Ellie.

Dumbfounded at such lies, Ellie could only look at Mr. McGuire. Yet, she didn't refute his remark. Instead, she slowly nodded her head, feeling even more entangled in this web of deception.

"Very well," the deputy said. "Was he alone or with someone?"

"He was alone," Craig told the man. "I *am* sorry to hear of his demise."

Mumbling, the deputy nodded and jotted something down on his notepad before walking away. In stunned silence, Ellie could only stare at the man who faced her. "Why did you say that?" she whispered to Craig. "There was no need. I had something important to tell him."

"Do you think they'd believe you? After all this time and you not coming forward, they would have detained you for questioning," he whispered back.

Once more Ellie felt stunned. Questions bombarded her mind as she thought about last night. *He knows, but how could he? Did he see what happened?* "How did you know?" she finally asked.

"I saw what happened," Craig replied softly. "I was about to open the door when I heard the commotion. I looked through the glass just in time to see you defending yourself and this Harvey fellow falling through the gate."

"But *why* didn't you say something?" Ellie asked in dismay.

"I waited until you left and then I saw the gate," Craig admitted. "I knew that would cause all sorts of questions, so I fixed it."

"How *did* you? And why didn't you tell me earlier?"

"I'm quite handy with a screwdriver and during my frequent travels, I've learned where they keep their spare parts, so I helped myself," he confessed. "And I didn't want to upset you, by letting you know I saw what happened."

When hearing the man's explanation, Ellie realized she *should* feel grateful. *Perhaps he's right. After all this time the deputy might well have detained me for questioning. Hard telling how long and maybe they wouldn't have believed me at all...*

"Thank you, Mr. McGuire. I *do* owe you a debt

of gratitude for helping, but I *don't* understand why you're doing all this for me," Ellie told him.

"I found no reason why you should disrupt your plans for the likes of that man who was obviously a low-life," Craig told her. "And you, my dear, have nothing to be ashamed of. I feel you did the world a favor, so put the whole episode out of your pretty head."

Pretty head? Does he really think I'm pretty? For the first time in her young life, a man had called her pretty. Suddenly, despite her earlier dilemma, Ellie felt elated. "Since you've been so kind, I guess I should listen to what you wanted to tell me earlier," she told him.

Glancing at his watch, Craig smiled and leaned back in his seat. "I would be much obliged, my dear," he said, looking pleased.

———————

Several hours after Craig had left the train, Ellie still felt excited. *He said I'm pretty enough to be a model! And I'd be in all that California sunshine. Just imagine, could I really get paid for wearing beautiful clothes? Could it be true that handsome men would be interested in dating me?*

In her hand Ellie held a business card. "Kate's Girls…Modeling and Dating Service…Beautiful Girls for all Occasions," it read in gold letters. On the back was Craig's name and telephone number. *It sure sounds exciting, yet, I can't change my plans. I have to keep my end of the bargain. But who knows, if*

Rudy doesn't work out, perhaps I will give this Kate a call, Ellie thought, stuffing the card in her purse.

CHAPTER THREE

Thankfully, Ellie changed trains in Los Angeles. For twelve hours she would have a sleeper-car where she could have a shower and a bed to sleep in. Due to the cost, Rudy arranged for her to have this luxury for only twelve hours every other day.

Although it was small, the privacy of her compartment made up for the cramped space. "Oh, this is heavenly," she muttered a short time later, feeling the hot shower run over her.

The farther Ellie traveled the less she thought about Harvey Combs. No longer did she feel guilty about what happened. *He caused his own death, yet, what would Aunt Marie think? Will I ever tell her what happened?*

After her shower, Ellie put on her nightgown and braided her wet hair into one long plait. When looking through the drawer of the small bedside table, she was surprised to find an unopened package containing a pink toothbrush. "Whoever left this behind, thank you!" she blurted with glee.

In no time she had brushed her teeth and was ready for bed. Then, pulling back the covers, she crawled in and pulled them over her. *Oh, this feels good,* she thought, stretching out.

Despite having to give up the bedroom compartment, Ellie was grateful for the shower and restful sleep she'd enjoyed. Once again, a friendly porter helped her to a window seat in one of the coaches.

Feeling excited, she was enthralled with the scene outside her window; the west coast and wide expanse of the Pacific Ocean.

As the train snaked its way along high cliffs and through small coastal towns, Ellie had a view of the coastline. She felt mesmerized by the endless rows of gentle waves lapping at the miles of sandy beaches. Then, the flat smooth shoreline changed to jagged rocks. The gentle waves were now thunderous breakers whose unrelenting barrage crashed against the rocky buttress, covering them in foamy whiteness that would recede, only to have another onslaught seconds later.

It's breathtaking! I never would have seen anything like this in Kansas, Ellie thought, watching the vast sea of blue.

From her window, Ellie felt transfixed as her eyes swept across the changing landscape. From the roaring ocean's surf, to quaint little towns, to vast fields of vegetables, she eagerly stored the images in her memory.

"Are you enjoying the ride, miss?" the sociable conductor asked as he passed by Ellie's seat.

"Oh yes, thank you," she replied, pulling her eyes from the view to glance at the middle-aged man. "But, I'm not sure what I'm seeing at the moment. Could you tell me what those are?" she asked, pointing to the seemingly endless hillsides passing by her window.

"Those are vineyards or grape arbors," he answered kindly. "This is wine country and you'll see these for miles. Wineries, elegant homes and vast fields of rich black soil make this part of California famous," he added.

One day I will live here. If only it were today, Ellie thought dreamingly. "It's all so beautiful, thank you for telling me," she told the man before he sauntered down the aisle.

Laying her head back against the seat, Ellie let her mind wander. She imagined herself in pretty clothes, living in a beautiful house and being loved and cared for by a wonderful husband. When seeing an elegant home in the distance, she imagined that she lived there. Certainly, this was far from the dust ravaged farms of Kansas and the daily degradations.

Will that man be Rudy Davis? Will he ever bring me here? Ellie wondered.

No one will want you! You're nothing but a hick girl, so don't get so high and mighty! Suddenly those degrading words pushed their way into Ellie's psyche; cutting and tearing at her already dismal self-esteem. *Dad said I was no good, but not always. Sometimes he told me I was his special girl,* Ellie thought, closing her eyes against the sickening memories.

Trying to clear her mind of those abusive years, Ellie thought about Aunt Marie, and their long talks. Once more she heard her aunt's words of encouragement and praise. *You're very special, Lizzie. Don't ever forget that you're a lovely young lady, smart and level-headed.*

Not only had Aunt Marie restored some of Ellie's lagging self-confidence, but she also taught her basic communication skills and manners. Certainly, such things were thought to be a waste of time by her dad. Sadly, due to Morton Cooper's continuous badgering of his wife, she, too, told Ellie such skills were unnecessary. Yet, as she traveled, Ellie was grateful for those months of mentoring from her aunt. *Somewhere out there, Lizzie, you'll find happiness and a great new life waiting just for you.* With each new day, those words were precious morsels that Ellie clung to the farther she traveled.

It was also during those times of sharing their deepest feelings that Ellie expressed her hatred toward her own father. *'I promise you, Lizzie, one day he'll regret what he did to you,'* her aunt had told her. *'He's evil and cruel, and one day he'll die a very lonely man.'*

Well, he's seen the last of me, of that I'm certain! Ellie told herself, vowing never to see Kansas *or* Morton Cooper ever again.

For three days the train wound its way north and still Ellie was in awe of the view from her window. Eagerly she awaited her scheduled compartment for a shower and a real bed. Some passengers nodded and said hello, but no one was as friendly as Craig McGuire had been.

While keeping a close watch on her meager traveling allowance, she went to the dining car only once a day. Instead of enjoying a full meal, Ellie simply ordered a bowl of soup or a few pieces of fruit. Mentally, she would assess her funds to make sure she wouldn't arrive in Homer, Alaska penniless, despite the gnawing hunger she felt most of the time.

It was raining when the train arrived in Bellingham, Washington. Like an ominous cloud, fear suddenly replaced the excitement Ellie felt earlier. As the train slowed she saw streets and sidewalks filled with people. Whether they were in cars, on bicycles or walking, each one seemed in a hurry.

For the first time this Kansas farm-girl was in a big city—alone. *Oh, I wish Aunt Marie was here with me. How will I ever find the ferry boat from here?* Ellie thought frantically, wishing she could stay on the train.

When the train stopped at the station, Ellie nervously gathered her things and prepared to disembark with the others. Soon, she was hearing happy greetings as loved ones found each other. Friendly handshakes were exchanged between passengers as they parted company. But for Ellie, there was over-whelming loneliness and a feeling of uncertainty.

I must do this; there is no one else. Aunt Marie said I can do anything I put my mind to. I am not a hick or a hayseed despite what Morton called me, Ellie thought. *I'm on my way to a new and exciting life, and I'll do what I have to. I'm intelligent and Aunt Marie said to be assertive.*

With her aunt's words resounding in her ears, Ellie squared her shoulders and stood to her feet. "Excuse me, sir. Would you mind helping me with my things?" she asked of the porter approaching her.

"Of course, miss," he replied with a smile. "Are you meeting someone?"

"No, I'm afraid not, but I am looking for the ferry boat to Alaska. Could you possibly tell me how to get there?" Ellie asked, handing him her ticket.

"Certainly, miss," he said a moment later, giv-ing it back to her. True to his word, when he had helped Ellie disembark, he motioned for someone. In no time, a red-headed young man stood in front of them.

"Bruce, see that this young lady gets to the dock. She's taking the afternoon northbound," the porter quickly instructed. "He'll see that you get to the right one, miss," he assured Ellie.

"Thank you, sir. I'm most grateful," she replied, retrieving a quarter from her small handbag for a tip. Like before, Ellie quickly subtracted the twenty-five cents from her meager assets. With a smile and nod the porter left. "Is the dock far from here?" she asked Bruce, trying to befriend her new guide.

"Yeah, it's a hike, but we have plenty of time," he told her. "Follow me." With that, Bruce picked up Ellie's luggage and headed down the station's platform. Threading her way through the crowd, Ellie hurried to stay close behind Bruce, the rather gangly young man whom she now relied on.

By the time they neared the dock, Ellie was grateful to be leaving the noisy old car she was riding in. Not only was the muffler dragging, but the engine back-fired on several occasions, causing a puff of black smoke. It was obvious most bystanders thought the faded-blue Ford should be scrapped for its metal, instead of clamoring down the otherwise quiet streets.

"I appreciate you bringing me here," Ellie shouted, making herself heard over the loud noise. Some blocks away she saw the dock and a small crowd. "Bellingham is a much bigger town than I've ever been in."

"It was for me, too, but I'm getting use to it," Bruce yelled back as he pulled into a parking space. "I'm from Wallace, Idaho, a mining town. Ever heard of it?"

"No, but my third-grade-teacher's name was Mrs. Wallace," Ellie replied loudly, only to realize a second later how ridiculous that sounded. *That was stupid! What's my teacher got to do with a mining town?* Bruce's silence only added to her embarrassment.

Despite her gnawing hunger, Ellie retrieved fifty-cents from her handbag and handed it to Bruce when he had unloaded her luggage. *Five dollars and ten cents,* she quickly calculated.

———————————

Although the rain had stopped, low-hanging dark clouds still remained, bringing an eerie feeling as Ellie boarded the *Bellingham Princess*. Never before had she been on a boat and this one seemed huge to her.

She again felt entranced by the strange new sights and was in awe of the massive ferry. Vehicles, large and small, were being loaded; she noticed some passengers wearing clothes made from animal skins, while others wore suits and stylish hats. Seeing these reminded Ellie of the diverse region where she'd be living.

I'm almost there to meet Rudy, my future husband. Then what? Will he still want me after he sees me in person? What if he doesn't? Again, she thought about the business card she carried.

Before long they were underway. The huge paddlewheel slowly gained speed, churning the water as the ferry proceeded through Bellingham Bay. "Be sure to watch for whales, folks," the boat steward announced a short time later. "They'll be a ways off, but the dolphins will be right along side."

Sure enough, it wasn't long until Ellie saw the playful gray porpoises swimming near the bow of the boat. Soon, other passengers joined her in craning their necks to see the water antics of the popular mammals.

Although the ferry had some accommodations, Rudy wrote that he couldn't afford for Ellie to have one, therefore, she must 'make do' by sleeping on a deck chair. She soon noticed others also shared the same dilemma.

Adding to Ellie's hardship was the lack of food. With her money nearly gone, she couldn't afford to pay the inflated prices of the ferry's small restaurant. Tired, hungry and feeling unsure of her future, Ellie's adventure had turned sour.

Here and there she over-heard conversations between other passengers which made her feel apprehensive about where she'd soon be living. *It sounds harsh, wild, and rowdy, but what did I expect? Should I go back, but to what? There's nothing for me, not even in La Junta. And if I call Kate McGuire how would I get there? I barely have five dollars!*

Then Ellie thought of why she left. *I've come here for a new life and I will make it work. I want Aunt Marie and Mother to be proud of me, not disappointed that I gave up. Anyway, Rudy is waiting for me and we'll be married and he'll take care of me,* she thought confidently.

The afternoon slowly inched by. Yet, instead of conjuring up problems that may not exist, she tried hard to concentrate on the beautiful scenery in the distance and the abundance of birds and wildlife. *What kind of man is Rudy Davis?* Ellie couldn't help wondering.

On the huge middle deck, Ellie found a place away from the dozen or so others who'd also be 'roughing' it. Although her stomach growled from hunger, Ellie decided to save her dwindling money until the next day. Perhaps then she would splurge on a bag of chips or maybe even a hotdog.

When night come, Ellie not only found the deck chair uncomfortable and hard, but she soon discovered her quilt was far from adequate against the cold night air. Before dark, the boat steward lowered a heavy, clear-plastic curtain over the open sides and secured them in place. Despite wearing her warmest clothes and winter coat, Ellie still shivered from the cold.

After she secured her luggage beside her, Ellie tried to get comfortable in the rather wobbly chair. With her knees pulled up, she lay on her side and huddled under the quilt.

As she closed her eyes, she became aware of sounds around her. The steady rhythm of the paddle wheel as it churned through the water; the wind whistling around the plastic curtains; the sound of someone snoring some distance away.

Due to her long trip and having had little sleep, Ellie soon found herself being lulled by the normally irritating noises. Just as she was about to fall asleep, she heard a new sound; distinct and alarming. *Is someone choking?*

"You didn't *really* think you'd get away with it,

did you?" someone said in a raspy voice. "I warned you and now you'll see I wasn't kidding."

Upon hearing the threatening words, Ellie opened her eyes, but was too scared to move. Looking straight ahead she saw the silhouette of a man a short distance away. He was bending over someone who slept in a chair; something was in his hand. She saw him quickly glance around just before he drove his fist into his victim's stomach; a sudden agonizing cry was heard.

In fear, Ellie covered her mouth, muffling the gasp that escaped her lips. *He killed that person! Right in front of my eyes!* Her heart began pounding and in disbelief she watched as the man straightened, towering over his victim. Then, he looked her direction.

Am I next? What if he knows I saw him? What should I do? When the man headed her way, Ellie closed her eyes, fearing he would surely hear her heart pounding as he drew near. When he arrived at her chair, he stopped. Trying to feign sleep, Ellie fought hard to maintain her breathing in a slow, steady rhythm. With the quilt up around her ears, her face was hidden as she huddled on her side, away from his obvious scrutiny.

"You better forget what you saw," he warned, before walking on.

It was another sleepless night for Ellie. Not only did the numbing cold keep her awake, but witnessing someone's murder had filled her with despair. *It happened again! Another tragedy and I can't tell any-one. Not for fear of being questioned, this time it's my very life that's in danger! He knows who I am, but he could be any face in the crowd. Oh, but I'll remember his voice,* Ellie decided, recalling its distinct grating tone.

From shear exhaustion, Ellie finally dozed off only to be awakened by a scream a short time later. Now daylight, someone had discovered the body.

A hubbub of activity quickly ensued as small groups of people gathered to discuss the poor man's demise. The ferry's captain and boat steward were bombarded with questions as to what action would be taken to find the killer.

"Ladies and gentleman, if I could have your attention please," a voice blasted over the loud speakers. "With the discovery of an apparent homicide this morning, we've been ordered, by the authorities, to change course. Since the one responsible for this act is obviously still among us, we won't be docking, but rather, we'll anchor off shore while everyone is questioned. We appreciate your cooperation in this matter, thank you," the man concluded.

By now, Ellie was filled with renewed anguish. *What will I say when they question me? Will they believe me if I say I saw and heard nothing? But if I tell the truth, will I be the next victim?* Ellie wondered in fear. *How can this be happening to me, again?*

By mid morning, a large boat came along side. 'Police' was written in large black letters. Now at anchor, the ferry sat more than a half mile off shore. Certainly, no one would survive the frigid waters if they tried to swim, at least not without the appropriate gear.

One by one, the three detectives who came aboard began questioning the passengers. Nervously, Ellie awaited her turn. Over and over she rehearsed her answers, but each time she heard Aunt Marie's words resounding in her ear.

'Lying never pays, Lizzie. We only dig ourselves a deeper hole we can't get out of. And, worst of all, we lose our credibility with those around us.'

But what if it means my life? Doesn't that make a difference? Ellie argued, trying hard to find some reason for sticking to her plan. *But, could I live with myself if I lied, knowing I let a murderer get away?* For the first time, Ellie realized what her aunt meant by 'proving your character.' *'Our character is the very fiber of what kind of person we are. It exposes the essence of our inner self.'* Again, Aunt Marie's words echoed through Ellie's mind, bringing a surge of truth she couldn't deny.

Finally, it was her turn. When her name was called over the loud speaker, Ellie took a deep breath, squared her shoulders and ignored the pounding in her chest. Then suddenly, before she could reach the door to the interrogation room, a man stepped in her path, startling her.

"I do hope you'll be having a pleasant trip, Miss Cooper," the man said, glaring at her. Fear washed over Ellie when recognizing the same gravelly voice from last night. In that brief moment she studied his face, seeing a large scar on his right cheek; a broken front tooth; one eye somewhat larger. "It'd be a shame to hear that a young thing like you had disappeared," he added, leaning his face within inches of hers.

Stepping back to avoid the man's putrid breath, Ellie looked at him with surprising calm. Whether due to her long and stressful trip or ravenous hunger, Ellie wasn't sure, but when hearing the man's threats, a feeling of rage welled up inside her. "Get out of my way!" she blared, shoving past him.

Hurrying for the door, she opened it seconds later and announced to the men sitting in their makeshift office. "See that man out there...he's the one you want. I saw him murder that man last night and now he's threatened me!" she yelled, pointing through the window.

For a brief moment the men only stared at Ellie, then to the man she identified. "Don't let him get away! He's your killer!" Ellie shouted when seeing the man disappear amid the crowd of passengers.

"He won't get far," the older looking detective commented. "Are you sure of this? Are you *sure* he did it?"

"Yes, I'm positive! He knows I saw him and now threatens to kill me, too!" Ellie wailed, suddenly feeling weak. "Please, you *have* to find him or I'll be his next victim." Just then the room started spinning, but before she could reach the nearby chair, Ellie collapsed in a heap on the floor.

For a moment after she opened her eyes, Ellie wasn't sure where she was. Then she remembered. *I fainted, but how did I get here? What is this place?* From where she lay, Ellie scanned the small room. Nearby was a cabinet with glass doors containing bottles of liquid and neatly stacked white packages. She saw no one. "Hello...is anyone here?" she called out as she tried to sit up. When doing so, she again felt dizzy and lightheaded.

Just then a man stepped into the room. "Hello, Miss Cooper. Are you feeling better?" he asked, approaching her side.

"I thought I was, until I sat up," Ellie replied, holding her head. "How did I get here? And who are you?"

"I'm Detective Chad Ryan, Miss Cooper, and I carried you here. Until we catch the man you identified, you'll be safer here in the infirmary," he said.

"You haven't *caught* him yet?" she wailed, grimacing against the sharp pain in her head.

"Miss Cooper, please, you mustn't worry about him," Detective Ryan told her. "We'll get him, but in the meantime, what about you? Are you traveling with anyone? A friend, family member, husband perhaps?"

"No, I haven't *anyone* with me," Ellie sighed, closing her eyes. Suddenly, she felt renewed loneliness and fear which only added to her many suppressed emotions that now erupted. "I'm traveling to Alaska to marry a man I don't even know; I haven't eaten in days because I have no money and I'm sleeping in the cold on a stupid old chair. Now I've witnessed a murder and the killer knows I saw him and threatened to kill *me* if I told! But I *had* to tell; I couldn't let him get away, could I?" she blurted through sudden tears. Then, looking up at the solemn-faced young man beside her, listening, she felt embarrassed.

"Miss Cooper, I *am* sorry for your misfortune. This explains why you fainted. You need food! I can't fix everything, but I *can* fix that particular problem," he told her. "You just lie still, I'll be back."

Upon the young man's departure, Ellie felt even more ashamed. *What is wrong with me? I shouldn't be telling everyone my business! He'll think I'm nothing but a big baby, crying about my problems. Oh Aunt Marie, if only you were here!* Ellie mourned, wiping her tears with her sleeve.

It seemed no time until Detective Ryan was back, carrying a tray of food. "They don't have much variety, but I brought what they had," he told Ellie, setting the tray in front of her.

Stunned, she saw a steaming bowl of vegetable soup, crackers, buttered toast, apple pie, coffee, and milk. "Oh, I brought these too." Reaching in his coat pocket, the young man retrieved four chocolate candy bars and placed them on the bedside table. "Something for your sweet tooth," he said with a smile.

For a moment Ellie could only stare at the banquet she saw, feeling overwhelmed by the man's kindness. "I don't know what to say," she finally whispered, looking up at him. "Thank you just isn't enough, but if you'll give me your address I'll send you the money, I promise," Ellie told him.

"Nonsense, you just think of it as a reward for coming forward about the murder. After all, you've saved us many long hours of investigation in tracking him down," he assured Ellie. "Now, you enjoy your lunch and I'll be back to ask you some questions. In the meantime, I'll see if there's anything new on our suspect."

With a lopsided grin, the pleasant young man once more left Ellie alone. Finally, for the first time in days, there was food in front of her. Like a refugee she began devouring it and wondered about the young detective. *Why is he being so nice? Is he married? What does it matter, I'll never see him again when this is all over,* Ellie decided, somewhat sadly.

When she had finished everything but the candy bars, Ellie laid her head back and closed her eyes. No matter how hard she tried, she couldn't help thinking about that kind, handsome young man.

CHAPTER FOUR

It was sometime later when a female voice began coaxing Ellie from her deep sleep. "Miss Cooper, can you hear me? I'm sorry to wake you, but I have a gentleman here who needs to ask you some questions."

Opening her eyes, Ellie felt embarrassed as she sat up, trying to clear the sleep from her mind. "Yes, yes, of course," she stammered, rubbing her face. "I'm sorry." When looking up, she saw an attractive red-headed woman in a white uniform. "Are you a doctor?"

"No, I'm a nurse. My name is Roxanne, but you can call me Roxie. This is my domain," she said as her eyes swept the small room. "Are you feeling better?"

"Yes, thank you. Much better since I've eaten, thanks to Detective Ryan," Ellie replied, seeing the man standing in the doorway. "I'm ready to answer your questions now."

"Then I'll leave you two. When I get back, Miss Cooper, I'll check your blood pressure to make sure you're okay to leave," Roxie said before leaving.

With a notebook in hand, Detective Ryan pulled up the nearby chair and sat down. "Now, Miss Cooper, tell me what you saw last night," he began.

For the next several minutes, Ellie relived the horrifying scene she had witnessed. She felt sick to her stomach when explaining the chilling event that left one man dead. "I was terrified he would kill me, too," Ellie said, recalling his stern warning. "And this morning, he was brazen enough to threaten me in broad day light! You *have* caught him, haven't you?"

"Not yet, but I'm sure we will very soon. We're searching each deck thoroughly," he assured Ellie.

"Then I'm still in danger," she replied, realizing the man had nothing to lose. "What if he finds me here? I can't protect myself."

"In case we don't find him by nightfall, we'll have someone posted at the door, making sure you're safe, Miss Cooper," he told her, looking up from his notes. "I'll make certain."

While Detective Ryan jotted down pertinent information from his witness, his mind was also on her earlier revelation. *She's traveling all this way alone to marry a man she has never met? What is she running away from?* Chad wondered, feeling certain she was inviting misery if she carried out her plans.

"I think that about covers it," he told Ellie a moment later. "You are very observant, Miss Cooper, and your description is sure to help convict this man."

"Please, just catch him before he finds me," Ellie begged as her eyes bore into his. "I won't feel safe *anywhere*, now that he knows my name. No matter where I go, I'll wonder if he's after me."

"Miss Cooper, I hope you'll forgive me for speaking my mind, but I feel I must say something, if I may?" Chad asked, wondering at his concern.

"Yes, of course, say what's on your mind," Ellie replied, looking puzzled.

As he searched for the right words, Chad thought about the cases he'd been on. The cases involving abuse and yes, even homicide, committed by men against their female partners...married or not. Thoughtfully, he looked at the floor, feeling the inquisitive stare of the young woman to whom he was about to give advice. Certainly, not official business, but rather, it was her personal life he was delving into.

"Miss Cooper, I really wish you'd reconsider your plans," he began as his eyes met hers. "I know you've come all this way, but do you honestly want to marry a man you've never met? Someone you know *nothing* about?"

Making no comment, Ellie lowered her eyes as she nervously interlaced her long slender fingers.

For the first time Chad noticed her hands. *No rings or nail polish,* he thought as he awaited her rebuttal.

"I *must* continue on, Detective," Ellie finally said. "Rudy sent me money and he's expecting me to show up. Besides, I have nowhere else to go."

"You can't go back home? I mean, being around friends or family has got to be a better option than marrying a stranger," Chad argued.

"No, it isn't!" Ellie blurted, surprising him. "Sometimes home is the *last* place we want to be. I will never go home...not ever! I came here for a new life, and I *will* find it. If not with Rudy, then I'll get a job and make my own way."

When hearing Ellie's strong retort to his suggestion, Chad realized his suspicions were right. *There's a lot she isn't telling; she feels trapped. Maybe I can give her another choice,* he thought, deciding to try.

"I understand, Miss Cooper. I'm sure you feel obligated to this Rudy fellow," Chad told her. "But, if you change your mind, I know someone who is in need of a trustworthy person like you. The job involves travel and a chance to learn things. Are you interested?"

"Who'd want me? I *barely* finished high school," Ellie protested, shaking her head. "Cooking, cleaning and feeding farm animals. That's all I know."

"Don't demean yourself, Miss Cooper," Chad hurriedly refuted. "You can obviously learn and it's quite clear you're trustworthy. If not, you wouldn't be so concerned about the money Rudy sent you, although it wasn't enough to make your trip pleasant."

Before Ellie could comment, Roxanne poked her head around the door. "Hey, I'm sorry to interrupt, but your partner wants to see you," she told Chad. "I think they have your man cornered and they need your help."

"Thanks, Roxie. I'll see you both later," Chad said as he gathered his notes and hurriedly left the two women. If their suspect was indeed caught, it would mean leaving the ferry and taking him to jail. In that case, he would have to work fast to convince Miss Cooper to change her plans.

After Detective Ryan left, the nurse took Ellie's blood pressure. "It checks out just fine," Roxanne assured her, removing the cuff from her patient's arm. "Anymore dizzy spells?" she then asked.

"Not since I ate," Ellie replied. "The food was delicious and I'm very grateful to that nice detective."

"How long *had* it been since you'd eaten?" Roxanne asked.

"I had a cup of soup a while back," Ellie admitted, standing to her feet. "Things are much more expensive than we planned for, so I'm afraid what money I had didn't go very far." Before Roxanne could comment, the door opened and Detective Ryan stepped inside the room.

"We got him, so you can relax now, Miss Cooper," he told Ellie. "He's a slick one, but this ferry didn't give him many places to hide."

"Thank you, *thank you* for catching him," Ellie blurted, feeling relieved. "What will happen now?

Where will you take him?" Exiting quietly, Roxanne again left Ellie alone with Detective Ryan.

"Back to Bellingham, where he'll be arraigned and charged with murder," he informed Ellie. "They'll need you to testify in court, Miss Cooper. Since you're the only witness it's vital that you do, or he could get off scot-free."

"You mean this isn't *over* and I have to come back to Washington? But how do I get here and where do I stay?" Ellie gasped, feeling life was becoming even more uncertain.

"When the time comes, you'll be notified and arrangements will be made for you. Your expenses will be covered since your testimony is so important. Please don't worry," Chad kindly informed her. "I'll just need your address of where you'll be so the court can contact you."

For a moment, Ellie could only look back at the young man as her mind filled with a hundred questions. "I'm not *sure* of my address, I mean, with me arriving late Rudy may think I changed my mind. In that case, he may not want me when I *do* show up," Ellie said softly, feeling a wave of despair.

"Then, would you consider my offer, Miss Cooper? You'd be appreciated, plus you'd have a place to live *and* get an hourly wage," Chad told her.

For the first time, Ellie thought seriously about changing her plans. "What is this job...*exactly*?" she asked, thinking it sounded too good to be true.

"It's working for my brother, Doctor Matthew

Ryan; Matt for short," he began, keeping his eyes on Ellie. "He's a missionary doctor *and* a bush pilot. He needs someone dependable that he can train as his office girl. So far he's had several that didn't like to work."

"I know what a doctor is, but what's a missionary and a bush pilot?" Ellie asked, not having heard of either one.

"Well, Miss Cooper—"

"Please call me Ellie," she interjected.

"Thank you…Ellie," he said, "and I'm Chad." Although he seemed rather surprised at her question, he began. "A missionary is someone who tells others about God. They usually travel to different parts of the world from where they live, but not always. And, a bush pilot is also a special kind of person," he explained kindly. "They fly small planes to remote places, delivering mail, supplies, and in Jeff's case, he shares his expertise in medicine *and* his deep faith in God. Most areas in Alaska have no roads or landing strips, so his plane is equipped with pontoons to land on water in the summer, and skis for ice and snow in the winter."

As she listened, Ellie was intrigued to learn more. For years she had wondered about the God she'd heard people talk about. Yet, the only time God's name was allowed to be used around their house was in her dad's profanity. Whether animal or human, each was certain to hear his vile words aimed at them before the day ended.

Once, when she was ten, Ellie was invited to attend a Christmas program at church with their neighbor. But, after the nice lady had endured her dad's verbal wrath, she made her quiet exit and never returned. If nothing more than to defy her father's wishes, Ellie knew she wanted to learn everything she could about God, that entity that so repulsed Morton Cooper.

"Can you tell me more about your brother?" she asked.

"Matt is kind, big-hearted and loves people," Chad told her. "And you'd love his wife, Lucy. She's his nurse, but right now she's his girl-Friday, too. She'd much rather help Matt deliver babies, set broken bones *and* share their faith with people. They'd both appreciate having you."

"They sound very nice," Ellie said, finding the whole idea quite tempting.

"Where do they live?"

"In Anchorage, but they fly down to the lower forty-eight quite often. Of course, they'd take you along, too, on those fun trips," Chad quickly added.

As she listened, Ellie found herself imagining such a life. *Working for someone like that and getting paid for it? Getting to fly in an airplane?* "But how do you know they'd want me?" she asked, feeling inadequate for such a job.

"I'll call Matt and if he isn't flying somewhere on an urgent matter, he'll probably meet you at the dock in Homer. If you both agree it's what you want, he'd take you home to Anchorage," Chad explained enthusiastically. "Does that mean you'll do it?"

As Ellie studied the young man's face, she couldn't help but wonder at his urging. "Why are you doing this for me?" she suddenly asked. "You know nothing about me."

"I've seen enough to know you're genuine and not a con artist," Chad replied. "Plus, if you grew up on a farm, I'm sure you know how to work."

"And, if it didn't work out, what then? I mean maybe I *won't* be able to learn everything I need to. Then what do I do? Where do I go?"

"Don't worry, Ellie, if that were to happen, I'm sure Matt and Lucy would have no trouble finding someone who'd hire you on their recommendation. They know plenty of people, *and* they'd make sure you were well taken care of," Chad said assuredly.

"May I think about this for a few minutes?" Ellie asked. "I can't just jump this direction without giving it some thought, now can I?"

"Of course not, besides, we have to wrap things up with our suspect before we take him away. I'll be back in about twenty minutes. Will that give you ample time to decide?" he asked, glancing at his watch.

"I guess it will have to be," Ellie said, suddenly filled with excitement. In a daze, she watched Chad leave the room as her eyes lingered after him. All the while she teetered on the threshold of a new adventure. *Should I do this? Do I dare make such a move without Mother's or Aunt Marie's approval?*

———————————

By the time Chad Ryan returned to the infirmary,

Ellie had made up her mind. "Now, Ellie, should I make that call to my brother and tell him about you?" he asked, standing in the doorway.

"Yes … well, I mean, you can *tell* him about me, but I really feel I should continue on as planned," Ellie told him. "It's not right taking Rudy's money and then not carrying through. But, if it doesn't work out with him and your brother still wants to talk to me, then I'll get to Anchorage *somehow*."

For a moment the young man only looked back at her, seemingly disappointed. "As you wish, Ellie," he replied, "but I'll need Rudy's address. For the court," he quickly added. "And here's Matt's telephone number." While Ellie fumbled in her small purse for Rudy's letter containing his address, Chad retrieved a business card from his wallet and handed it to her.

"Thank you so much for your help," Ellie told him, feeling somewhat sad to be leaving his company. "Will you be in court too, when I testify?"

"I'll certainly make a point of it," he answered kindly. "Perhaps by then you'll be working for Matt, and we can all have a nice dinner together."

When hearing his remark, Ellie was surprised at the soft flutter she felt in the pit of her stomach. "I'd be delighted," she replied, returning his smile.

"In the meantime, this is for you. And I'll accept *no* excuses," he said, handing her a ten dollar bill.

"Oh no, you've done *too* much already!" Ellie protested, feeling shocked at such generosity. Before she could say anything more, Chad quietly backed from the room and closed the door, giving her a lopsided grin.

———————————

Still feeling stunned over Chad's charitable behavior toward her, Ellie watched him and the other detectives as they led Jack Barton away in handcuffs. Just before they loaded the man onto the police boat, the murderer found Ellie in the crowd and aimed an icy sneer her direction. "Don't sleep too soundly, Missy! I'll get you yet!" he yelled at her.

A sudden chill ran up Ellie's spine when hearing the man's new threats. *He won't know where to find me. Certainly, after I testify, he'll be sent to prison for a good long time,* she told herself.

Brushing aside the memories of the past several hours, Ellie's mind was now on another challenge... meeting Rudy Davis, the man she was supposed to marry.

CHAPTER FIVE

Because of the murder and the ferry's delayed arrival, everyone was assured those meeting its passengers would have been notified of the time change. After two more miserable nights on a deck chair, Ellie finally heard those long awaited words. "Homer, Alaska, next stop."

Peering through the window on the main deck, Ellie saw the town in the distance. Suddenly she felt nervous. Somehow, this romantic adventure had lost its appeal. *I'm just tired; I'll feel better when I've had some sleep,* she decided, still thinking about Chad Ryan *and* his surprising offer.

The dock held only a scattering of people when the captain slowly eased the *Bellingham Princess* along side the wooden pier. In no time, those leaving the ferry had their belongings in hand and were saying goodbye to those whose destination was Anchorage.

For a moment, Ellie heard a small inner voice nudging her to proceed, too, and find Dr. Matt Ryan. Yet, she brushed it aside as she stood in the shadows looking for the familiar face from her magazine. *Is Rudy one of those people?*

Just then, the thought of marrying a man she didn't know caused a chill of uncertainty to sweep over her. *I'm not the first one to do this! Besides, I made a deal. If it doesn't work out, then maybe Dr. Ryan would hire me. What makes you think you could learn such a job?* Ellie's thoughts argued, remembering her poor high school grades. *I can do this! I will make it work with Rudy since we need each other.*

Taking a deep breath, Ellie picked up her luggage and lumbered off the ferry toward the unknown.

By the time the ferry was unloaded and had pulled from the pier, Ellie still waited. Her earlier fear was now terror. *What if he doesn't show up? Did he abandon me?* In frustration, Ellie plopped down on her suitcases to wait.

A short time later, she pulled Dr. Ryan's business card from her purse. *Do I dare call him? What if Chad hasn't had time to tell him about me?* For now, Ellie knew she had no recourse but to wait for Rudy.

It was two hours later when a faded red pick-up skidded to a stop in front of Ellie. An immediate cloud of dust swept over her. As she coughed and wiped her eyes, a man emerged from the vehicle and staggered toward her.

"Miss Cooper...I presume?" he slurred, removing his hat and bowing at the waist. "I do apologize for my delay, but since *you* kept *me* waiting, I didn't think you'd mind."

Now on her feet, Ellie could only stare at her intended husband who was obviously drunk. Yet, she was grateful he had arrived, regardless of his condition. "Yes, I'm Ellie Cooper," she told him. "I was beginning to wonder—"

"No, Miss Cooper, you must *never* wonder about me," he began, leaning his face close to hers. "I come and go as I please, so don't *ever* ask me *any* questions. Got it?" he asked, waving his finger in front of her face.

Not only did the man reek of whisky, but his body odor added to his disgusting appearance. Stepping back, Ellie could only stare at Rudy Davis, seeing little resemblance to the man in the magazine she had gazed at so often.

If I had enough money, I'd get me a room and send you back to that bar you came from! Ellie thought with disgust. But, instead of verbalizing her anger, she picked up her luggage and headed for the tailgate of the battered old truck. "Do you live far from here?" she asked, lifting her suitcases inside.

"You'll see, soon enough," Rudy told her, plopping the hat back on his head and climbing in behind the wheel. "Get in." When Ellie opened the door, several beer bottles rolled out, hitting the running board before landing on the ground. "Leave um!" Rudy shouted.

"No!" Ellie yelled back, retrieving all four. After tossing them in the bed of the truck, she climbed in beside the man. His only response was a sideways glance as he began pumping the accelerator, coaxing the grinding engine to start.

"It's flooded," Ellie told him a short time later, smelling gasoline. "Let it sit for a minute, or hold the foot-feed clear to the floor."

When hearing her remark, Rudy stopped and leaned back against the seat. "Well, if I didn't get me a Miss know-it-all," he slurred, glaring at her. "If you think you can do any better, do it!"

With her temper rising, Ellie got out and stomped around to the driver's side. "Okay, I will!" she blared, pushing Rudy out of her way. After climbing in behind the steering wheel, she tromped down on the accelerator and held it as she pushed the starter button.

Seconds later, while it cranked and backfired, the old truck finally started. While the engine coughed and sputtered off the excess fuel, Ellie kept it running but said nothing to Rudy.

"Well, I'll be," he said somewhat disgustedly, shaking his head.

Although she had gotten the vehicle running, Ellie once more let Rudy behind the wheel, much to her displeasure. After grinding the gears and racing the motor, he finally headed up the dirt road. Once more, Ellie was filled with doubt and fear of what lay ahead.

"I'll be a minute," Rudy said when stopping at a small store a short time later. In an unsteady gait he staggered inside and out of sight.

Quickly, Ellie glanced up and down the narrow dirt street, hoping to see a telephone booth. *I'm sure I'll be calling Dr. Ryan...unless things improve drastically,* she decided, doubting such a miracle would happen.

As she studied the area, Ellie saw no one except for a few children playing some distance away. Minutes later, Rudy reappeared carrying a small bag of what appeared to be groceries.

By the time they arrived at Rudy's cabin, not five minutes later, he had loudly burped several times without a hint of embarrassment or polite word of pardon. Overwhelmed with disgust, Ellie had to admit her intended husband wasn't only a drunkard, but his manners matched the pigs she'd fed everyday on the farm.

On the off chance Rudy's poor manners were due to his intoxication, Ellie soon realized his living conditions also closely resembled the smelly animals. A sickening odor greeted Ellie when Rudy opened the door to this two-room shack and motioned her inside.

Filth was apparent. She saw dirty dishes, clothes and papers strewn everywhere along with empty beer bottles. The small stone fireplace overflowed with ashes and the tiny kitchen sink held cold, slimy-looking water. *What have I gotten myself into? He's an animal! No sane person would live like this!* Ellie moaned, shaking her head.

From the first room, she wandered into the bed-room, separated by a curtain instead of a door. A small closet was along one wall where three dingy looking shirts hung askew on bent-wire-hangers. Opposite the closet, a coat and a pair of muddy boots had obviously been thrown in the corner.

I know these haven't been washed in months, maybe years! Ellie thought when seeing the filthy looking sheets and blankets on the unmade double bed. One small window was the only source of light in the dreary room. Going to it she looked out. *Nothing new about that,* she shrugged, seeing the unpainted outhouse sitting among the trees some distance away.

As she reentered the kitchen area, Rudy looked at her. "You can fry me up some bacon and eggs for supper tomorrow," he told her, "and I got you some soap so you can wash things up around here."

As she stood listening and watching Rudy empty the bag of groceries into the ancient looking refrig-erator, Ellie could say nothing. Instead, she realized life had once more dealt her a rotten hand.

He doesn't want a wife; it's a slave he's looking for. He couldn't even clean up his stinking mess before I got here; he had to go get drunk! Ellie fumed as she suddenly wondered how soon she could reach Dr. Ryan.

"Where's your nearest pay telephone?" Ellie asked, trying to curb her ire.

"Telephone, what'd need that for?" Rudy slurred, frowning.

"Because I want to call someone, and I'll need some change," she replied.

"The only telephone is down the street, but it won't do ya any good."

"Why won't it? It's a public pay phone isn't it?" Ellie asked.

"Yeah, but some drunk ran into it a few nights back, so it's broke."

"Was that drunk you, Rudy Davis?" she blared, now feeling trapped.

"No, no, no, it wasn't me," he said shaking his head. "Not this time."

For now, Ellie knew she had no choice but to make the best of her ordeal. Without a telephone she had no way of contacting anyone. "If you have a pillow I'll sleep over there," she said, pointing to the sway-back sofa.

"Suit yourself," Rudy replied, shrugging his shoulders. "I'll leave some change for the laundry; there's a place to wash clothes down the road. I'm leaving early so you'll have all day to get things done around here," he told her.

If I weren't so tired I'd slap your lying face for bringing me way up for nothing but to clean up after you. Love and adventure; what a joke, Ellie thought, turning to retrieve her quilt from her suitcase.

"Don't ignore me while I'm talking to you!" Rudy yelled, startling her. "I'm *telling* you what I need done!"

Tired or not, Ellie saw red. Turning, she slowly started toward him, staring in his face as she opened and closed her fists as her arms hung stiffly at her sides. "I'm *not* your slave, nor am I a child to order around. I've had enough of that to last me a life-time, so don't do it again!" she shouted, stepping up to within inches of his face.

For a moment Rudy looked at her, seemingly unsure of what to do next. "Now, I'm going to get some sleep so don't wake me up in the morning!" she concluded loudly.

"If you aren't the *crabbiest* woman I've ever laid eyes on!" Rudy blared, kicking over an already rick-ety chair. With that, he turned and left, slamming the door behind him.

When Ellie woke the next morning, she could barely move. She felt stiff and the long skirt she slept in was wrapped around her legs. Sleepily, she untan-gled herself and sat up, trying to work the kinks out of her body. Her stomach growled causing her to realize she hadn't eaten since she finished the last candy bar yesterday before leaving the ferry.

Getting off the sofa, she went to the refrigera-tor and looked inside. *A quart of milk, three bottles of beer, a dozen eggs and a pound of bacon; what kind of provider is that?* Ellie fumed, deciding Rudy was a selfish skin flint.

After a trip to the outhouse, she changed into a pair of jeans and a flannel shirt. *Now, I need a fire*, she decided, opening the wood cook stove. A few sticks of kindling sat in a pail beside the stove and outside behind the cabin, she found some larger pieces of wood.

In no time, she had a fire blazing and bacon frying in a beat-up skillet, the only cookware besides a warped kettle. Seeing these brought sudden memories of the farm and what she'd left behind. *From the frying pan into the fire, is that what I've done? It appears so,* Ellie thought sadly, retrieving the eggs. *Rudy can't expect me to work on an empty stomach, so I guess he'll have to find something else for his supper.*

The longer Ellie worked, the more enflamed she became at such filth. Over and over in her mind she recited the words that had enticed her to this miserable place to marry a man of such low character.

'*Come to the new frontier; meet the man of your dreams for love and adventure. Share the beauty of unspoiled wilderness and pure air. Enjoy its splendor as you and your handsome mate conquer life's challenges!*'

"Is *that* what they call this? Filth, inconveniences, a drunk ordering me around? I'd say this is just more punishment!" Ellie ranted as she swept a mound of dirt into the battered dustpan. "I won't be doing this for long! I'll be finding me *some* way to get to Anchorage," she promised herself.

After scrounging around, Ellie found a dilapidated basket into which she piled the dirty clothes. With the detergent and handful of change Rudy left her, she headed for the laundry mart, a short distance down a mostly deserted and unpaved street.

Squatty looking houses sat sporadically. To Ellie, the small fishing village was more depressing than the Kansas flatlands she had escaped from months earlier. Sitting on the south end of the Kenai Peninsula, Homer was far from what Ellie had envisioned. Yet, it wasn't nearly as disappointing as Rudy, the man she had come here to marry.

It was three o'clock that afternoon when Rudy arrived. "I'm home, woman," he yelled as he flung open the door and stepped inside. Following behind him was another man obviously in the same stage of inebriation. Each one carried an open bottle of beer.

In the next instant Rudy stopped and looked around. "Wow! Would ya *look* at this place?" he sang out as his eyes scanned the newly cleaned cabin. "I *do* believe I found me a wife!" he said laughing as he slapped his friend on the back. "I *told* ya I was gettin' married."

When he saw Ellie his eyes moved over her jeans and baggy shirt. "Woman, can't ya wear something that fits ya? I don't like baggy clothes; I wanna see what's under all that," he smirked, staggering toward her.

"You'll *never* see what's under all this," Ellie blurted, pinching her shirt sleeve. "And you're *not* getting married, at least not to me! I cleaned this mess because I couldn't stand the smell, but I *won't* be doing it again."

"Now wait just a dog gone minute," Rudy blared. "I paid good money to get you up here and I expect *you* to hold up your end of the deal."

"We *have* no deal! You're a drunken slob! I waited hours at the dock for you to show up, drunk and smelly!" Ellie yelled back. "Do you think *any* woman would put up with you? I'm leaving just as soon as I can find someway out of here!"

In silence, Rudy stared back at her, seemingly lost for words. Then, he staggered toward her. "No one, much less a woman, tells *me* what to do," he seethed through clenched teeth. "I see *you* need a good lesson."

Already Ellie had a plan. With each layer of filth she'd scrubbed away today, her anger increased. Now, when hearing Rudy's remark, it stirred inside her like a volcano, ready to erupt. From all the years of wrangling stubborn farm animals, Ellie had learned to be quick on her feet. With her fists at her sides, she waited.

Within a few steps of her, Rudy grabbed the neck of his beer bottle for an apparent weapon. It was then that Ellie's right fist shot out and landed a hard blow to Rudy's left jaw that sent him sprawling backwards onto the floor. The beer bottle he held became airborne and flew against the fireplace. The sound of shattering glass filled the cabin. From the corner of her eye, Ellie caught a glimpse of Rudy's friend leaving quietly, closing the door behind him.

Seemingly stunned, Rudy lay on his back staring up at Ellie. His face held a twisted sneer as he then staggered to his feet. "So, ya wanna play hardball, is that it? Well, let's get after it," he muttered, glaring at her.

Once more he came at her and like before, Ellie surprised him. This time with a quick, powerful kick, she slammed her right foot into Rudy's chest. Again, the room echoed with the sound of destruction as his body was hurled into the wooden table and chairs, leaving them useless except for firewood.

This time Rudy lay there amid the debris, making no attempt to get up. Inching forward Ellie looked down at him.

Suddenly, things felt surreal. Here, in a strange part of the world she once expected to call home, Ellie's rage had resurfaced. Just like her assailant on the train, Rudy Davis, too, had sparked that volatile reservoir of emotion Ellie harbored. That festering storehouse of pain caused by years of abuse had again left its mark.

CHAPTER SIX

A crescendo of excitement filled the log cabin as Mimi Minooka gave the final push that delivered her baby into the world. "Great job, Mimi, you did it! Congratulations, you have a big healthy boy," the doctor and nurse told the exhausted first-time-mother and her husband, Luke.

Seconds later, the infant's hardy cry filled the room as he was gently placed in the warm blanket and Lucy's waiting arms. For a moment Matt looked at his wife, knowing the heartache she felt for being childless.

The baby's cry brought a unified sense of relief to everyone, now that the ten-hour ordeal had finally ended. Minutes later, the new parents were gazing at their eight-pound-five-ounce, full-faced, dark-haired baby, carefully touching his tiny fingers and toes as though they were made of delicate china. "Thank you, my lovely Mimi," Luke whispered to his wife. "You are so brave," he added as tears glistened in his eyes. Despite her weariness, Mimi managed a soft smile as she looked up at him.

"You rest now and take it easy for a few days. I'll be back in two weeks to check on everyone *and* bring your supplies," Matt told the couple as he patted Mimi's hand. "Good job, you have a fine, handsome son."

"Thank you, Doc," Luke said, grinning ear to ear. "We're naming him after you, for all you've done."

With a smile and nod, Matt shook the man's hand and mentally said the name. *Matthew Minooka.* "I'm honored, Luke. Thank you."

As Lucy cleaned up the area and helped Mimi get comfortable, she gave instructions to the new mother. In the kitchen, Matt rolled down his shirt sleeves and took a gulp of coffee Luke poured for him minutes earlier.

Thank you, Lord, for another happy ending; for awhile I wasn't sure it would be, he sighed, knowing small-built women like Mimi often needed C-sections to deliver such a big baby. *This might have ended tragically so far from a hospital*, Matt thought, feeling relieved Mimi and son had survived the ordeal.

Stepping to the window, Matt let his gaze wander over the lush array of vegetation. Beside the path he saw Peony bushes covered with growing buds. Near the cabin was a large lilac bush. *Those will be pretty in a few weeks*, he decided, feeling grateful for warmer weather.

A thick carpet of mountain grass surrounded

the Minooka home and at the edge, standing like majestic guards, were Hemlock, Aspen and Birch trees, each wearing their fresh attire of shimmering leaves.

———————

It was Matt and Lucy's third year in the North Country. Here, the couple was achieving their dreams. Not only were they helping people with basic medical needs, but sharing the Gospel and leading lost souls to Christ had become most rewarding and appreciated. Using his skills as a bush pilot, Matt had countless opportunities to meet people.

While attending Harvard Medical School, Matt also studied the Bible, fulfilling a promise to his dying mother. It was during this time that his faith grew, bringing a call on his life to be a missionary doctor. While harboring a hidden desire to use natural cures, Matt's beliefs only escalated when seeing his patients suffer from debilitating side effects, caused from toxic chemicals in pharmaceutical medicines.

However, when he began prescribing herbs and natural remedies he was branded as a 'renegade' doctor who was out of touch with reality. Yet, at no time in his life, while growing up in Wyoming, had he cowered to critics. *'Follow your heart and go where God leads you,'* his mother had often told him.

Therefore, when a letter arrived from a fellow classmate urging Matt to move to Alaska, he jumped at the chance. With his pilot's license in hand and many hours of flying time under his belt, he and his bride, Lucy, headed for the 'new frontier.' Equipped with a deep compassion for people and a strong faith in a Creator who generously supplies natural cures for mankind, they arrived in Anchorage.

Knowing the abundance of medicinal herbs and roots in the area, Matt often spent his Saturdays with his native friends scouring the woods for his supply of harmless cures.

Although the pay was far below his peers who worked in hospitals or did private practice in large cities, it didn't matter. The never ending supply of fresh or smoked salmon, moose or caribou meat and other such items, held a far greater reward when added to the vast beauty they enjoyed.

Because of the remote areas, some of Alaska's residents live hundreds of miles from the nearest town, making two-way radios vital for communication. When calling, they made known their need of supplies, medical care or request for help in emergencies. It is then they rely on the bravery of the bush pilot.

With Alaska's three million small lakes and snowy landscape of winter, planes appropriately equipped have easy access to landing. Since coming here, Matt made his rounds to the remote areas to help people any way he could.

For his prior visits and delivering baby Minooka, Dr. Ryan received fifty dollars plus a bag holding several packages of meat. "Our many thanks," Luke told him, giving a smile and hearty handshake.

After telling the Aleut Indian couple goodbye,

Matt and Lucy left the cabin and headed down the well-worn path to the lake where their plane sat waiting.

It was early June and the day felt exceptionally warm; certainly higher than the average temperature of sixty-two. Soon, the plane was in sight. Just as they neared their Four Passenger Cessna, they heard a vicious growl from the nearby bushes. Then they saw it; a large grizzly bear stood on its hind legs looking at them.

"Get in!" Matt said as he quickly opened the door for Lucy. "It's a sow with cubs I suppose, and she's warning us to stay away," he told his wife.

"I can't *imagine* living out here with all these wild animals!" Lucy blurted as she hurriedly crawled inside the plane. "They're braver than I am."

"They've learned to adapt; to live with nature," Matt replied when safely inside the plane.

Moments later, they were skimming across the clear, mountain lake and in no time were airborne. Then, tucking a pillow under her head, Lucy closed her eyes for a quick nap while they made the short flight to Anchorage.

As they leveled off, Matt scanned the scene below. The vast spruce forests, the numerous lakes and surrounding mountains brought the usual feeling of exhilaration as he headed his plane south-west toward home.

Once more, Chad felt disappointed at not reaching his brother. Several times he had called, but no answer. Since leaving Ellie Cooper, the younger Ryan found himself thinking about her. Certainly, it wasn't her beauty for her drab appearance did nothing to entice the opposite sex. Yet, there was something about her that drew the young detective.

At twenty-five, Chad Ryan had recently completed the Law Enforcement Academy. Although his handsome features and clean-cut appearance had females of various ages clamoring for his attention, Chad rarely dated. Instead, he poured all his time and energy into his studies, knowing high grades would guarantee him the placement of his choosing.

With the ferry murderer, Jack Barton, behind bars and awaiting trial, Chad did all he could to hurry the process along. As the state's only witness, Ellie would be there and for Chad that brought a distinct feeling of gladness. *Maybe she'll be working for Matt by then, too,* he thought, secretly hoping she'd decide against that Rudy Davis fellow after all.

For Ellie, life appeared in shambles. When Rudy finally got to his feet, he said nothing. Instead, he glared at her as he slowly staggered out the door. Seeing the look of hate in his eyes, Ellie knew he'd be back. Not only was he humiliated for being beat by a woman, but his friend had witnessed it. Certainly, no man would let such embarrassment go without retaliation, least of all a man of Rudy's caliber.

For that reason, Ellie hurriedly packed her things to leave. Like before, she would wear her long skirt and heaviest coat. *I'll probably be sleeping outside tonight,* Ellie thought with disgust. *If only I could get to Anchorage and find Dr. Ryan. Surely he and his wife would put me up for the night. I wonder: did that nice detective really tell his brother about me like he said?* "It doesn't matter, right now I have to get out of here and find someplace to hide," she mumbled as she grabbed her two suitcases and headed for the door.

As she stepped outside Rudy's cabin, Ellie was surprised to see a woman approaching. "Hello, miss, may I have a word with you?" she asked, looking at Ellie. "My name is Carla and I was told you might need a place to stay. It does appear I was informed correctly," she added, eyeing Ellie's luggage.

"Well, yes, I'm afraid I do need a roof over my head, at least until I can find a ride to Anchorage," Ellie replied, "but *who* told you about me?"

"My brother, Billie," Carla said. "He's friends with Rudy and he told me what happened here. He's trying to keep that hothead out of trouble so he wants you out of the way. I guess he's afraid Rudy might come after you."

"Yes, I'm afraid he's plenty mad, so that's why I'm leaving," Ellie told her. "I *would* appreciate having someplace to stay. Thank you."

As she studied the woman, Ellie wondered what such an attractive woman was doing in Homer.

With delicate features, the petite woman wore her brown hair short in a flattering style. Her long denim skirt and matching jacket looked expensive, as did her boots. "Do you live close?" Ellie asked, seeing no vehicle.

"Just up the street; let me help with those," Carla said, taking one of Ellie's suitcases in hand. "Billie didn't catch your name, Miss—"

"Cooper, but please call me Ellie. I can't thank you enough for your offer," she told the woman as they headed down the dusty street. "I came here to marry Rudy, but he's *nothing* like the magazine ad."

"Oh honey, you're not the first girl who fell for Rudy's bologna," Carla said, shaking her head. "He might be nice if you can catch him sober, but so far that day hasn't happened. I wish Billie wouldn't hang around him so much, but he feels like Rudy's protector somehow, like today," she added.

As they walked, Ellie's mind filled with questions. *Why would Carla invite me, a stranger, into her home? Does she have a family besides Billie?* Not wanting to appear nosey, she didn't ask, instead, she knew she'd learn the answers soon enough. In silence they walked and were soon on a new street.

"That's it, up ahead," Carla said pointing a minute later. When noticing the large house facing them, Ellie caught her breath.

"Oh, it's *beautiful!*" she remarked, seeing the well-kept, two-story structure. "I see other small houses, but this one looks like a mansion." For the first time, Ellie thought about the beautiful houses she'd seen from the train. This one reminded her of those large, stately homes she dreamed of having one day. "Do you have a big family?" she couldn't help asking.

"I guess you could say that," Carla replied as they neared the front porch. "I have other young ladies living here. We all work together."

Before Ellie could ask what kind of work they did, Carla led the way up the front steps and opened the door. For a moment, Ellie stopped to admire the door's oval glass. On it was an intricate lacy design etched in white, leaving only a small amount of plain glass to see through. Nowhere had Ellie ever seen such an elaborate door.

"Girls, we have a visitor," Carla called out from the foyer. "Make sure you're decent before you come down," she hurriedly added. "Ellie, I want you to make yourself at home, my dear. I'll show you upstairs to your room, but first, would you like some tea?" she asked.

"That would be nice," Ellie replied feeling entranced. Slowly her eyes drifted upward, seeing the beautiful wallpaper with tiny bouquets of red roses; the shiny wooden banister of dark wood and the curved stairway; high overhead hung a shimmering crystal chandelier.

Everything was clean and beautiful. Suddenly, Ellie felt as though she'd stepped inside a fairytale where nothing bad could happen. At her feet, hardwood floors glistened in the sun as it filtered through the window's lace curtains. In awe, she slowly walked into the next room, seeing furniture upholstered in elaborate material. Lovely lamps, end tables and sofas were scattered throughout the spacious room. A shiny dark piano sat in the corner. For Ellie, the long ago dream of taking piano lessons resurfaced, and a vision of her playing such a beautiful instrument flashed through her mind.

As her eyes swept across the room, Ellie knew she wanted to stay. Not just tonight, but permanently. Finally, the sound of giggling behind her brought her back to awareness.

"Girls, this is Ellie," Carla told the group of young women. "She'll be staying with us tonight, so make her feel welcome," she said, before leaving the room.

Instantly, like schoolgirls, many of them gathered around Ellie and offered a hand of greeting. After stating their names of introduction, they asked questions of her. As she looked at them and tried to give short answers, Ellie guessed most were around her own age. "What do you girls all do here together?" Ellie finally asked, thinking surely she could stay and work too.

Glancing at each other, the girls seemed hesitant to answer. "We're in the entertainment business," the one named Irene finally said. "We have gentleman clients who come on a regular basis and they pay us to entertain them."

"I see the piano, do you sing and dance?" Ellie asked, knowing she had no such talent.

"If that's what they want," Irene answered, bringing a round of giggling from the others. "We try to accommodate in every area. With a little alteration here and there, *you* could make some money," she added, lifting Ellie's long mane off her shoulder. "How's that sound?"

"Tea is served," Carla announced before Ellie could answer. Carrying a large silver tray, the woman placed it on the coffee table. Just then, the Grandfather clock across the room chimed five times. "Are everyone's chores done? We do have clients starting at six you know," she then added.

With that, the young women left the room. Only Irene stayed behind. "I was just telling Ellie she might want to join us. I think some of our gentlemen would like some *fresh* entertainment," Irene told Carla.

"How old are you, honey?" Carla asked.

"Eighteen. Is that old enough to work here?" Ellie asked, hoping it was.

"I'll tell you what, you think about this tonight, and if it still interests you tomorrow, we'll talk more," Carla replied. "Right now, let's have our tea and you tell us a little bit about yourself. Where you're from and why you ended up in Homer."

For the next fifteen minutes, Ellie told the two women about finding Rudy's ad in the magazine and why she left Kansas. Yet, at no time did Ellie reveal the extensive sexual abuse she'd suffered at the hands of her dad. She wanted only to bury it, never to speak of it again.

"I'm sorry you had to come all this way for the likes of Rudy Davis," Carla told Ellie, patting her hand. "But, maybe it won't be a total loss after all. And now, I'll show you upstairs."

Just like the main floor, the upstairs was eloquent and neatly furnished. The room Ellie would use was decorated in blue, her favorite color.

"The nearest bathroom is three doors down on the right," Carla informed her. "There are towels and washcloths on the shelf if you'd like a hot bath. I only ask that you do it now, before our clients arrive. Oh, and I'll bring you up a supper tray later," she added before leaving.

Glancing at her watch, Ellie knew she had to hurry to finish before six o'clock. As she hurriedly retrieved her nightgown and slippers from her suitcase, she thought about this beautiful house and the fact she may possibly get to stay. *But I have no talent; certainly nothing any client would pay money for,* Ellie decided, feeling disappointed. *Oh, but that bath will feel good!*

By six o'clock, Ellie had finished her bath and was now fighting to stay awake. Not only was she exhausted from her long trip, but her ordeal with Rudy only made it worse. Now she faced more decisions. *What if I can't work here? How will I get to Anchorage to find Dr. Ryan? And what if I can't learn that job either?* Ellie wondered as she pulled back the bedcovers. *I can't think about this now, maybe in the morning,* she decided, crawling into bed.

If she hadn't felt so tired, she would have stayed awake just to look at her surroundings. *This is the most beautiful place I've ever seen. One day I will have a house like this,* Ellie vowed silently as she closed her eyes.

Sometime later, a knocking sound coaxed Ellie from her deep sleep. "I have your supper tray," an unfamiliar voice called out. "Are you awake?"

"Yes, please come in," Ellie said sleepily, sitting up in bed. "I guess I dozed off," she told the young woman she recognized from that afternoon.

"Carla made this for you and since I have a lull in business, I was elected to bring it up," she said, setting the tray on the bed.

"Thank you, Miss—?"

"Just call me Terri. We only use first names around her."

"Thank you, Terri. I appreciate everyone being so nice," Ellie said, pulling the tray toward her. "What kind of talent do *you* have? I mean, that your clients will pay money for?" she hurriedly asked, hoping to learn more.

"Just the normal kind," Terri replied. "The kind *any* woman has. Men want only *one* thing, honey, and they're willing to pay good money for it. So we're more than happy to accommodate their needs," she said. "Enjoy your supper." With that, Terri left Ellie alone.

As she stared at the now closed door, Ellie felt stunned. Suddenly, she knew. *They sell their bodies? This beautiful house is used for such disgusting things as that?*

Instantly, she was back on the farm, reliving the horrors of abuse she endured for years. She remembered how her dad would catch her in the barn while she was milking cows, or out by the haystack, or weeding the garden. It didn't matter. When he wanted *his* needs met, everything else was forgotten.

Again, she tasted gall as anger erupted, choking her with rage. Then, as she thought about the despicable acts done in this beautiful room, the colors began fading before her eyes. Soon, all hint of delicate blue was gone, replaced by stone gray, looking lifeless and cold. *How could they let men touch them like that? They're like animals and no amount of money is worth it!*

For Ellie, her appetite had vanished. In its place was a plan to get away. *I must get to Anchorage, somehow.* "I'll walk if I have to," she muttered.

CHAPTER SEVEN

The house was finally quiet. All night Ellie had buried her head between the two pillows to block out the sounds she heard coming from across the hall. Yet, at times, she heard a man's loud voice speaking, using vile and degrading names for his apparent entertainer. These words made Ellie gag as she remembered her abusive past.

Finally, when everyone had apparently gone to sleep, Ellie crawled out of bed and got dressed. Since she had no idea when her next meal might be, she decided to eat the cold hamburger and bowl of soup.

After making the bed, Ellie cautiously opened the door. With her suitcases in hand, she quietly left the room. Instead of it being a place of comfort and rest, it had been a torture chamber. Again, having had very little sleep, she wondered how she'd manage another day of uncertainty.

Carefully, Ellie descended the stairs, giving one last look at the house that no longer held the stunning appeal it did yesterday. Today, it was only a symbol of disgrace and the waste of young women. *Women just like me are being used in this horrible place,* Ellie thought sadly.

Somehow, Ellie felt sure each one would change their lives if they could. Yet, without an education or someone who really cared about their well-being, what chance did they have? Suddenly, she was grateful for a young detective who cared enough about her to offer a way out of a dismal future.

I have to find Dr. Ryan. Somehow, I will make a better life, Ellie vowed as she opened the door of the brothel and stepped outside.

The driver of the old truck held tight to the steering wheel as he glanced at Ellie and grinned. "Hang tight, miss. We still have a long ways to go," he told her, shifting to a lower gear.

The engine whined as it worked hard to plow through the deep mud. The overnight rainfall had turned the dirt road into what reminded Ellie of the pigs-wallow on the farm. Just then, she thought of the many times in Kansas when she had gotten out and helped push a vehicle through the mud or snow. And now, if need be, she'd do it again. Yet, she'd hate to ruin her most comfortable shoes and favorite long skirt.

Slowly, the truck inched its way up the road toward Anchorage. "Is it mud the *whole* way?" Ellie had to ask, wondering why anyone would make such a hard trip in these conditions.

"Yup, after a rain like this," the man told her, peering intently through the windshield. "It's slow going, but we'll make it."

Despite her jostling inside the truck, Ellie felt grateful for the ride. Normally, she'd be too shy or afraid to accept such an offer from a stranger, but this morning she felt only relief when the man and his truck suddenly appeared beside her on the road. With less than two dollars in her purse, Ellie had no choice but to rely on this stranger for help; somehow she felt certain he meant her no harm.

From side to side, the truck slid back and forth across the road. At times, Ellie felt sure they would slide into the ditch, leaving them helpless. Often she gasped while bracing herself for the inevitable. Yet, surprisingly, the man would maneuver his truck through the slimy substance, seemingly having no doubt they'd get through the miles of mud.

While trying not to worry, Ellie welded her eyes on the beautiful snow-capped peaks in the distance. *What if Chad hasn't told his brother about me? What do I do then? Where will I sleep tonight?* She could only wonder.

———————————

Before leaving for work that morning, Chad dialed his brother's telephone number while uttering a quick prayer that he'd finally get an answer. "Morning Matt, I didn't wake you, did I?" Chad greeted, feeling relieved to hear his voice.

"Hi Chad, no, I've been up for a while," Matt replied in his usual happy tone. "This is a surprise; I thought maybe you'd forgotten about us," he added teasingly. "So how are you?"

"Doing great, and yeah, I know it's been awhile, I'm sorry. Time flies, but I *have* been calling you for two days," Chad said in his defense.

"Oh, well, we've been delivering babies, stitching up wounds from a knife fight. You know how it is," Matt told his younger brother. "We have no set office hours since Lucy has been going with me a lot more. So what's up?"

"I know you wanted to hire a girl for your office. Is that still your plan?" Chad asked as his thoughts turned to the young woman he'd met days earlier. "If it is, I found someone I'm sure you and Lucy would like."

"Yes, we *do* need someone. Who do you have in mind?" Matt asked, sounding interested. "Tell me about her."

For the next several minutes, Chad told his brother about Ellie Cooper and how they'd met. Also, about her plans to marry a man she met through a mail order catalogue. "Ellie was nearly starved, yet she refused to change her plans because she felt obligated to this guy who obviously doesn't care a wit about her welfare. If he did, he would have sent enough money for her trip to be comfortable," Chad ranted while trying to contain his anger.

"Does she have *any* training? More importantly, is *she* interested?"

"No training, but I know she's interested," Chad answered. "If she hadn't felt indebted to this Davis fellow, she would have let me call you right then. I'm sure of it. She wouldn't talk about her past, but did say she'd never go home again," he added, feeling his usual curiosity.

"Where is she now?" Matt wanted to know. "How do I find her?"

"I gave her your card. If it doesn't work out with this guy, she said she'd call you," Chad replied. "Somehow, I feel confident that she will."

"From all you've told me about her, Lucy and I would certainly like to talk to her," Matt remarked. "We *do* need someone we can trust. Too bad we don't know *if* she'll be calling. But, we'll try to stay by the telephone as much as possible the next few days, just in case."

"Thanks, Matt. I know you'll like her," Chad said, wondering at his own interest in the young woman. "We need Ellie in court as our witness to this murder, so I *do* have to find her."

"Is it *only* the murder case, or do I sense other reasons for you needing to find her?" Matt asked his brother. "You've shunned the ladies so long it's good to hear this spark of interest in the opposite sex. It's not good for man to be alone, you know," he added, feigning his authority.

"Yeah, I know," Chad said chuckling. "You and Lucy just *can't* wait to see me settled down." Certainly, up until now, Chad had given little thought to dating much less getting married. First his training and now his job had taken precedence in his life. "It would be nice to have someone waiting for me instead of paperwork and an empty apartment," he admitted.

"Like I've always said, dear brother, God has that special one waiting for you somewhere and at the right time, the two of you will cross paths," Matt replied in his serious tone. "You'll both know when the time is right."

"Hey, I guess I'd better get going," Chad said, cutting short the same lecture he'd heard many times before. "Let me know if Ellie calls, okay?"

"Will do, and Chad, thanks for your help," Matt told him. "If Ellie is everything you say, I'd like to give her a chance, despite her lack of training."

"Thanks, Brother. I feel she just needs someone she can count on. I think you and Lucy could help her a lot," Chad said as the call ended.

Suddenly, it wasn't his job or the day ahead that occupied Chad's mind. Instead, it was a young woman wearing loose-fitting clothes and oversized glasses. Despite her obvious attempt to hide behind her attire, Ellie Cooper had revealed much of herself to the candid eye of the young detective.

During his four years of criminal law and psychology, Chad knew victims of abuse would often hide behind walls of their own making. Whether they felt guilty, hurt or angry, he knew most victims wanted to be inconspicuous by making themselves unattractive. Others, he had learned, become promiscuous due to their feeling of shame and low self-esteem. Somehow, he sensed Ellie had been abused badly. If that were the case, he knew Matt and Lucy would be the most likely couple to break through that barrier Ellie now hid behind.

Whatever it took to heal Ellie of her past, Chad knew it would be worth the time and effort. Certainly, he wanted to be around to see the end result.

By the time the mud-spattered truck arrived in Anchorage, Ellie knew the driver's name was Burt and his occupation was fishing. She knew he was half French and half Alaskan Indian and had lived most of his forty-eight years in or around Anchorage. Although Burt was eager to share his background with Ellie, she, on the other hand, revealed little about herself.

With the long ride finally over, Ellie sighed with relief. Her body ached and every nerve felt raw with tension. *Anchorage, so what's next?* she had to wonder. "Thanks for the ride," she told Burt, prolonging her exit from the vehicle.

"Do you have someone waiting for you?" he asked kindly. "It's a big town to be alone."

"I have a number of a doctor. I was told he might hire me to work in his office," Ellie replied, feeling obligated to explain. "Hopefully I'll find him."

"What's his name?" Burt asked. "I might know him."

"Ryan...Dr. Matt Ryan," Ellie replied, doubting their paths had crossed.

"Oh, of course, he's a bush pilot," Burt answered

with a smile. "Most people know all the bush pilots since we usually need one sooner or later."

"I have his address. Perhaps you can tell me how to get there," Ellie said, retrieving the business card from her purse and feeling pleased at such news.

"It's too far to walk so I'll take you," Burt offered after reading the card. "I won't be long."

"Oh *thank you*, that would be wonderful," Ellie said, feeling sure her legs wouldn't carry her even a short distance.

After Burt had exited the vehicle, Ellie laid her head back against the seat and closed her eyes. Despite her exhaustion and the very real chance Dr. Ryan would be off in his plane somewhere, Ellie tried to think positive. *I've come this far so I can't quit now,* she told herself.

Still, she felt very alone in the world. *No one knows where I am. Mother and Aunt Marie think I'm in Homer getting married to Rudy,* Ellie thought, feeling grateful to have escaped such a fate. *If this job doesn't work out, what then? Chad said his brother would help me find a job, but I have no training.*

A wave of despair washed over Ellie. Then, when thinking about the uncertainties facing her, she let down the wall she hid behind. To her, tears were a sign of weakness, yet here, alone and afraid, they fell unhindered.

By the time Burt returned to the truck, Ellie's tears had stopped. In their place was a tinge of hope that things would work out, somehow.

Since receiving Chad's call, regarding the young woman named Ellie, Lucy had felt excited. Several times she had offered a prayer for God's protection over the girl, wondering if she was the one they'd been waiting for.

When she learned Ellie's past seemed troubled in some way, Lucy hoped even more that she would call. In recent years, she'd felt a burden for troubled young women. Whether it was her motherly instinct or a calling from God, she only knew it was a profound longing.

Since Matt had promised Chad they'd stay close by the telephone in case Ellie called, Lucy stayed behind while her husband made his rounds to those needing supplies. This would also give her time to do some much needed paperwork and tidy up the office. Each time the telephone rang she hoped it was Ellie, yet, each time she felt disappointment.

It was nearly three o'clock that afternoon when she heard the familiar tingling of the bell, alerting her that someone had entered the front door. "I'll be right out," Lucy called as she filed one last report on a patient. A moment later she closed the filing cabinet and headed out front.

"May I help you?" she asked the young woman who stood just inside the door. It was then that Lucy noticed the tired and somewhat scared look on the girl's face. Then, she knew. "Are you Ellie?" she asked softly as she approached the visitor.

"Yes, but how did you know?"

"I've been expecting you, or at least your phone call," Lucy admitted, feeling overjoyed that she had arrived in person. "I'm so *happy* to see you." Reaching out her hand, Lucy grasped one of Ellie's and smiled. "Chad called about you. I'm Lucy and I'm so glad you've come."

"You are? I mean, I was wondering if Chad had *really* called you," Ellie said, looking somewhat surprised. "I should get my things. They're outside in the truck," she quickly added.

"Let me help," Lucy offered as Ellie opened the door. Just then a man was seen carrying two pieces of luggage toward them.

"I decided you must have found someone at home," he told Ellie as he sat the two rather seasoned suitcases on the ground.

"Thank you, Burt, for everything," Ellie told him. With a kind nod, the man turned and headed back toward his truck. "He drove me here from Homer."

It was obvious to Lucy that God was watching over Ellie. Certainly, she might have found plenty of men who weren't as kind. Many times they read or heard reports about a body of a young woman being found dead along the road. Sadly, most had been raped and murdered. The thought of anyone suffering such a fate sent chills up Lucy's spine. "Let's go in," she urged, taking Ellie's suitcases in hand.

Within minutes, Ellie was enjoying delicious sandwiches and hot tea. While she devoured everything in front of her, she scanned the neatly kept kitchen and found herself mesmerized by Lucy. Never before had she met such a kind and friendly person, and soon found herself envying everything about the lovely, dark-haired woman.

"I'm thrilled to have you here, Ellie," Lucy reiterated as she took a seat across the table from her. "We have plenty of room for you to stay here, even if you decide this isn't the type work you're looking for."

"I'm not sure you'll want *me*," Ellie replied, shaking her head. "Did Chad tell you I have *no* training for such work?"

"Yes, he did. But, *anyone* would need training, no matter who they are," Lucy answered kindly. "I'll teach you a little at a time; nothing complicated."

"Thank you for taking a chance on me," Ellie said, feeling at ease with the woman. "Chad said you were very nice and I can see that already. He was right about other things, too," she added, remembering his remark about Rudy.

Although she hadn't mentioned her disappointment in Homer or the obvious mistake she'd made, Ellie felt sure Chad had told his brother and Lucy about her planned marriage. Now, looking back, she wondered how she could have ever agreed to such a proposal. "I came to Alaska for a new life, and if you and Dr. Ryan are willing to give me a job, I promise I'll do my *very* best," Ellie vowed determinedly.

"What more can anyone ask?" Lucy replied, reaching out to pat Ellie's hand. "Now, let's get you settled in your room, shall we? I know you must be tired after all your travels," she added with a soft smile.

Leaving her seat, Ellie quickly gathered up her dirty dishes and took them to the sink, thinking what a pleasant task it would be to wash dishes in such a cheerful looking kitchen. "Thank you for the tea and sandwiches," she told Lucy. "And yes, I am a bit tired."

After insisting she carry Ellie's luggage, Lucy led the way up a flight of stairs. "This old house needed lots of work when we arrived, but Matt is real handy and loves to work with his hands," Lucy explained as they made their way. "He hired an electrician to rewire everything and a plumber, too, but he did everything else. And, I helped out here and there."

"It's very nice," Ellie remarked, knowing that was an understatement when comparing it to what she'd lived in all of her life.

"Here we are," Lucy said when they'd stepped inside the room.

A gasp of surprise came from Ellie as her hand flew to her mouth. "Oh, it's be*autiful!*" she blurted a second later. Slowly she turned, letting her eyes drift across the spacious pink and white room. Frilly white curtains hung at the double windows. A four-poster bed with a pink bedspread sat at one end of the room, flanked by two, white bedside tables. Each table held a small pink lamp and a dainty figurine. On the floor was a large braided-rug with varying shades of dark rose and lavender. Beneath it, Ellie noticed shiny wood floors.

The top half of the walls were painted white

while the bottom half was covered in wallpaper with delicate pink flowers. At the other end of the room was a white vanity dressing table with mirror and padded white bench; a matching chest-of-drawers sat nearby. A high-back rocking chair in dark wood completed the furnishings. Never, had Ellie dreamed of having such a lovely room to call her own.

"I'm so glad you like it," Lucy said having placed the suitcases on the floor. "Matt said I could decorate this room in my favorite color, so here it is."

"Blue is my favorite color," Ellie commented, unable to pull her eyes free of her surroundings. "But now seeing this, I think pink is."

"This is *your* room, Ellie, for as long as you want to stay," Lucy said.

When hearing this, Ellie felt overjoyed at her good fortune. Hours before, she'd had no idea of her future. But now, after meeting Lucy and seeing this lovely room, she felt renewed hope. "How can I ever thank you for all this?" she asked, meeting Lucy's eyes. "You have no idea what—" A sudden lump in her throat kept her from saying anymore.

"Oh, you dear, sweet girl," Lucy said softly, putting her arms around Ellie. "No matter what disappointments you've had in the past, from now on things will be different, you'll see."

CHAPTER EIGHT

After Ellie had unpacked her belongings, she took a hot bath. Unlike the last time, she had no reason to hurry. Instead, she lingered while the soothing aroma of lavender and chamomile coaxed the tension from her mind and body. Dreamingly, she envisioned her life filled with happiness and fun. No longer would she doubt her future.

Where would I be now if I hadn't met Chad? On the street, no doubt, Ellie decided, cringing at the thought. Once more, the face of the young detective appeared in her mind's eye. His lopsided grin, his piercing blue eyes and gentle manner brought a strange flutter to Ellie's insides. Then, when thinking about seeing him again in court when she testified, she wondered at the excitement she felt.

Because of her shameful secret about her abuse, Ellie made no close friends. The wall she hid behind assured her no one would ask questions regarding her family. Although loneliness was her constant companion, she felt it was better than the embarrassment she'd feel if anyone learned the truth. *Can I forget about all that now? No one here knows my past and I'm never going back! I'll pretend it never happened,* Ellie thought confidently.

While her new guest was upstairs getting settled, Lucy called Chad's office in Bellingham. Although he was out, she left a message with the secretary, informing him of Ellie's arrival.

As she made supper, Lucy thought about the days ahead. Somehow she sensed, as Chad did, Ellie was harboring deep hurt. *Dear Lord, give me the wisdom I need to help this girl. You know what she's been through and only you can heal her wounds,* Lucy silently prayed.

Due to the late hour and knowing Ellie was tired, Lucy suggested the two of them not wait for Matt's return. Minutes later, they were sitting down to meatloaf, scalloped potatoes, salad and hot rolls.

"Dear Lord, I thank you for this day and for bringing Ellie here safely. And thank you, too, for this food and bless it to our body. In Jesus' name, Amen," Lucy prayed. "Now, my dear, I'm sure you're wondering about things here, so I'll fill you in," she told Ellie. While they ate, Lucy told about the work she and Matt did and the joy it brought when helping people.

There would be plenty of time for deeper, more

revealing conversations, yet Lucy sensed Ellie had no desire to talk about her past.

————————

During the next few days, Lucy showed Ellie around town, acquainting her with the area and places of business she and Matt most often patronized. Each time they were out, Lucy surprised Ellie with something special. It was during their stop for lunch at the 'Silly Penguin,' a place known for its delicious hamburgers and chocolate malts, that Lucy gave Ellie her surprise. The first day it was a beautiful scarf; the next, a pair of shiny silver combs for her hair. Again, as they finished their lunch, Lucy handed Ellie a small box.

"Not another present!" Ellie said, looking surprised. "You've done *far* too much already, but thank you," she said smiling. Carefully, Ellie loosened the ribbon binding the square package. As she lifted the lid, her eyes widened in shock at what she saw.

"In case you want to write your friends and family back home," Lucy told her. "I wanted you to have something nice to write on."

"Oh, I've *never* had anything so lovely," Ellie gasped, taking a piece of the stationary in her hand. "My name is on it! And the envelopes match the paper...*and* a pen!" she wailed in dismay. "Where did you ever find it?"

"I ordered it and I couldn't wait for you to see it," Lucy admitted feeling overjoyed at Ellie's response. "And this goes with it," she added, retrieving a small address book from her purse. "You'll be making lots of new friends and this is for all those addresses and telephone numbers."

For a moment Ellie said nothing, instead she slowly fanned the pages of stationary as though they were delicate leaves. "Pink, blue, yellow, they're *all* so pretty," she said softly, meeting her gaze. "Thank you, Lucy."

"You're welcome. *Thank you.*"

"Thank me for what?" Ellie asked looking surprised. "I've done nothing."

"Oh yes, thank you for coming here," Lucy said. "You could have gone home when things didn't work out in Homer. But instead, you took Chad's offer to find us here, and we're *all* very glad you did."

"I would *never* have gone home!" Ellie blurted, shaking her head.

For the first time Lucy saw the obvious hurt Ellie was harboring. Not since her arrival had she talked about her family or why she had left them to marry a stranger. But now, after seeing this small crack in Ellie's stolid veneer, Lucy wanted more than ever to help this hurting young woman.

"I'm so sorry for what you've been through," Lucy said laying her hand on Ellie's. "No matter what happened in your past, I promise you, that is *not* what your life is supposed to be. God has a special purpose for all of us, including you, Ellie."

When hearing that, Ellie only stared back at her, seemingly in shock. "But, why would God want *me* for anything?" she then asked.

"Because he loves you," Lucy said choking back her tears at Ellie's obvious low self-esteem. "You are very special to him, Ellie. No matter what *anyone* has said or done to you, God *loves* you and will never *stop* loving you."

"How does God even *know* me? There are so many other people."

"God created us and knows *everything* about us. He knew us while we were being formed in our mothers' wombs, the Bible says," Lucy explained kindly. "We can't hide anything from him. He alone knows our deepest sorrows and *all* the unfair and terrible things that have happened to us. And, God will heal and comfort us if we'll let him," she concluded.

"I was never allowed to hear about God, except in anger," Ellie remarked. "We didn't go to church so I know *nothing* about such things."

"I'm sorry for that, but it's not too late," Lucy assured her. "Starting tomorrow, how about you and I having our own special Bible study? Later, down the road, perhaps we can invite other women to join us," she offered feeling excited. "Does that sound okay to you?"

"I'd like that," Ellie replied. "Thank you."

"I couldn't ask for a better student," Lucy said feeling pleased at the smile she saw on Ellie's face. "But right now, I think we'd better get going since Matt said he's bringing home a surprise tonight, for both of us. What do you suppose *that* might be?" she asked as she retrieved money and paid the bill.

"Maybe a dog or a kitten," Ellie offered cheerfully as they walked outside. "I can't imagine what else it would be."

"Me either, so I guess we'll just have to wait and see," Lucy remarked as they climbed inside her Jeep. *Thank you, Lord, for bringing Ellie into our lives*, she quickly prayed. *Help us give her the home she never had …*

Each day Lucy and Matt had noticed a definite change in Ellie's demeanor as they did everything they could to make her feel welcome. At first, Ellie seemed unsure of their sincerity, but now, as she spent time with her, Lucy felt overjoyed a their growing friendship. *I can't wait to see what a wonderful future is in store for her,* Lucy thought as they headed home.

It was hard for Ellie to contain her excitement as she ran upstairs to her room. Not only was she thrilled over her beautiful bedroom, but her newest possessions from Lucy only added to her happiness.

"I must write to Aunt Marie and Mother," she said softly as she admired the lovely pages of her stationary. "They'll be so surprised hearing where I am."

For a moment Ellie thought about how her life had changed. *I was coming here to get married! But now look at all this,* she cheered silently as her eyes drifted around the delicately furnished room. *Lucy said God has a special plan for my life. Is this it? Will I get to live here and learn everything I need to know about a doctor's office? I hope so, because I never want to leave here, not ever. I'll live with Matt and Lucy from now on.*

While Lucy thickened the gravy, Ellie sat the table with the usual three place settings. They expected Matt any minute and as usual, they'd have supper all ready by the time he walked in the door.

"Lucy, thank you for *everything*," Ellie blurted, setting a tray of pickles and olives on the table. "You don't know what this means, being able to live in a nice house, having nice things. I don't know *where* I'd be if I wasn't here with the two of you."

"Oh my dear, we're just thankful you and Chad met each other and he told you about us," Lucy replied, stirring the skillet of steaming brown-gravy. "I feel you were *meant* to be here with us and God orchestrated all of it."

"I couldn't agree more," Matt replied from the doorway, surprising both women. "It sure smells good in here! Oh, by the way, you better add another plate, we have company."

Just then, Chad appeared behind his brother. At seeing him, Ellie felt a sudden weakness in her legs and a flush on her face. This time he wasn't wearing a suit and tie, but rather a red form-fitting knit pull-over and blue-jeans. Unlike before, Chad's well-tone physique was easily noticed. His blond hair appeared longer and its natural curl was obvious to Ellie.

"I have to agree, it *does* smell mighty delicious.

Hello, ladies," he then greeted as his eyes met Ellie's.

"Chad, we expected a puppy!" Lucy teased as she hurried to give her brother-in-law a hug and kiss on the cheek. "But, I guess seeing Chad *is* better than a getting a dog or a kitten, wouldn't you agree, Ellie?"

"Oh *yes*, I mean, of course it is," Ellie stammered, trying to hide her excitement. "Hello, Chad. This *is* a surprise."

"Well, I couldn't very well pass up a chance to see such lovely ladies, now could I?" Chad replied with a grin. "Matt said he was heading my direction, so I took some time off and hitched a ride."

"You *mean* you get to stay a few days?" Lucy asked excitedly. "This calls for a celebration. My, aren't we *glad* we baked that chocolate cake today?" she said, winking at Ellie.

"Well *I'm* glad you did, since that's my favorite," Chad said, retrieving a black olive from the table and plopping it in his mouth.

"Well, let's get washed up, because *I'm* hungry," Matt told his brother. When the two men had left the kitchen, Ellie realized her heart was racing and she suddenly felt giddy.

He didn't come to see me, she chided herself. *He likes being with his brother and Lucy and it's been a while. So why am I getting all excited?* While trying to squelch her happiness, Ellie helped Lucy get supper on the table. Yet, she couldn't help wishing she had fixed her hair with the new silver combs as she had planned earlier.

As they all ate supper, Lucy couldn't help noticing the flush on Ellie's face each time Chad looked at her. *All the times we've invited him up for a visit he had an excuse, but now he's staying for several days? I do believe he's found a new reason for coming,* Lucy thought, grinning to herself.

"By the way, we have a court date," Chad said, spooning a second helping of salad and roast on his plate. "We got lucky and the venue isn't so crowded so we start in three weeks."

"Three weeks? You mean I'll need to be there *that* soon?" Ellie asked as her eyes widened in surprise. "How will I get there?"

"The state will take care of everything. Your plane-fare, hotel room, meals and they'll even give you a voucher in case you need a cab," Chad replied, meeting Ellie's gaze across the table. "Like I said before, you're our *only* witness and it's vital that you testify. Also, the victim's family is quite well-known around Bellingham, so *they'll* make sure your accommodations are top notch. They're already asking questions about you and if there is anything you need," he informed Ellie.

"They *are?* What kind of questions?" Ellie asked again in surprise.

"Oh, they want to make sure you have a place to stay and enough to eat, so you won't be tempted to sell out to one of Jack Barton's cronies. Sometimes, witnesses get scared and change their mind about testifying. Or, if they're having financial hardship and offered money, they take it. After all, this *is* a murder case and money talks."

"I've never heard of such things," Ellie remarked shaking her head. "You mean people *really* do that? They let a *murderer* go free because of money?"

"Oh yes, I'm afraid it happens quite often," Chad replied. With that remark, everyone grew silent. For Lucy, she saw the look of dismay on Ellie's face and wondered at her innocence.

She's obviously been through a lot of sadness in her young life, yet, she's naïve in many other ways, Lucy thought. "I *do* believe it's time for some of that cake," she said, breaking the silence. With that, Ellie jumped up and started clearing away the dirty dishes.

"I can help," Chad offered leaving his seat. When hearing that, Lucy was amazed at the change of attitude she saw in her brother-in-law. There was no doubt he was looking for ways to impress Ellie. And from the look on Ellie's face, she was taking it all in…

During coffee and dessert, Chad and Matt told Ellie about growing up near Jackson Hole, Wyoming. Their stories soon brought rounds of laughter as they teased each other about their boyish escapades. "One day I'm going back there," Chad confessed. "It'll always be one of my favorite spots on earth."

"Yes, those Teton Mountains are breathtaking," Matt said with a nod. "We had a chance to sell the homestead after Mother died, but there's no way we could do that. Our folks worked long and hard on that place. We lease out the land and pay someone to look after the house."

"Do you and Lucy visit it often?" Ellie then asked.

"Not recently, but it's time we make that trip again soon," Matt replied. "How about next summer, little brother?"

"You don't have to twist my arm, I'm ready!" Chad said, grinning.

Next, Matt told about his recent frightening encounter with a bull moose. "He put an end to our dig *that* day," he said. "We decided we could find Chickweed another time."

As they talked, Chad found himself watching Ellie. With intense interest, she listened, but said nothing. For Chad, he remembered his conversation with his brother earlier that afternoon. *They agree with me, Ellie is one sweet girl and Lucy does seem mighty attached to her, just like Matt said,* Chad thought, wondering at Ellie's past. *I could do a background check, but for what reason? I have no right poking around in her business. She's not a thief. On the contrary, her bravery helped nab a murderer. Because of her, Jack Barton will be put away for a very long time. No, when she's ready she'll confide in Lucy and that's good enough for me,* he decided, feeling increasing interest in this mysterious young woman.

"I think that's enough exciting reports for one evening," Matt said a few minutes later, winking at his wife. "Now, I'm sure you ladies would like us out of your hair so Chad and I'll go down and get the paint I ordered. Tomorrow, we start putting some color on this place," he said, slapping Chad on the back. "And your visit, little brother, has come at *just* the right time."

"We'll help, too," Lucy offered. "Just get us some new paintbrushes."

"Are you volunteering Ellie without her permission?" Matt teased, putting his arm around Lucy's shoulder. "Maybe she'd rather *not* sling a paintbrush."

"Oh no, I don't mind," Ellie quickly replied as she filled the sink with hot, soapy water. "I've never painted, but would like to learn."

"Okay, if everyone agrees, we'll get an early start in the morning and see just how much we can get done in the next two days," Matt told them. "Let's go, Chad." With that, Matt stepped out into the entryway.

"Thank you, ladies. Supper was great," Chad remarked before leaving. "I *do* envy that brother of mine, getting a home-cooked meal every night."

"It comes with marriage," Matt blurted, poking his head around the corner. "It's high time you start thinking along those lines if *you* want home cooking on a regular basis."

Although he laughed at his brother's remark, Chad had to admit marriage didn't sound so farfetched to him now that his training was over and he had a good job. No longer was his nose in a book learning about the criminal mind or studying for exams. "I guess you're right," he said grinning, as he looked Ellie's direction.

———————

Known for its long summer days, Alaska had nearly nineteen hours of daylight by late June. Although it was hard getting used to at first, Matt and Lucy now appreciated the extra time for doing jobs, like painting. As he and Chad headed toward the hardware store to get the paint, Matt glanced at his brother.

"My, you seem quite smitten with our Miss Ellie," he remarked, having observed Chad's attentiveness toward her.

"She's very nice. I do like her," Chad replied. "I think she's carrying a heavy burden though *and* I doubt any of us will be privy to it anytime soon."

"Lucy thinks so too," Matt said, "but I disagree. If we keep showing her love and support, she'll open up. I'm sure whatever she's dealing with will have to surface before long."

"I hope so," Chad answered. "She's a *real* gem."

When hearing that, Matt was convinced his brother had more than a passing interest in Ellie. "Next week, Lucy will start training her around the office. They'll take it slow and start out with filing and other easy projects. We don't want to overwhelm her in any way."

"And, with the trial starting in three weeks, I'm sure Ellie will be nervous about that, too," Chad remarked. "It's good if Lucy goes easy."

As they silently rode, Matt again felt grateful

for Ellie being in their lives. Not only did it fulfill Lucy's desire to help young women, but losing her sister four years earlier had left a void that perhaps Ellie could fill.

———————————

As Lucy and Ellie finished up the supper dishes, they said little about Chad. For Ellie, she wanted only to think about the way he looked at her and the way it made her feel. Privately, she would dwell on her growing attraction to him, yet, feeling sure she would never be more than a friend to Chad.

"I'm so pleased Chad came to visit," Lucy remarked as she finished drying the last kettle. "We see so little of him and he never spends more than one night, so this *is* a treat."

"It's probably because he has more time now," Ellie replied, wiping off the counter. "He's obviously been busy with training."

"His training ended six months ago, so that's not it," Lucy refuted. "No, I'm sure *you* have something to do with it." When hearing this, Ellie felt a flush on her face and quick flutter of excitement wash over her.

"Yes, he's concerned about the trial, I'm sure," Ellie answered, not daring to think it could be anything more. "They're making sure I'll still testify against that horrible man."

"Perhaps, but I choose to think differently," Lucy said smiling. "Are you concerned about that, I mean the trial and all?"

"A little, I guess," Ellie said truthfully. "I've never

been in court before or had to talk in front of people. I wish *you* could come with me," she blurted out without forethought. "I'm sorry, Lucy, I know that's not possible with all you have to do," she hurriedly apologized. "I'll be okay."

For a moment Lucy said nothing, but a smile touched her face. "I'm honored that you would want me with you, Ellie. And, you know what, it might work out. I'll do *anything* to help you, no matter what it is," Lucy said solemnly. "I hope you know you can tell me anything, sweetie. Whatever your fears or concerns may be, I'm always here. And, if you need me during the trial, I'll do my *very* best to be in that courtroom," she concluded.

When hearing Lucy's kind words, Ellie suddenly wanted to tell her everything. She wanted to reveal her feelings for Chad, her insecurities about so many things, and yes, even the abuse. Yet, just as quickly, that wall of secrecy was there, preventing such personal revelations.

"Thanks, Lucy, I know you will. I think I'll go up to my room now and write some letters. Please tell Chad and Matt goodnight for me, okay?"

"Of course, dear, and you have a good night, too," Lucy told her. With that, Ellie turned and left the kitchen. Somehow, she knew she had to get her mind off Chad, and perhaps writing to Aunt Marie and her mother would help.

CHAPTER NINE

Writing the letter to her mother and aunt proved difficult for Ellie since her thoughts weren't far from Chad. As she jotted down her news, she would wistfully remember the man's intriguing eyes and sweet smile and how he looked at her that evening.

I've got to quit thinking about him! Ellie scolded herself. *He's handsome, smart and successful. I'm just a farm girl, plain and uneducated. Certainly nothing he'd be interested in.* "I wish he hadn't come," she muttered, rereading her letter.

Dear Mother and Aunt Marie,

I am sorry for the delay in writing, as I'm sure you've been wondering about my arrival and marriage to Rudy. I am not married to him, nor ever will be. He is far different than the magazine boasted. However, I am living with a wonderful doctor and his wife in Anchorage. They have opened up their beautiful home to me and I will be learning office work. How I arrived here is quite surprising and details are far too lengthy to explain on paper.

Dr. Matthew Ryan and his wife, Lucy, are most generous and caring toward everyone they meet. They say I can stay here as long as I want. I have a beautiful pink and white bedroom with lovely furnishings.

Chad Ryan, Matt's brother, is a detective. He comes for visits sometimes and is also very nice.

I miss you both and I hope this finds you doing well. I am very happy here as Matt and Lucy shower me with daily kindness. I look forward to hearing from you.

With Love, Ellie

If only I could say more about Chad, she sighed, folding the letter. *But what would it be? That he's handsome, smart and witty? No, I can't brag about him or they'll know I have a crush on him,* she decided.

For Ellie, she had never had a boyfriend or been interested in one. She knew having a close friend, boy or girl, would lead to those intimate conversations of sharing. She knew that's what close friends do. But for her, she'd risk no such relationship. Yet, as the days passed, she wanted to confide in Lucy. After all, she was kind and loving, much like Aunt Marie.

As she addressed the envelope, Ellie thought about the days ahead. She wondered about the trial and its outcome, but mostly, she thought about Chad and how much she liked being around him.

———————————

The next morning, after a hardy breakfast, the four began the chore of painting the large structure which wasn't only a home, but also a spacious office used for treating patients. Dressed in old clothes, each had a bucket of paint and a newly purchased paintbrush.

"Okay ladies, if you'll do the window frames, Chad and I'll start on the gables," Matt said motioning upward. "Let's get started," he urged as he and Chad climbed up the scaffolding.

This was the first time Ellie would be exposed to painting. After all, Morton Cooper thought such extravagance was only a waste of money which meant all farm buildings, including the house where they lived, consisted of rough brown boards. As for the interior walls, they, too, wore a drab, grayish color that only added to the depressed environment. For Ellie, experiencing the beautiful room that was now hers, she wanted more than ever to rescue her mother from the prison she called home.

———————————

For Ellie, their day of painting was one of the most enjoyable times she could remember. Not only was she helping transform the house from a dirty tan color to a soft buttercup yellow, but she heard Chad's voice, his laughter and often his gaze was on her. That, most of all, brought a feeling of elation to Ellie as she carefully spread the thick, smooth paint around the windows.

"You're doing a mighty fine job, Ellie. Are you *sure* you've never done this before?" Chad asked as he scanned the window frame she just finished.

"I'm sure, but Lucy's a very good teacher," Ellie replied, feeling the usual flush on her face. "I think painting is fun."

"And we're glad to have your help," Matt said as he joined them on the ground. "Now, how about letting me take you all out for a nice steak supper? I think you ladies need a night out of the kitchen."

"I think that's a *splendid* idea," Lucy remarked, pulling the kerchief from around her head. "Don't you think so, Ellie?" With a nod and smile, Ellie had to agree she, too, would appreciate an evening of no cooking and doing dishes.

An hour later everyone had cleaned their paint-stained hands, taken a shower and was ready to go. "That's a big step," Chad told Ellie, helping her inside Matt's Suburban.

"Thank you," Ellie said, feeling lingering warmth from his touch. With her seated, Chad then closed the door and hurried around to climb in beside her. Matt did the same for Lucy before getting behind the steering wheel. The sweet smelling aroma of men's aftershave soon filled the inside of the vehicle.

What gentlemen, Ellie thought to herself, realizing how different these men were from any she'd been around.

Small talk ensued between the others, but for

Ellie, she only wondered at the strange new feelings she was experiencing from spending time around Chad.

***

As was usual for a Friday night, Anchorage had its abundance of rowdy men looking for a good time. Although the Northern Lights Steak House was known for its quiet ambience and good food, the lounge next door had its share of drunken brawls among its patrons. Tonight was no different.

Shortly after the Ryan party was seated at a table near the fireplace, two other couples entered the restaurant. Despite the dim light obscuring their faces, their boisterous comments were soon a concern for the proprietor of the upscale eatery. It was obvious he wanted to curtail any further outbursts before escorting them to a table.

With Matt and Chad nearby, Ellie felt completely safe despite being aware of the stares aimed in their direction. Keeping her eyes lowered as the newcomers passed by their table, Ellie was shocked to hear a familiar voice.

"Well, would ya look whose here; if it ain't Miss Ellie Know-it-all!" Rudy bellowed out as he stopped near their table.

At hearing the remark, Chad was instantly on his feet. "I'd advise you not to say another word," he warned, glaring down at Rudy who stood several inches shorter. "Now be on your way."

"My, oh my, so she's found *another* sucker to take care of her, huh?" Rudy slurred as he looked from

Ellie back to Chad. "I just might have her arrested, for fraud, since she bilked me out my hard-earned cash."

"And, perhaps she'll sue *you* for false advertising," Chad hurriedly remarked, leaning his face within inches of Rudy's. "Do *you* have a lawyer?"

When hearing that, Rudy took a step back as his bloodshot eyes strayed across the faces at the table. Then, with no further remark, he staggered off to join his friends.

While watching the scene unfold, Ellie felt a roller coaster of emotion. One minute she was embarrassed for being the object of such a confrontation, and in the next, she was overjoyed for the way Chad stood up for her.

"I'm sorry, Ellie. This shouldn't have happened," Chad told her, laying his hand on hers. "That kind of scum never knows when to stop."

"Are you okay?" Lucy asked, studying Ellie's face. "We can leave if this is too uncomfortable for you."

"Oh no, please. I'm fine, really," Ellie replied, refusing to let Rudy Davis ruin another minute of her life. "Thank you, Chad, for what you did."

"Anything for you, Ellie," he said, smiling at her. For a moment longer his eyes were on Ellie's face. Then he spoke. "Are we ready to order? I'm famished." Only then did he remove his hand from Ellie's.

At Rudy's table loud outbursts of vulgar language were heard. Once more the proprietor warned them to quiet down, yet, within minutes, they were all asked to leave. It was hard for Ellie to contain her joy when seeing Rudy got what he so deserved.

Soon the waiter took their orders, and twenty minutes later sizzling hot steaks with baked potatoes, corn, salads and hot rolls were served. Everything was delicious, especially when accompanied with the lighthearted conversation.

For Ellie, the day had gotten better and better. *It's this wonderful food, the warm fire and being included in all this,* Ellie decided, wishing the evening would never end. *It's because of Chad and you know it,* her thoughts suddenly blared. For the first time, Ellie had to wonder if this was what love felt like.

On Saturday, the painting was finished, except the back porch. "You get more paint and I'll do this next week," Lucy told Matt.

"That I can do, my pet," he replied, putting his arm around his wife's shoulder. With that, he quickly dabbed his paintbrush on Lucy's nose, causing a round of laughter to erupt from everyone.

Feigning her anger, Lucy chased Matt around the yard with her paintbrush in hand. "I'll get you back!" she teased, "I'll starch your underwear!"

As she watched, Ellie couldn't help but envy the obvious love between Matt and Lucy. *I hope I have such a marriage one day,* she thought, glancing at Chad. *You might as well forget that one,* Ellie quickly decided.

Sunday meant church for everyone, unless Matt was called away on an emergency. Today, because Chad would be joining them, Ellie wanted Lucy's advice on what to wear. "This one is lovely and I don't remember seeing it," she told Ellie, removing an outfit from the closet.

"Mother made that for when I married Rudy," Ellie explained, knowing there was little chance of it now being used for such a purpose.

"Please try it on," Lucy urged, removing the light-weight jacket and dress from its hanger. Made of beige colored linen, the long sleeve, high-neckline dress was trimmed in lace with delicate eyelets. Its fitted pattern accentuated Ellie's figure; certainly, it was far different than her usual attire.

"You're *beautiful*," Lucy cheered as Ellie donned the matching waist-length jacket to complete the outfit. "Oh my dear, you look stunning, and I can't think of a better time to wear it," she said excitedly. "No doubt, *all* eyes will be on you today." Smiling, Lucy left the room.

Now alone, Ellie stepped in front of her mirror for the first time. Not since the day her mother finished the dress had she put it on. Removing her glasses, Ellie then pulled her hair back and held it. For a moment, she studied the image looking back at her.

A feeling of gratitude washed over Ellie for having inherited her mother's smooth olive complexion. *Not so bad I guess; I could have Morton's ugly face with his deep pitted scars and beady eyes.*

Pushing memories of her dad from her mind,

Ellie leaned close to the mirror. *Brown eyes, thick dark lashes, arched eyebrows. Aunt Marie says I look like my maternal grandmother. I wish I could have known her,* she sighed, feeling somewhat sad for having so few living relatives.

For the next few minutes, Ellie brushed her hair and then carefully placed the silver combs. *Why am I doing all this? Chad certainly doesn't notice what clothes I wear,* Ellie decided before heading downstairs.

However, when arriving in the kitchen, Ellie was not prepared for the whistles and cheers that suddenly erupted. "A princess has been unveiled," Matt announced as he draped his arm over Lucy's shoulder.

"Yes, and a *beautiful* one at that," Chad whispered as he slowly left his seat and stood, looking at Ellie. "You *must* be Cinderella or I'm dreaming," he added, sitting his coffee cup on the table.

A blush came to Ellie's face. When hearing Chad's words of praise, she *felt* like a princess and quickly decided she was wrong about Chad not noticing her attire.

Monday arrived far too soon, especially for Ellie. When dressing that morning, she put on her best pair of blue jeans and a baggy white sweater. Other than the dress she wore yesterday and some long skirts, her entire wardrobe consisted of loosely-fitted clothes.

Somehow, Chad's flattering remarks had caused

Ellie to rethink her years-long vow to hide behind over-sized apparel. Yet today, there were no such comments and for Ellie yesterday was just a dream.

"It's been fun, ladies," Chad remarked as they finished breakfast. "And I'll see *you* in three weeks. Do you have any questions about the trial?"

"How will I know where to go?" she asked, already wishing the ordeal was over. "Do I have to see that awful man again?"

"Someone from the prosecutor's office will contact you and I'll pick you up at the airport. And yes, Jack Barton will be in court, too, but I'll be right there beside you," Chad assured her. "So there's no need to worry."

"Ellie has asked me to accompany her to the trial and if at all possible I'll be there," Lucy told Chad. "I'm sure she'll do just fine, but a friendly face in the crowd might help ease her uncertainties a bit."

"Like I said, I'll be right there," Chad reiterated as his gaze rested on Ellie's face. "I won't leave her for a minute."

"Are we ready?" Matt asked, entering the room. "Time to get going; too bad it's the first day of training, otherwise you ladies could come along."

"That's okay, we'll go when there's time for shopping," Lucy replied. "You two have a safe flight," she added throwing her arms around her husband's neck for one last kiss.

It was then that Chad looked at Ellie and smiled. "Take care, and don't be afraid of all that medical jargon," he advised. "You'll do just fine," he added softly as his gaze lingered on her face. "Anyway, it won't be forever."

Once again, Chad's words brought a flutter of excitement. *How does he do this to me?* Ellie lamented, lowering her eyes.

"We'll keep supper hot, but let us know if you'll be very late," Lucy told Matt. "And you be sure and do this again, real soon," she told Chad giving him a hug. "Ellie and I are always glad when handsome men show up," she teased.

"I'll soon have my pilot's license, and when I get my own plane, I'll be here so much you'll get tired of me," Chad said teasingly, returning the embrace.

In a matter of minutes the two men were gone, but for Ellie, Chad's remarks echoed through her mind. *Is he teasing or does he really plan on being here more?* Right then, she could only wonder how to keep her heart from making a fool out of her whenever Chad was around...

It was nine o'clock that morning when Lucy and Ellie entered the office to start their day of training. Although Matt was normally out of the office on Mondays, unless grounded by bad weather, their patients knew Lucy was there to handle minor ailments. Lucy hoped for a quiet day to devote to Ellie.

"First I'll show you where things are kept," Lucy said going to the large supply cabinet. "Everything for the office is in here: pens, paper, staples and folders for new patients, whatever you'll need. And on this side, we keep the examining room's supplies along with linens, small blankets and such."

Step by step Lucy explained how to make charts for new patients and where they were filed. "Everything regarding the patient is kept in their file; reports, insurance information, office visits; anything with their name on it."

While she explained, Lucy noticed how Ellie listened intently, nodding her head but saying nothing. "Do you have any questions?" Lucy finally asked.

"Oh no, so far I understand," Ellie replied. "I think I'm going to like this."

By the time they stopped for lunch, Ellie was familiar with the office and where all supplies were stored. When Lucy had her make a mock file for a patient, they both cheered when she did it exactly right.

"You're a fast learner!" Lucy raved, patting Ellie on the back. "After lunch we'll use this," she said, removing the cover from a typewriter.

Suddenly, Ellie remembered the 'special favor' she had to do for her dad before he allowed her to take typing class in high school. The usual wave of nausea swept over her again as she thought about that repulsive act. Yet, her vow to escape to a better life drove her to comply with his despicable demands.

Each time he forced himself on Ellie it heightened her feeling of hate. Now, as she stared at the new Smith Corona typewriter, she felt a hint of reward for the anguish she had suffered.

"Do you know *how* to type?" Lucy asked looking at Ellie.

"Yes, yes I do," Ellie said. "I love typing but I've never had a typewriter to use, not since high school. This is wonderful," she added softly, running her fingers over the keys.

"You can use this anytime, Ellie. It's not just for office use, so if you'd like to write personal letters, you feel free," Lucy told her.

"You mean it?" Ellie spouted feeling overjoyed at such a privilege.

"Of course, sweetie. Just to let you know, I'm hinting to Matt that one of those new electric ones would be great as soon as they're available. Now, we can both *suggest*," Lucy teased as they giggled like school girls.

For Ellie, she felt excited despite her emotional upheaval regarding Chad. "I believe I *can* learn this job," she said, nodding her head. "Thank you for giving me this chance." With that Ellie threw her arms around Lucy's neck.

The afternoon flew by while Ellie typed labels and addressed envelopes for Lucy. She was nearly finished with her last envelope when she heard someone enter the front door. Lucy was sitting at Matt's desk.

"Help...please, is anyone here?" a male voice yelled. "We need help."

With that Ellie and Lucy both jumped to their feet. "Yes, we're here," Lucy said as she rounded the corner of the waiting room. What is it?"

"It's the baby!" the man gasped frantically. "It isn't due yet. Can you stop it from coming?"

"Well, babies have their own timetable sometimes, but we'll see what we can do," Lucy assured the young looking man. "Ellie, let's get her into one of the rooms." Quickly, Ellie took hold of the woman's right arm while Lucy took the left. "Don't worry, dear, it's going to be all right. We're here to help you."

Then, Lucy's last words registered in Ellie's mind. *We're here to help? What do I know about babies?* Ellie thought frantically.

Within seconds, they had the petite young woman in one of the examining rooms and up on the table. "While I'm checking things out, Ellie, you go get that young man some coffee, okay? I'm sure he could use it," Lucy said calmly. "I'll be out to see him shortly," she added.

With a nod Ellie left the room and headed for the kitchen. Quickly, she filled a cup with the dark steamy liquid. "I brought you some coffee," she said, offering the cup to the rather frazzled looking man. "Do you take cream or sugar?"

"No, black is fine, thanks," he said reaching for it. "How's my wife?"

"Lucy will be right out to talk to you," Ellie replied, taking a seat across the room. "She's a very good nurse and I'm sure everything will be just fine," she added confidently. "Do you live nearby?"

"No…yes…well, I mean, we just moved here," he stammered. "The baby isn't due for three weeks. I have a new job, but I don't start till next week. We were unpacking when Julie's pains started. I sure hope she'll be all right."

"I'm sure things—"

"Ellie, I'll need your help," Lucy said as she entered the waiting room. "Now, Mr.—?"

"Reynolds…Josh Reynolds," the man replied, getting to his feet. "Is Julie okay?"

"She's doing fine, Mr. Reynolds, but I'm afraid your baby is a little anxious to make his or her appearance," Lucy said hastily. "There's no time to get her to the hospital, so we'll make due right here. Ellie, come with me."

As she hurried after Lucy, Ellie's mind began to fill with the many births she witnessed on the farm. On one occasion she remembered watching the veterinarian help her favorite milk cow give birth to her first calf. Finally, the long night ended successfully, but if not for the vet's help, Ellie doubted whether the cow or calf would have survived.

But now, she was about to help deliver a human baby. *This is far from being an office girl!* Ellie thought as they reached the examining room.

It was obvious this small room would soon hear the cries of a newborn. "You're doing great, Julie," Lucy told her patient. "You keep pushing like that and this will be over in no time."

At that moment Ellie heard the painful exertion

that accompanies any birth. Whether it was cattle, horses or dogs—the distress was all the same.

Despite being nervous, Ellie felt the usual excitement of such an event. Intently, she followed Lucy's instructions and soon gathered the required items from the supply cabinet. "Very good, Ellie, and now I need you to stand by with that blanket. This little one is *about* to make an entrance. Okay, sweetie, one last push," Lucy coaxed.

With a moan, the young woman gritted her teeth against the pain and did as Lucy said. A thrill washed over Ellie. "What a miracle!" she whispered as the baby was delivered. Seconds later came the baby's robust wail.

"It's a girl!" Lucy said as she wrapped the baby in the blanket. Then, she laid the newborn on Julie's stomach. "Go make the announcement, Ellie, while I finish up."

For no apparent reason, Ellie's eyes clouded with tears as she headed for the waiting room. For the first time she had to wonder about the future. *Will I ever get married and experience motherhood?* Right now, it was hard to imagine her life ever being that settled…

CHAPTER TEN

With news of a baby being delivered in Dr. Ryan's office, many stopped by to congratulate Lucy. The next day local newspapers wanted pictures and an interview. "I had help," Lucy told the reporters. "This young lady, Ellie Cooper, helped me out and by God's grace we had no complications."

Questions were then directed at Ellie, regarding her relationship to Dr. Ryan and his wife. "They've become wonderful friends and have offered me a job working in their office," Ellie told the three who sat taking notes. As she spoke, Ellie saw bright flashes of light from the two cameras aimed at her.

"Where's your home?" one of the men asked, taking Ellie by surprise.

"Here, my home is here," she replied without forethought.

"Where did you live before coming here?" another asked.

"I'm from Kansas," Ellie replied, "but I won't be going back." With that, Ellie looked at Lucy for support.

"Gentlemen, I'm afraid we *do* have an office to run, but we appreciate your interest," Lucy told them kindly. "Have a wonderful afternoon."

With that announcement, the men quickly gathered their notes and cameras and after a nod of thanks were soon gone. "My, they are inquisitive," Ellie remarked, shaking her head.

"Yes, but I suppose this *is* refreshing after all the terrible things they have to report about people," Lucy replied.

When the newspapers came out, it brought another wave of interest. Chad, too, called with his words of praise. "You *are* cool under pressure—we know that from the ferry experience," Chad told her that afternoon.

"Thank you, but in this case, I'm glad Lucy was around," Ellie replied.

"Besides deliver babies and give interviews, what *else* do you two lovely ladies spend your time doing?" he said with a smile in his voice.

"We work, visit *and* she's teaching me the Bible," Ellie boasted. "I'm afraid I'm a beginner in that too, since I never went to church. I have *lots* of questions, but Lucy is very patient with me."

"I'm real happy to hear that, Ellie," Chad said, sounding serious. "That's the most important Book any of us can read. I didn't always think that, but I learned the hard way. That's a long story we'll cover some other time," he quickly added. "I look forward to seeing you soon, Ellie."

"Me too," she replied as the call ended. As she sat holding the receiver, Ellie felt the usual excitement. *He's only a friend so why do I feel this way?*

———————————

Due to the publicity of delivering a baby and Ellie's training, the painting of the back porch had been delayed. But today, while Matt was out gathering herbal medicine, Ellie and Lucy decided to get it done.

The day was clear with no threat of rain, so after an early breakfast they began. "I'll do up along the eaves," Lucy told Ellie, climbing the ladder.

No matter what type of work they did, the two enjoyed doing it together. Today was no different and in no time they were engrossed in their project. Despite the strong smell and occasional smear of paint, they were having fun as they exchanged light conversation.

Then, as she turned to dip her paintbrush, Lucy's paint bucket toppled from where it sat. "No!" she yelled in horror as she watched it plummet toward the ground *and* Ellie who knelt beneath her, painting the trim.

With a thud, the bucket landed on Ellie's right shoulder, knocking her off her feet as a wave of yellow paint drenched her. "Dear God, what have I done?" Lucy yelled scrambling off the ladder. "Oh Ellie, I'm so sorry! So *very* sorry!" she wailed, kneeling down beside her. "Lord, let her be all right!" she pleaded, seeing Ellie lying motionless and her broken glasses on the ground. Then, grabbing a clean rag, Lucy began wiping paint from Ellie's face.

"Oh, sweetie, I can't *believe* I did this to you!" Lucy cried with remorse as Ellie sat up with a moan. Paint was everywhere: on Ellie's face, clothes and dripping from her hair.

"I'm okay, just a little...*yellow*," Ellie remarked, wiping paint from her eyelids. Seconds later, Ellie reached out and smeared paint on Lucy. With that, all seriousness disappeared amid a round of laughter.

After a shower and two more hours of trying to get paint out of her hair, Ellie gave up. "It's time to get it cut," she told Lucy, lifting her sticky locks between her fingers. "There's just too much."

"I'm sorry," Lucy lamented once more. "I can't believe I'm responsible for this!"

"Oh Lucy, accidents happen," Ellie said kindly. "I don't blame you; *I* might have been the one on that ladder."

"Thank you for being so gracious. I promise I'll get you new glasses, new clothes and your hair fixed anyway you want it," Lucy vowed.

A short time later, the two women were headed for Marco's Cut & Curl. The painting of the back porch would have to wait until another day.

This was Ellie's first trip to a *real* beauty shop. As a child her mother had cut her hair, but as she grew older, Ellie refused even a trim.

As they stepped inside the door a strong pungent odor greeted them, stinging Ellie's eyes. "It's a permanent wave," Lucy whispered.

Several women were getting their hair fixed, one sat waiting. "Don't you worry, I can fix this up for you," a woman named Frieda assured Ellie after seeing her paint-streaked hair. "It'll be just a few more minutes."

While she waited, Ellie glanced through the newest hair-style magazines, deciding on what she wanted. "Would this look good on me?" she asked Lucy who sat beside her.

"My dear, with that face, you'd look *good* in anything," Lucy replied, bringing a warm feeling to Ellie. "I can't believe what a lovely face was hiding behind those glasses!"

"Thank you, but I've never thought of myself as pretty, in *any* way," Ellie confessed, thinking of all the humiliating names aimed at her.

"Okay, Ellie, let's get started," Frieda said a little while later.

"I think this is what I'd like," Ellie said, showing Frieda the style she selected. Then, after taking the chair in front of the large mirror, Ellie closed her eyes to await the end result.

Seconds later, she heard the scissors and felt her hair being cut, but was unaware of those coming or going, and who was watching.

What if I don't like it? How long till it grows out? I'll

wear my tam or a scarf, Ellie decided, feeling confident she could somehow disguise this mishap.

While she waited, Ellie heard voices around her, yet she refused to look. She heard comments about her thick hair; some praised Frieda for the job she was doing. Still, Ellie sat quietly fearing her new hairdo.

"Okay, dear, I think we got it," Frieda said much later. "Is this what you had in mind?"

Taking a deep breath, Ellie slowly opened her eyes and looked in the mirror. For a moment she could only stare at the image she saw. In disbelief she leaned closer, feeling sure they had somehow tricked her. *This isn't me!* Ellie thought, seeing that one staring back at her.

"I love it!" Lucy blurted as she approached. "You're gorgeous!"

"Yes, indeed," a male voice commented, "Hollywood *must* be missing one of their starlets," he went on. When looking around, Ellie saw a handsome, well-dressed man resting his arm casually on the reception desk. For a brief moment his eyes bore into hers. Quickly, she took note of the silver at his temples; otherwise, his hair looked dark and wavy.

"Thank you, everyone," Ellie said, feeling embarrassed for being the focus of attention. "And yes, I do like it, *very* much." Before Frieda could remove the cape from around Ellie's shoulders, the stranger approached.

"Hello, Miss Cooper," he said politely, surprising Ellie. "I read your name on the scheduling book, if you're wondering," he quickly added. "My name is Marco De Ville. I *must* tell you how pleased I am that you allowed us to attend to your needs," the man said with a slight Spanish accent. "Because of your misfortune with yellow paint, my dear, there'll be *no* charge. And I'll be giving you a nice tip for doing such a *fine* job for this young lady, Miss Frieda."

Again, Ellie was too stunned to speak. "How truly kind of you," Lucy told the man. "But the whole thing was *my* fault, so I really—"

"Nonsense," Marco interrupted, "I insist. For how often does a man have the pleasure of seeing the unveiling of a lovely butterfly?" he whispered as he lightly touched Ellie's hair. "Again, Miss Cooper, it has been a great pleasure, I assure you. I *do* hope I see you again."

No one spoke as Marco gave a polite nod and smile before he turned and walked away. A hush hung over the room as glances were exchanged between the few who'd witnessed Marco's surprising reaction to his newest patron.

How can getting my hair cut cause all this? Ellie wondered, feeling a strange surge of excitement at studying her image in the mirror.

Then, still pondering her feelings, Ellie quickly gathered her purse and jacket. "I have to agree with Marco, your transformation *is* quite amazing," a somewhat familiar voice remarked.

Ellie froze. There, in a nearby chair sat Carla, looking at her. Instant memories of that night in Homer filled her mind. That horrible night Ellie had learned how young women sell their bodies for money.

Sudden nausea rose up in her throat as she hurriedly left the shop. Once outside she gasped for fresh air, remembering the vile acts forced on her. *Is there no place I can go where I'm not reminded?*

"Sweetie, are you okay?" Lucy asked, putting her arm around Ellie's shoulder when she'd joined her outside.

"No, I feel sick," Ellie said truthfully. "Let's go home, please."

———————————

As they headed for home, Lucy felt puzzled over Ellie's sudden change of demeanor. "I'm afraid all those paint fumes were too much," she said, noticing her pallor. "I'm so sorry. What can I *possibly* do to make this up to you?"

"Oh Lucy, it's not you. Please, you *must* believe me," Ellie begged. "There is so much you don't know, but I guess I'm ready to tell you now."

There was a tone of sadness in Ellie's voice Lucy had never heard before. *Will she finally let down that wall? Is she ready to share what has hurt her so badly? Dear Lord, please help her, let her know how much she's loved,* Lucy quickly prayed. "When we get home, I'll make us some tea and then we'll talk, okay?"

"That sounds good," Ellie replied as she rested her head against the seat. "I *do* owe you an explanation of why I ended up here."

Nothing else was said as they rode, yet Lucy felt tears stinging her eyes. *How quickly our plans change.*

Lord, I'm so glad you're in control of things, and nothing surprises you!

For Lucy, she had learned four years earlier how fragile life was. Yet, she had no fear of the unknown, not anymore. She knew beyond any doubt, God would see her through any crisis, even unto death.

———————

Thirty minutes later, Ellie and Lucy were seated at the kitchen table. The spicy sweetness of Cinnamon tea drifted from the blue, porcelain teapot that sat between them. "I've kept things from you," Ellie began, taking a deep breath. "If Chad had known, he would have run the other direction instead of telling me about this job."

"Chad isn't like most men," Lucy said, adding lemon to her tea. "He looks for honesty and trustworthiness in people. He saw that in you, Ellie. Despite the many hardships you encountered while traveling here, you insisted on going through with your arrangement with Rudy Davis. *Whatever* you've done or been through, no one in this family will ever judge you."

For the first time Ellie was ready to tell Lucy everything. The dirty secrets she carried had become too heavy to carry alone. *Perhaps, if I tell her, I can finally put them behind me,* she decided, taking a deep breath.

"It *is* time I tell someone," she whispered, biting back her tears. "Since I was six, my dad, Morton Cooper, made me do things. They were horrible and disgusting, and if I refused he whipped me until I gave in. He threatened to hurt me *and* Mother if I told anyone. I hate him, Lucy, I *really* hate him!" she yelled as she began sobbing in anguish.

"Oh sweetheart, I'm *so* sorry," Lucy wailed, leaving her seat. In the next moment, she had wrapped her arms around Ellie, comforting her as she cried. "No one will ever hurt you like that again. Let it go, sweetie. It's time to let it all out," Lucy urged softly.

After hearing Ellie's admission of abuse, Lucy felt sick to her stomach. Sick for what Ellie had suffered *and* for the guilt she obviously felt. "This is not your fault," Lucy told her. "Please remember, you are the *victim* of a perverted, sick human being. Thank God you got away from him."

"Thanks to Aunt Marie," Ellie said wiping her eyes. "She figured it out and rescued me. She threatened to have Morton arrested if he didn't let me leave with her."

"And your Mother, did *she* stay with him?" Lucy then asked.

"She was devastated, but yes, she stayed. Mother is crippled and felt she couldn't make it on her own," Ellie explained sadly. "Aunt Marie wanted her to come and live with her, but Mother wouldn't think of imposing on her sister. One day, *I* want to take care of Mother and get her away from that man!"

As she listened, Lucy saw the pain on Ellie's face as she talked about leaving her mother to fend for herself. *I wish I could do something to help that poor woman, but right now it's Ellie I must help,* Lucy reasoned, knowing the long-term affects of living through such trauma.

"You've taken the first step toward healing, sweetie, by talking about this. And there *is* something more you can do. May I suggest you try what worked for me?" Lucy gently asked.

"Certainly," Ellie said, looking puzzled. "What is it?"

"When you're ready, start writing down your feelings on paper. Pretend you're writing to your dad. Tell him *everything* you ever wanted to say. How he made you feel; how he stole your childhood. I don't know why, but when we do this it somehow releases all that anger inside us and promotes healing."

"How do *you* know this?" Ellie questioned, frowning.

"I did it once, too, when my sister died," Lucy told her, remembering the pain four years earlier.

"Oh, I'm *sorry*. What happened?" Ellie asked in obvious surprise.

"She died from Leukemia," Lucy began, feeling the usual lump growing in her throat. "Kate was my younger sister. She was beautiful, talented and we all loved her very much, but my father was obsessed with her. When Kate got sick, I overheard him tell my mother, 'Why couldn't it be Lucy instead of Kate?' I was devastated," she confessed as memories washed over her. "Not only was I losing my sister, whom I loved dearly, but I started feeling guilty for being healthy *and* I knew my father resented me."

"What happened? Did your father ever apologize?" Ellie asked.

"No. When Kate passed away, he secluded himself away from Mother and me and became a recluse. Dad let his business partner run the company, but he rarely left his room to even share a meal with us. A year later, he died from a massive heart attack. The doctor said he grieved himself to death," Lucy revealed, choking back her emotion.

"How *terrible*," Ellie wailed. "Did you write down how *you* felt?"

"Yes, a counselor friend of mine suggested it, and it helped immensely," Lucy replied. "I had many issues to get off my chest; more than I ever suspected. Oh, I cried a tub full of tears while I did it, but that was good, too. And, I prayed for strength to get over my bitterness."

"Was it easier after that, about your sister?"

"Oh, I still miss Kate *terribly* and always will," Lucy admitted. "She *was* a special person, but each time I wrote something down, I asked God to heal that part of my anger *and* my heart. The day finally came when I was able to forgive my father."

"I don't *want* to forgive mine! You've shown me in the Bible that we need to forgive people, Lucy, but how *can* I?" Ellie blurted.

"Oh, I don't blame you for feeling this way," Lucy softly replied. "You've suffered more than any ten people should, but hating him only lets him win. Hate is like a cancer that eats away at us and makes us sick. It fills us with bitterness until there's no room for happiness in our lives. But, forgiving others will set us free. And yes, we *must* forgive others if we're to be forgiven."

There was silence as Lucy waited for Ellie's rebuttal. Tears spilled from her eyes as she finally spoke. "I *can't* forgive him for what he did, Lucy, at least not yet," she whispered.

"I understand. It'll take time, but one day, with God's help, it'll happen," Lucy said assuredly. "Right now, I want you to know you are loved more than you could *ever* imagine. We can't let the past ruin our present *or* our future," she added, taking hold of Ellie's hand.

"Thank you, Lucy," Ellie said softly, wiping her tears. "I'll do my best. There's still more, I'm afraid." With obvious emotion, Ellie closed her eyes seemingly to gather her thoughts as Lucy waited.

"I'm responsible for a man's death," Ellie confessed as her voice began quivering. "It happened on the train while coming here. It was horrible, Lucy! That first night, I passed a man on my way back from the restroom. As I excused myself to get by him, he turned and grabbed me. He tried kissing me, but I fought him off and when he wouldn't stop, I kicked him and he fell off the train to his death," Ellie hurriedly admitted as her words faded amid tears.

Once more, Lucy felt despair for what Ellie had endured. "Oh, my dear, what horrors you've been living with!" she gasped in shock. "Yes, it's sad a life ended in such a manner, but you were defending yourself. The man brought it on himself. What happened? Did the police question you?"

Silently, she sat listening as Ellie explained what happened next and the fear she felt. She talked about the fellow passenger, Craig McGuire, who lied to protect her. "He convinced me I did nothing wrong, but I still feel ashamed," Ellie wailed, dabbing her tears. "How could I keep such a secret?"

Reaching across the table, Lucy took hold of Ellie's hand as she searched for some word of comfort for this hurting young woman. *Dear God, what do I say? How can I help lift this burden she's carrying?* Lucy hurriedly prayed. Just as quickly she had the answer.

"God knows your heart, Ellie," Lucy whispered. "He knows how terrible you feel about this; he knows, too, you had no plan to harm that man. You *did* try to tell someone. *Any* woman would have defended herself, *and* be justified for her actions, just as you are," she concluded.

"Thank you, Lucy, I believe you," Ellie replied. "I'm so tired of it all, but no matter where I turn it slams me in the face. Just like today."

"Did something happen at Marco's, Ellie? Please, tell me what made you so upset," Lucy urged, feeling overwhelmed at what she was hearing.

"Yes, I have to tell it all," Ellie began. For the next while, she explained about Carla's brothel in Homer and the night she had spent there. "It was Carla at the beauty shop today. I saw her and it reminded me of what those girls do," she said, fighting a new round of tears. "But how *can* they?"

"I don't know," Lucy replied sadly. "Perhaps they feel trapped with nowhere else to go or they're desperate for money. Maybe they're looking for love, *any* kind of love. One day, Matt and I want to provide a home where these desperate young women can come to," she explained. "I'm not sure how it will come about, but if God is in it, it *will* work out."

"I'm sure *many* would leave such a life if they had a choice," Ellie replied.

Somehow, after verbalizing her past to Lucy, Ellie felt a sense of relief. That night sleep evaded her as she tossed and turned. Words and phrases tumbled through her mind. Lucy's words; words that made her feel good and others that left a longing inside her. *'God loves each one of us beyond anything we can imagine,'* Lucy had told her. *'He knows our every thought and desire, and promises to carry all of our burdens if we let him.'*

For Ellie, she was beginning to understand. That small voice inside her grew louder each day, wooing her with gentleness and love.

It was 2:00 a.m. when Ellie climbed out of bed and went to her window. Now, with another hour before sunrise, she could still see the moon and stars. *All this didn't just happen, everything needs a Creator,* she thought, seeing the sprawling vastness overhead.

As she gazed heavenward, Ellie pondered Lucy's

words. *She says God has a special purpose for my life. What would it be?*

Just then, Ellie remembered those times when she would escape to her hiding place. When her dad wasn't looking, she would sneak away to a small grove of willow trees a short distance behind the farmhouse. It was her place of solace. There, she would lie in the shade on a hot summer's day and fill her mind with wonderful thoughts of adventure—all those things she'd do when Morton Cooper was dead.

Back then I wanted to be a great poet and learn to play the piano; or be an equestrian with beautiful horses; I wanted to travel the world to far away places and see everything I could. But now, I just want peace in my life, Ellie sighed, turning from the window.

Before crawling back into bed, she sat down at her vanity and turned on the lamp. There, she studied her reflection in the mirror. *What does God have in mind for me? Will Chad be in my life? Will I ever get married?* Ellie wondered as she ran her fingers through her hair. "I do like it short," she whispered.

Like her grandmother, Ellie was blessed with a natural curl. Now, after losing its bulk, her dark brown hair was a mass of shiny curls. *Tomorrow, Lucy said I'll get new glasses and some new clothes. Ready or not, it's time for a new me; and after talking to Lucy, I think I'm ready for a whole new beginning,* Ellie decided, somehow feeling excited about the future.

CHAPTER ELEVEN

The next morning as planned, Ellie got a new pair glasses; this time they were smaller more attractive frames. Still, she would wear them only when necessary, for reading.

All day long Ellie thought about what she wanted. She longed for that peace Lucy and Matt talked about and obviously enjoyed. No longer did she want to fight her battles alone, she wanted Almighty God on her side. For weeks, she had read about his Promises and was now ready to fully trust what the Bible said. Somewhere deep inside, Ellie felt God *did* have a special purpose for her life and whatever it was, she didn't want to miss out.

"I'm ready for that clean, new heart," Ellie announced when she and Lucy began their Bible Study that evening. Sudden tears glistened in Lucy's eyes as she reached for Ellie's hand.

"Thank you, Jesus," Lucy whispered. Then, with

their heads bowed, Ellie began her simple, yet heartfelt prayer.

"Dear Jesus, I know I'm a sinner and deserve death. But you came to die in my place, so I could be saved. Your precious blood was the sacrifice for my sins. You rose from the grave to live forever more. Thank you, Jesus, for giving me the free gift of eternal life. Forgive me and cleanse my heart and make it brand new. In Your Precious Name I ask it, Amen."

Tears of joy began spilling down Ellie's face when the sudden weight of guilt and sorrow lifted from her shoulders. "It's true! I *do* feel clean from the inside out!" she announced as Lucy threw her arms around her.

"What a *glorious* week this has turned out to be," Lucy cheered. "If I accomplish nothing else in this life, I'm so *thankful* for this moment," she said, with her face beaming with joy.

"Thank you, Lucy, for all you've done. I'll *never* forget it," Ellie said, feeling blessed beyond words. Suddenly, Ellie felt her life had meaning...and purpose. Now, she couldn't wait to see what God had in mind for her.

The day had arrived. Tomorrow, Ellie would fly to Bellingham for the trial. In many ways she was eager to see Chad, yet she felt apprehensive, but didn't know why.

"I'm sorry, Ellie, but it looks like Matt and I'll be tied up with this for several days," Lucy said as she hurriedly packed boxes with a variety of medicine. "Two small children have already died and from the reported symptoms, it sounds like whooping cough. *Whatever* it is, we need to stop it before it's an epidemic."

"Of course, you *must* go and do all you can," Ellie agreed, feeling concern after the radio message that morning. "This is much more important and besides, Chad will be there with me."

In haste, Ellie helped Lucy pack up what supplies they would need for their stay in the remote village. While they worked, Lucy informed her that Dr. Watts had agreed to cover their patients while they were gone. "He isn't a Naturopath, but he's *somewhat* open minded about such things and he's helped out before," Lucy told Ellie. "He's just up the street, so we put a notice on our office door, letting our patients know."

Within an hour, Matt and Lucy were packed and ready to go. "We'll call Chad as soon as we get back," Matt told Ellie, giving her a fatherly hug. "Our prayers go with you. We know Chad will look out for you during the trial, so please don't worry," he added.

Then it was Lucy who cheered Chad's protection. "He thinks you're pretty special, my dear. I'm sure he'll watch over you *very* carefully. And, you won't be in court *all* the time, so do have some fun, too, okay?" Lucy added with a smile.

As she watched Matt and Lucy leave for their plane, Ellie was alone for the first time since coming to Anchorage. The house felt empty and as she headed upstairs to her room, she felt a strong need to talk to her family.

I wish Mother or Auntie would write, Ellie thought, hoping the mail would arrive before she left for the airport the next morning.

Because of a restless night, Ellie was up early. The same uneasy feeling persisted. *I do wish Lucy was here,* she thought for the hundredth time. *How will I ever get through this without her support?* Seemingly, a tape recorder went off in her head and she heard Lucy's words. *'God helps us do the impossible, if we ask him in faith believing.'*

"Okay, Lord, I'm asking, *please,* help me be strong and not afraid during this trial, even when seeing Jack Barton," Ellie prayed while making breakfast.

Soon, she'd made two pieces of toast and filled her cup with steaming hot coffee. While eating, Ellie's thoughts turned to her family. *I do hope Mother and Aunt Marie are okay. Surely they had my letter long before now, so why haven't I heard anything?*

After she'd eaten and cleaned up the kitchen, Ellie went upstairs to get ready. Although thoughts of the trial drifted in and out of her mind, she tried to enjoy her bath and the pleasant lavender aroma.

Yet, despite her good intentions, Ellie couldn't shake the strange ominous feeling that hovered over her. "Oh, it's just because I'm on my own again, without Lucy," she muttered softly, letting out a deep sigh.

Later that morning, Ellie took great care as she dressed in her new long beige and tan skirt with matching beige blouse. Her brown-colored shoes matched her small handbag. As she studied her image in the full length mirror, she liked what she saw. *New look, new life, new heart, too!* "Thank you, Jesus," Ellie muttered softly, feeling overjoyed at such blessings.

Right on time, Mr. Bass, the neighbor who'd be driving her to the airport, arrived. And much to her delight, so did the mailman.

"Oh, thank you," Ellie said, taking the stack of mail. "I'll just be a minute," she told Mr. Bass who was headed for his Packard with her suitcase. With a smile, the kindly man nodded as Ellie ran back inside the house.

Quickly, she thumbed through the mail hoping to see a letter with the familiar scrawl of her Aunt Marie. Instead, an envelope with bold, beautiful handwriting caught her eye. *What lovely penmanship you have, Attorney Sarah Grayson,* Ellie thought when noticing the return address. *Wow! All the way from Virginia, well, Lucy does know lots of people,* she reasoned, laying aside the letter and heading for the door.

Just then the telephone rang which Ellie debated to answer. "Good morning, Doctor Ryan's office," she greeted in haste.

"Ellie, thank God I caught you," Chad replied, seemingly out of breath.

"Chad, I was just leaving. What is it?" she asked, sensing urgency in his voice.

"You sound rushed."

"I have some bad news, Ellie: Jack Barton escaped early this morning."

Instant weakness nearly caused Ellie's legs to buckle. Hurriedly, she sought a nearby chair; she felt the blood drain from her face. Holding her breath, she tried to grasp what she just heard.

"They were transporting him downtown for trial, but someone was waiting with a car, and guns. They shot two deputies and made their getaway. An eye witness gave a vague description of the vehicle, but nothing else I'm afraid," Chad continued, seemingly in a far-off voice.

Barely listening, Ellie's mind was instead filled with Jack Barton's vile threats and the hateful look he had aimed at her on the ferry.

"Ellie, this means we have to move you somewhere safe," Chad told her. "I'll be there tonight as soon as I get a flight. Stay inside and lock all the doors. Ellie, did you hear me?" he then asked.

"Yes, yes I heard you," Ellie whispered, feeling numb with disbelief.

"Please, stay out of sight and try not to worry. I'll see you soon, and Ellie, I promise I won't let *anyone* hurt you," Chad concluded as the call ended.

When the line went dead, Ellie sat, trying to understand how her life had changed in an instant. *What now? Is that murderer on his way here to make good his threats? What if he finds me before Chad gets here?* Suddenly, the newspaper articles with her picture and address printed for all to see came to mind. *No doubt he knows exactly where I am,* Ellie reasoned.

"Miss, we should be leaving if we're to make it on time," a voice called out from the doorway, startling her.

"Oh, I'm sorry, Mr. Bass," Ellie called back, "but I won't be going after all. Chad just called and there's been a change in plans," she added, slowly leaving her chair and going to the door.

"Then I'll get your bag, miss," the man kindly remarked. As she waited, Ellie quickly scanned the area for perhaps an unfamiliar vehicle, seeing none.

"Call if you need anything," Mr. Bass told her, handing her the suitcase. With a nod, Ellie closed and locked the door, then lowered the blind on its small window.

In a daze, she moved through the house checking all doors and windows making sure they were secure. "Dear God, I don't know how or why this happened, but Lucy said we should always keeping trusting, no matter what, so I am. Please, work this out somehow," Ellie prayed, heading upstairs to her room. *This is the reason for my unsettled feeling,* she decided.

———

As she dressed in a pair of jeans and denim shirt, Ellie thought about the sudden turn of events. *It'll work out. Chad will get here tonight, and take me somewhere safe. The police will find that horrible man and then I'll come back to testify. I'm not worried; it'll work out just fine,* she reasoned confidently.

Vowing to stay optimistic, Ellie glanced in the mirror and fluffed her dark shiny curls, wondering what Chad would say about her new look. *Quite a change from his last visit,* she thought, feeling eager to see his reaction.

Glancing at her wristwatch, Ellie noted the time. *Eleven o'clock. I have all day to wait for Chad. He said to stay inside so I'm missing all that beautiful sunshine out there,* she lamented, peering through her window to the clear blue skies. *If I leave here I'll need more clothes, but what should I take? Where will he take me and for how long?* Ellie had to wonder.

After deciding on what she'd need, she neatly packed the larger suitcase, appreciating the many new clothes she had, thanks to Lucy and Matt.

Two hours later, Ellie had her things ready and had eaten a sandwich for lunch. *I'll take a nap to help pass the time,* she thought, yawning. Crawling atop her bed, she stretched out and closed her eyes. *I'm not going to worry about any of this,* Ellie vowed, pulling her favorite quilt over her.

After the briefing at headquarters regarding Jack Barton, Chad's anger grew. *Two good men dead because of that scum! And now they think he's headed for Anchorage, probably to find Ellie,* he moaned as he drove. The thought of Barton being anywhere near Ellie brought renewed furor to Chad.

Minutes later he arrived at his apartment to pack

a small bag. *Still an hour before my flight; if only I had my own plane,* Chad thought impatiently, knowing every minute put Ellie more at risk.

If that was Barton boarding that small plane, and if he's heading for Anchorage, then he'll get to Ellie before I do, Chad reasoned angrily. "I need to warn her about this." Seconds later he was on the telephone, dialing the familiar number to his brother's home.

He waited. When getting no answer, his heart began pounding as he imagined the worst. *Please God, don't let anything happen to our sweet Ellie. You know how special she is to all of us,* Chad pleaded.

———————————

"What a nice day for surprises; one down and one to go," Jack Barton sneered in his raspy tone, glancing at the piece of newspaper in his hand. "Won't it be fun seeing this little filly again," he added, bringing only a nod from Rex, his cohort and pilot. "Yeah, I got a special little treat for you, miss, just like I warned you," he gloated, studying the face in the picture. "Then, we're off to Jamaica where no one cares *who* we are."

Frowning, Rex threw Jack a sideways glance then again trained his eyes on the horizon. "I'm not so sure about being a nice day," he remarked, checking the gages. "I can't imagine taking this puddle-jumper through that," he added, nodding toward the growing bank of thunderclouds up ahead.

"I thought it was clear sailing," Jack told him. "What happened to all that sunshine?"

"I don't know, but flying through that was not

on my agenda," Rex replied. "We need to turn back and rethink our plans."

"You *know* they'll nab us as soon as we land. And, that isn't on *my* agenda!" Jack yelled, stuffing the newspaper article in his pocket. "Can't you fly around it?"

"No man, look at it! It's too wide to go around and too low to get under. I see no choice *but* to turn back," Rex said, shaking his head. "Let's fly to Seattle and hide out there. They won't expect us to stay that close to home."

"What *are* our chances, if we keep going?" Jack asked, gazing ahead.

"Have you ever seen a cork in a rain barrel? That'd be us, *before* this cork broke apart and hit the ground," Rex explained.

Shaking his head with disgust, Jack said nothing, but Rex knew he'd never give up on his revenge. No matter what, Jack got even. After all, he had plenty of money from the heist he pulled off years before, enabling him to find anyone he wanted. So, if weather delayed his plans to get that young Miss Cooper today, it was a sure bet he'd get her somewhere down the road.

CHAPTER TWELVE

A loud clap of thunder woke Ellie from her sound sleep. Snuggling under the quilt, she glanced at the bedside clock. *Three o'clock; Chad should be here in just a few hours,* she thought, stretching her arms over her head.

Within minutes, Ellie heard rain beating on her window and more thunder boomed overhead, causing an eerie feeling. *So much for a sunny afternoon,* she thought, wondering at its sudden change.

As she lay listening to the rain, Ellie's mind wandered. *How can we tell Matt and Lucy about all this? They're counting on me and now I'll be gone and won't be any help to them,* Ellie reasoned, knowing she'd miss them terribly.

Suddenly, she sat up in bed. *Aunt Marie. I must call her, too, and let her know all this and see why she hasn't written.*

Throwing aside the quilt, Ellie climbed off her

bed and slipped on her sandals before hurrying downstairs. "Aunt Marie knows nothing about the murder or the trial," she muttered, heading for the telephone. Within seconds, she was dialing her aunt's number in La Junta, Colorado.

In a daze, Ellie sat at the kitchen table. Her body trembled with emotion as her aunt's words resonated thought her mind.

'Morton's dead, Lizzie. Rose couldn't take anymore. He abused her until she shot him, but not before he broke her nose and some ribs. We knew he treated her like dirt, but no one realized all the beatings since you left. She was hospitalized in Syracuse for a time, but now she's recuperating here with me, dear, that's why I haven't called you. Rose wanted to tell you what happened and how terrible she feels for what you went through. Come home, honey, please. Your mother needs you.'

With her head in her hands, Ellie took deep breaths, hoping to calm the churning in her stomach. *He's really dead? He can no longer hurt anyone?* It was hard to believe her years-long wish had finally come to pass.

Memories of those torturous years, brought renewed grief. *Oh Mother, I should never have left you there alone with him. I should have known he'd take it out on you. Please, don't feel guilty for killing that monster! He might have killed us dozens of times,* Ellie's thoughts cried as sorrow settled over her like a cloak.

"Yes, I need to go back. Mother needs me more than ever. I'll take care of her, *somehow*," Ellie whispered.

It was six o'clock and still raining when Chad arrived. His flight was rough due to the storm, yet it brought a sense of relief. *If Barton took his small plane through this, he might be dead by now,* Chad reasoned, knowing that would prevent a tedious manhunt. When thinking about the families of the two deputies, Chad's heart went out to them as he said a quick prayer.

Now, before leaving his vehicle, he quickly scanned the neighborhood for anything looking suspicious. Seeing nothing unusual, Chad left the Jeep and made his way to the back door of Matt's office. Using his own key, he unlocked it and called out as he stepped inside. "Ellie, it's me, Chad. Are you okay?"

When hearing no response, he quietly closed the door and stood listening. Hearing nothing, he slowly walked through the waiting room and headed for the kitchen, some distance from the office. "Ellie, can you hear me?" he called out, not wanting to scare her.

"Chad? Yes, I'm here," he heard her say from the next room. With a sigh of relief, Chad continued on and was soon opening the door to the kitchen.

"I'm sorry I'm late, but the flight—" He stopped mid sentence when he saw her. Standing at the kitchen counter, Ellie looked at him as she dried her hands on a towel.

"Hello, Chad," she said softly, looking somewhat forlorn.

Feeling dumbfounded, Chad could only stare at the beautiful young woman looking at him. "Ellie, you've changed," he whispered, shaking his head. "You're *beautiful!*" Slowly he walked toward her, pushing thoughts of Jack Barton to the back of his mind.

"I tangled with some yellow paint, so I had to cut my hair," Ellie replied, "and my glasses had to be replaced, too."

"I'm glad," Chad said softly, studying her face. "You've been crying. Are you okay?" he asked, taking hold of her hand.

"It's been *quite* a day," Ellie remarked, tugging her hand free of his. Upon turning her back to Chad, she opened the cupboard and retrieved two coffee mugs. "I've made fresh coffee and I'm sure you're hungry, so I'll fix you some supper," she rambled on, keeping her back toward him.

"Ellie, please look at me," Chad told her, gently taking her arm and turning her around. "I don't need food; I need you to talk to me. Tell me, is it only Barton who has you so upset, or is there more?"

"I'm afraid it's much, *much* more," she whispered as her voice broke.

The pain and desperation Chad heard tore at his heart. Putting his hands on Ellie's shoulders, he looked at her. In that moment, he realized how much he wanted to protect her, to calm her fears and shield her from danger—of any kind. Lovingly, he then pulled Ellie into his arms, holding her close to his heart.

"Whatever it is, Ellie, we'll get through it, I promise," Chad whispered next to her ear. "You don't have to fight things alone, not anymore."

Briefly, Ellie stayed in the comfort of Chad's arms, then eased herself from his embrace and wiped her eyes. "Thank you, but I'm better now," she told him, avoiding eye contact. "Please, let's have some coffee and I'll tell you everything."

Like a spotlight in a darkened room, reality hit Chad full force. *I'm in love with this woman! Why couldn't I see it before? Now, with all this going on, do I dare tell her?* Chad wondered, taking a seat at the kitchen table.

As Ellie poured coffee she searched for the right words to tell Chad. *How do I tell him I'm leaving here, probably for good? And, how will I live if I never see him again?* Ellie lamented, biting back her emotion.

Now, seated across the table from Chad, her eyes welded to his as she began. "I telephoned my aunt this afternoon, to let her know about things, but before I could tell her, she revealed her own shocking news. My dad is dead. My mother shot him in self-defense."

Seemingly stunned, Chad only stared at her, saying nothing. "After I left home, he started beating my mother even more. Last week she found his gun," Ellie went on, still finding the news unbeliev-able. "Chad, I *have* to go back and take care of her. Mother is crippled from polio and she needs me. It's only me and Aunt Marie, so I have to do this," Ellie concluded.

Leaving his seat, Chad said nothing as he walked to the window and looked outside. "Are you sure of this, Ellie?" he asked a moment later.

"Yes, I'm very sure. I'll miss *everyone*, but I have no choice. You see that don't you?"

"Yes, I do understand. Ellie, I'm so sorry about all this; for your mother and the abuse that drove her to such lengths, but selfishly, I'm sorry most of all that you're leaving and I won't get to see you," Chad said, turning from the window. "I'll miss you more than I can say."

As he stood looking at her, Chad's face held an expression foreign to Ellie. There was sadness, yes, but much more. "There's so much I want to say to you, Ellie, but right now you have enough on your mind," he told her. "When do you need to leave? I'll buy your plane ticket."

"No, Chad, really, I have some money," Ellie refuted. "Matt and Lucy are paying me wages. Suddenly, she felt like a deserter. "Oh, how can I leave them after they've done so much for me?" she wailed. Fighting her tears, Ellie rested her elbows on the table and covered her face with her hands.

"They'll understand. Please, don't worry," Chad whispered, now standing at her side. "We all love you, Ellie, and only want to make your life easier.

Don't you know that?" he asked softly, taking a seat beside her.

Not only were his words tender and kind, but Ellie heard deep sadness, too. "Thank you, Chad. I've come to love each one of you more than I ever thought possible," she said truthfully. "I love it here. Please believe this: there's *no* place on earth I'd rather be."

Reaching out his hand, Chad took hold of Ellie's and cradled it gently between both of his. Lowering his eyes, he seemingly searched for a reply, but said nothing.

Although Ellie had gone up to her room hours before, Chad tossed and turned trying to get comfortable on the sofa downstairs. For him, the thought of not seeing Ellie again, at least until Jack Barton was caught and brought to trial, caused a feeling of gloom.

Why didn't I trust my feelings long ago? But, how could I know? I've never been in love before, Chad scolded himself for the hundredth time. *I'm sure she cares for me, but now she's leaving. How do I convince her I'd gladly take care of her and her mother if she'd let me? Certainly, there's never been anyone who has touched my heart like Ellie,* Chad realized, regretting he may never have the chance to tell her.

Please, watch over Ellie, dear God. You know how much she's hurting and needs comforting, Chad prayed. *I don't know what the future holds, but I do love that girl; just help me let her go, if I must…*

It had been hours since Ellie went to bed, yet, she hadn't slept. Instead, she lay staring at the ceiling, wondering what kind of future awaited her.

Dear God, having faith and trusting that things will work out for good is all new to me, so I'm having trouble understanding, Ellie prayed as tears fell on her pillow. *Why did it come to this, especially when I finally have a real home where there's love and happiness? You said there's a special purpose for my life, but how special will it be living on that dirt farm working my hands raw again? Dear Father in heaven, I just don't see much of a future for me at all!*

In despair, Ellie rolled over on her side and covered her face with her pillow as she sobbed. Sometime later she finally fell asleep.

As Ellie peered from her window the next morning, the gloom she saw outside matched her own. It was still raining. Although she slept, it wasn't nearly enough and already her mind was filled with yesterday's anguish.

Oh, I wish Lucy and Matt were home. How can I leave without telling them goodbye? Yet, if I wait too long, Jack Barton may come here and that could be disastrous, Ellie sighed, turning from the window.

Just then her eyes fell on her packed suitcases sitting beside her dresser. A sudden lump appeared in her throat as her eyes drifted around the lovely room she'd enjoyed since arriving. *Certainly, there's no such bedroom waiting for me on the farm,* she thought sadly.

No matter how hard she tried to feel positive, Ellie found no good reason to be glad, other than Chad's tender words. Yet, what did it matter? She was leaving and Kansas was a very long way from Washington. *I surely wouldn't want him to see the farm anyway,* Ellie decided, thinking of all the rundown outbuildings and depressing farmhouse. *Besides, I'll be far too busy with all those chores to have company!*

———————

All the while Ellie made her bed and got dressed, she thought of Lucy and Matt and how much she'd grown to love them. And now, as she headed downstairs, Ellie also knew life without Chad would be nearly unbearable.

"Good morning, Ellie," Chad greeted as she arrived in the kitchen. "Coffee's ready and I've made breakfast, so I hope you're hungry."

"Good morning, Chad. It smells good, but I'm afraid I haven't much of an appetite," Ellie replied, retrieving a cup. "I'll just have coffee."

"Please, at least have this little bit," Chad coaxed with a smile. "I know you didn't eat anything last night…besides, I hate eating alone."

Already he was setting a plate of freshly made French toast and crispy bacon on the table. "Since it may be a while before I can cook you that nice steak dinner as I planned, this will have to do," Chad said with a grin.

"I didn't know you *were* planning to cook me

dinner," Ellie replied, filling her cup with coffee. "So I'll miss out on that, too." At the thought of missing such good times, Ellie's fragile emotions erupted. Yet, before she could dash from the room, Chad took hold of her arm, preventing her escape.

"Ellie, I'm sorry if I upset you, please forgive me," he pleaded. "I never want to hurt you—I love you far too much for that."

Again, she felt stunned. Yet, unlike the horrible news of yesterday, this was quite different. "What…what do you mean?"

"I mean what I said, Ellie. I love you. I guess I have for some time, but wouldn't admit it, even to myself. Then last night, when I saw you upset and hurting, my heart ached with wanting to protect you. It was *then* I realized I'm in love with you. Please, let me take care of you, my sweet, innocent Ellie," Chad whispered, gently brushing his hand against her cheek.

For a moment Ellie closed her eyes, basking in Chad's touch, but then, without warning, she felt another hand taking liberty with her. Those hands she knew so well—the ones that violated her innocence so long before.

In response to those degrading memories, Ellie slapped Chad's hand away as she stepped back, freeing herself from his touch. "I'm *not* innocent, Chad. I haven't been for a very long time," she blurted. "Morton Cooper saw to that! He's dead, but what he did to me still lives on, in here," Ellie cried, resting her fingers against her temple. "Oh yes, I've spent hours thinking about you, hoping one day I'd be more than just your friend. But, now I realize my past has scarred my future. You deserve someone fresh and pure, Chad; someone who won't cringe at your touch. I can *never* be that someone."

As Chad looked back at her, Ellie noticed a glistening in his eyes as his lips grew tight with emotion. "I had no idea," he whispered in dismay.

"I should have told you long ago," she wailed. "Lucy knows, I told her everything. All the junk in my life; those dirty secrets I've lived with that keep coming back to haunt me."

"Don't give up on your future, Ellie, please. There are counselors, good people who are trained to help victims like you. I hear about them everyday," Chad told her.

"I doubt any such people live on the flatlands of Kansas," she refuted. "If they do, I'm sure they want cash, not laying hens or some bushels of corn."

"Don't worry about the expense. I'll gladly pay for *all* of it," Chad told her. "This isn't only *your* future, it's mine too."

For the first time, Ellie began to see how much Chad really cared. "How can you still want me in your life, knowing this?" she asked, shaking her head.

"That's what love is: getting through the hard times as well as the good. I won't give up without a fight, because I know the reward waiting on the other end. *You're* that reward, Ellie. I see us having a life together. Not as quickly as I wanted perhaps, but I'm willing to wait, my dear Ellie," Chad said tenderly, giving her an easy smile.

"I think your lovely breakfast is getting cold," she said, nodding toward the table.

"So it is," Chad replied. "Won't you please join me?" he offered, holding the chair for her. Just then a ray of sunlight filled the kitchen, chasing away the earlier gloom. "I believe God just lifted the blinds," Chad said with a smile.

For Ellie, she somehow felt it just *might* be a promise for the future.

CHAPTER THIRTEEN

It was mid morning. The arrangements were completed for Ellie's flight to Denver and the bus ride on to La Junta, where her mother and aunt eagerly awaited her return.

"I hate leaving like this," Ellie said, shaking her head. "Not telling Lucy and Matt goodbye seems so callus. Especially, after all they've done for me."

"They'll be disappointed, too, but they'd never want to put you in danger," Chad assured her. "Are we ready?"

"Yes, I suppose I am." With one last look around, Ellie choked back the threatening tears. Memories of her and Lucy fixing dinner, having tea and sharing conversation at the table filled her mind. "I'll never find another friend like Lucy," she said. "Please, tell them both how much I love them."

Just then a noise was heard outside. "Stay here," Chad whispered as he quickly headed for the front of the house. With her heart racing, Ellie stared after Chad and wondered if Jack Barton had already found her.

Emotions were high as Ellie and Lucy hugged each other. "Thank *God* we got here before you left," Lucy whispered. "We've witnessed several miracles the past few days, and this is one more."

"She's right," Matt interjected. "Our plane developed engine trouble and we almost didn't make it."

"You mean you might have crashed?" Ellie wailed in fear.

"No, there are plenty of lakes to land on, but getting engine parts way out there is pretty difficult," Matt explained. "Now young lady, thank you for bringing immeasurable joy to all of us," he told Ellie, giving her a bear hug. "You and your mama will be in our prayers and you can call us *collect* anytime, whether you need something or if it's just to talk, okay? We want to hear from you, *regularly*."

"Thank you both, for everything," Ellie said. "I can't begin to tell you how much you've changed my life. I love you *so* much."

"We love *you* like a daughter," Lucy said with eyes glistening.

"It's time to go," Chad coaxed softly, looking at Ellie. "I'll be in touch," he told Lucy and Matt. One last smile passed between them although any words were lost amid their emotion.

For Ellie, sadness surrounded her as she thought

about life without these who had come to mean so much. Yet, she'd be forever grateful knowing she wasn't alone. *Thank God I'm not leaving you behind,* Ellie thought as she climbed in the seat beside Chad.

For Lucy, the house felt empty without Ellie. To keep her mind busy, she decided to thumb through the pile of mail despite her extreme need for sleep. *Advertisements, electric bill, payment from Mr. Gleason,* she called off mentally as she glanced at each piece.

Then, she saw an envelope with her name written in somewhat ornate penmanship. "Sarah Grayson, Attorney? What might this be?" Lucy uttered while searching her memory for such a person.

After opening the envelope, she unfolded the professionally typed letter. At the top of the page, in bold lettering, was the letterhead containing the address and telephone number of Sarah Grayson, Attorney at Law. The letter read,

> *Dear Lucille Ryan:*
>
> *This letter is to inform you that you have been named in the Last Will and Testament of Miss Violet Covington.*
>
> *Please call my office at the telephone number listed above, or write to me at the available address.*
>
> *We look forward to dispersing the funds expeditiously. Thank you for your prompt reply.*

Most Sincerely,

Sarah Grayson, Attorney

In shock, Lucy plopped down in the chair behind her while her mind filled with memories of Violet Covington, the elderly woman she had once worked for. *Dear, sweet Violet. Always so concerned about others and oh, how she loved children and donated thousands to orphanages. I'm sure she named one or two of them in her will also. I never imagined she'd leave me anything!* Lucy thought, shaking her head.

With the letter in hand, she left her seat to go find Matt. *Dear God, thank you for Violet Covington, what a precious soul she was!*

"Well, sweetheart, give this Sarah Grayson a call," Matt told his wife after he'd read the letter. "I know you won't sleep until you find out about this."

"Oh Matt, just think, wouldn't it be *wonderful* if this money could start our savings toward making our dream a reality!" Lucy raved, throwing her arms around his neck.

"Yes indeed, truly wonderful," Matt replied, seeing the joy on Lucy's face.

"I have other news, too. I was going to tell you later, after all this paperwork, but now seems like a good time," he confessed with a grin.

"News? What might that be?" Lucy asked curiously.

"It's about Chad and Ellie. While we were unloading the Suburban, Chad admitted he loves Ellie," Matt explained. "He told her just today, but she's so scarred from her abuse she thinks she'll never have a normal life."

"Oh no, Matt, we've *got* to help her see that just isn't true!" Lucy cried, shaking her head. "We *know* God can heal any scar, no matter how deep it goes. I know she cares for Chad, too; it'd be tragic if her past interfered with their happiness."

"I know, honey. Chad said he'd pay for any counseling she needs, but I told him we have the best counselor *and* he's free," Matt told Lucy.

"Amen! We *must* help Ellie regardless of her being so far away, but how?"

"I don't know off hand, but it'll work out," Matt assured his wife. "Now, why not call that lawyer and see what's up, since we're both curious."

"Yes, indeed," Lucy replied as she hurriedly left his office.

As Matt watched her go he smiled to himself. *What a woman, a great wife and superb nurse! Lord, you truly blessed me by giving me such a helpmate as that,* Matt thought, resuming his paperwork.

It was nearing time for Ellie to board the plane. Choking back her tears, she looked at Chad. "Thank you for everything," she told him. "I *do* hope you catch that horrible Jack Barton," she said, feeling somewhat relived to be leaving the area.

"Yes, I hope so, too," he replied, returning her gaze. "When we do, we'll fly you here to testify. I'm sure going to miss you, Ellie," he went on. "Please, remember what I said, okay? My love for you is real and I'm not giving up on us." In saying that, he reached out and gently took hold of her hand.

As she looked in Chad's eyes, Ellie saw tenderness. "I appreciate everything you're saying, Chad, but how do I get past all those things that happened? Can I close out those memories or change who I am?" she asked, tugging her hand free of his.

"God *already* changed who you were, Ellie. He changed your heart and made you a new creation. His Spirit lives inside you now and he'll help you overcome anything, if you ask him," Chad told her.

"Are you *sure* of that?" Ellie asked, hoping desperately it was true.

"Certainly, it won't happen overnight, but *any* war takes time. And, that's what this is, Ellie, war. It's a battle between good and evil, for your future and a chance to have a normal life. I know about this," Chad assured her.

Before Ellie could comment, her flight was announced. "Take care of yourself. And, may I please hug you?" he asked then.

"Yes, of course," Ellie said, stepping toward him. Tenderly, Chad wrapped his arms around her for a warm embrace. Closing her eyes, she let the sweet scent of Chad's cologne fill her senses, preventing any reminder of those indecent touches she had endured so often.

Still holding the telephone, Lucy stared out the window. She could hardly breathe. Over and over she replayed the conversation just ended.

"Matt? *Please*, would you come here?" Lucy called out from her chair, not trusting her legs to hold her. "I *can't* believe this! How could that sweet little lady gather so much wealth?" she whispered in disbelief.

Soon, Matt was at her side. "It appears our prayers have been answered, sweetheart," she said, staring straight ahead. "It's all *quite* unbelievable."

"I'm listening," Matt replied, relieving her of the telephone.

"Violet leaves no family; her only sibling just recently passed away. Therefore, I'm the sole beneficiary of her estate," she said softly.

"That's quite amazing," Matt replied, joining her at the table. "Just how much *is* Violet's estate worth?"

"Three…million…dollars," Lucy pronounced slowly, feeling sure she'd awake from this dream any minute. "And, there's a house in California."

"Are you *sure* you heard correctly?" Matt questioned, looking stunned. "Just how long *did* you work for this lady?"

"Only two months the first time, after she'd broken a hip," Lucy informed him, "and then a year later, when she lost part of her leg to gangrene and diabetes. She offered me a very generous wage if I'd quit the hospital and work for her, which I did. I was with her when we met, if you remember," she told Matt. "Obviously, she never forgot me."

"How could anyone forget you, my pet," Matt said, reaching for her hand. "No one is more devoted and caring than you." With heightened emotion, Lucy could only smile as he kissed her hand.

"I know you're exhausted, so let's get some rest," Matt coaxed lovingly a moment later. "Tomorrow is another day, *and* it appears we have some plans to think about."

With her husband's arm around her, Lucy let him guide her toward their bedroom. Today, the pendulum of emotion had swung wide in both directions. And, for Lucille Ryan, the thought of attaining her lifelong goal was sure to keep her flying high for some time to come...

CHAPTER FOURTEEN

The flight to Denver, followed by the bus ride to La Junta, seemed endless to Ellie.

As she traveled, she thought about the day she had left. *Things certainly didn't turn out like I planned, but Lucy says our steps are directed by God. I'm beginning to see she's right. Meeting Chad like I did was a God thing, I just know it!* Ellie decided, realizing any number of other detectives might have been on that police boat. *Through him I met wonderful Lucy and Matt, not to mention these feelings I have toward Chad. But, now I'm coming back here? Well, there must be a reason, yet, how can Mother and I go back to that place of such horrible memories? Dear God, please, work it out so we won't have to,* Ellie prayed.

———————

Before the bus came to a complete stop, at La Junta's

bus station, Ellie saw her aunt waiting with the small group of people. At seeing the stocky built woman, sudden tears filled her eyes as she realized how much she'd missed Aunt Marie.

Feeling grateful the long trip was finally over, Ellie gathered her things and exited the bus. When her aunt's gaze drifted past her, she smiled to herself. *She doesn't recognize me without my long hair and baggy clothes.* "Aunt Marie, over here," Ellie called out.

"Lizzie? Is that you?" the woman gasped in surprise. "My goodness, *look* at you!" With a hurried glance her eyes swept over Ellie and seconds later both women were hugging each other excitedly. "Oh, my sweet Lizzie, I've missed you *so* much," Marie whispered.

"Me too," Ellie replied, having noticed the somewhat strained look on the woman's face. "It's good to see you, Auntie." Despite her many questions, Ellie decided they could wait until later.

Within minutes the driver had unloaded the baggage from the bus and Ellie retrieved her two suitcases. "I'm sorry you had to come back under these circumstances, Lizzie," Marie commented, taking one of the bags.

"Is Mother doing okay?" Ellie then asked as they headed for the car. "About what happened?"

"Yes *and* no," Marie answered. "Physically she's getting better, but emotionally she's a wreck. She blames herself for everything: your abuse and for staying with Morton after we begged her to leave—

even for her beatings and the ultimate act of defending herself."

"I can't go back there, Aunt Marie," Ellie blurted, suddenly feeling sick at the thought. "There are just *too* many memories."

"Well, neither of you *have* to go back," Marie told her. "We just learned yesterday that a neighboring farmer wants to buy the place. The real estate agent called and said this farmer is eager *and* willing to pay a good price."

"Thank you, Jesus!" Ellie shouted, bringing a look of surprise from Marie. "Oh, Auntie, I have so much to tell you and Mother."

"Well, *I'm* certainly eager to hear everything, starting with this marvelous new look you're wearing. It's high time we have some good news for a change," Marie said solemnly.

Standing in the doorway, Ellie covered her mouth to muffle a gasp. Despite knowing what happened she wasn't prepared for what she saw. "Oh, *Mama,* what did he do to you?" Ellie cried, hurrying to the woman and kneeling in front of her. Reaching out, she gently smoothed her mother's hair while choking back her tears.

Bruises and swelling dominated her mother's face and when Ellie looked in her eyes, they seemed empty and lifeless. "Hello," Rose greeted in a tone void of emotion.

"Hello, Mother," she could only whisper as despair settled over her.

At that moment time stopped as Ellie battled unseen forces inside her. *I hate him for this; I'm glad he's dead! I'll never forgive him for what he's done!* Ellie vowed, wishing she could have pulled the trigger instead of her mother.

Then, just as quickly, Ellie heard Lucy's words. *God will avenge his children, no matter what. He will repay for our suffering, but we must forgive others as he forgives us.*

Straightening to her feet, Ellie thought of Lucy. *Oh, I wish she was here. She'd make sense of all this, I know she would.*

The next few days were especially hard for Ellie as there appeared to be no change in her mother's emotional well-being. No matter how hard she and Marie worked at involving Rose in conversation, their efforts failed. Mealtime was just as difficult. After nibbling only a few bites, Rose would excuse herself and escape to the confines of her bedroom.

To get away and spend time alone, Ellie would often walk to the park and there, lying on the cool grass, she'd talk to that One who had come to mean so much. *God, I only have you to turn to, so here I am again, Lord, asking for help. Please, lift my mother out of this gloom she's in. Give her a life she's never had and a joy she's never felt,* Ellie prayed, trusting somehow there'd be an answer.

"What *are* we going to do?" Marie asked one morning as she prepared to take her dog Sam for a walk. "I felt sure seeing you again would do the trick."

"I don't know, but there's someone who might just have an idea," Ellie replied, leaving her seat. "Lucy is the wisest lady I know and if anyone can figure this out, she can. And, I'm going to call her right now." *Please, let her be home,* Ellie quickly prayed, dialing the operator.

"Dr. Ryan's office, may I help you?" Lucy greeted in her usual happy tone.

"Hi Lucy, this is Ellie," she said back. "It's so good to hear your voice."

"Ellie, what a *wonderful* surprise," Lucy cheered. "I've been thinking about you so much. How was your trip, dear?"

"It seemed long, but only because I was eager to get here," Ellie admitted, "but, I'm afraid Mother isn't doing too well. I'm hoping you might have some advice of what to do."

"Of course, if I can," Lucy told her. "Tell me about her." For the next few minutes Ellie explained about her mother and the depression that was worsening day by day.

"She won't talk, won't eat, and seems to have no interest in anything, not even her sewing," Ellie said. "We need a miracle, Lucy. I see no other way."

"Can she travel? I mean is she well enough to leave there?" Lucy asked, surprising Ellie. "If she can I have a suggestion."

"She sees the doctor tomorrow for her final

checkup, but after that I guess she could travel. Yet, persuading Mother to go *anywhere* will be difficult," Ellie admitted. "She's never had a vacation before or traveled anywhere. That's a luxury Morton didn't believe in."

"Then I'd say it's high time she has one," Lucy said excitedly. "And, I have just the right destination in mind for all of you. Now, my dear, hang on to your breeches because I have a splendid idea!"

As was her routine, Marie took her little dog, Sam, for a twenty minute walk every morning. When she neared her house on their return, Marie was surprised at what she heard. "Singing? Is that what I'm hearing?" she uttered, while tilting her ear.

Sure enough, the closer she got the more amazed she was to hear the happy sounds coming from her house. *What has happened to make Ellie sing and shout like that?* Marie wondered, feeling grateful that the gloom might have disappeared for at least a little while.

"Thank you, Jesus! What blessings you give us!" Ellie was shouting. Never before had Marie seen such adoration coming from her niece.

"What is it? What's happened?" Marie asked, unhooking Sam's lease from his collar. Just then, she noticed Rose setting on the sofa looking alert and actually smiling.

"Mother, Aunt Marie, everything's going to be all right! What the devil meant for harm, God has turned into joy!" Ellie blurted, taking hold of

Rose's hand. "I had barely gotten off the phone with Lucy when the realtor called. He's coming by with papers for you to sign, Mother, *this* afternoon. By next week, we'll have the money for the farm! A very *large* sum of money, I might add," she said excitedly. "And, we're *all* going on vacation...to California! It's all because of Lucy and Matt, those wonderful people I told you about."

"Are you sure of this, Ellie?" Rose asked, surprising Marie even further that her sister was actually joining in on conversation. "Why would these people take strangers on vacation?"

"Like I said, Mother, they're great people. The *most* generous and caring I have ever met, *and* because they love Jesus and everyone else, too," Ellie proudly announced.

Although she believed in a Higher Power, Marie felt sure no such Entity would care for her as an individual. "Do you believe in all that Jesus stuff?" Marie had to ask Ellie. "I heard what you were saying, so I'm wondering."

"Oh yes, Auntie, I believe," Ellie said, nodding her head. "I've been born-again and I know it's real! There is nothing like it and I want both of you to experience what I found," Ellie explained as her eyes glistened.

"Is that why you look so different?" Rose asked, studying Ellie's face.

"That's part of the reason, Mother. A bucket of yellow paint atop my head broke my glasses and ruined my long hair. But now I'm glad it did," Ellie confessed with a smile. Matt and Lucy are responsible for every change in me. They taught me the Bible, but most importantly, they live what it says. One day I hope I can do as much."

As she watched and listened to her niece, Marie had to admit there was a definite change in her. Not only outwardly, but inside, too. Gone was the girl filled with bitterness and shame that had boarded the train for Alaska. In her place was a beautiful young woman who seemingly glowed from within.

———————————

As promised, the sale of the farm closed and the money was dispersed. "I can't believe it's really over. It's like a dream," Rose said softly as she looked at the check. "Now, it's our turn," she added, putting her arms around Ellie.

"Oh yes, Mother, and we'll never look back," Ellie said, returning the embrace. "Now, let's get this in the bank, because *we* have to get ready for our trip to California!"

CHAPTER FIFTEEN

The flight arrived on time in San Francisco. Upon deplaning, Ellie was surprised to see a man wearing a dark uniform and holding a sign that read: Cooper Party. Approaching, they learned he was a chauffeur named Richard and would be driving them to their destination.

With a skycap handling their luggage, they were escorted to a shiny black limousine that sat waiting. Looks of amazement passed between the three women after being offered a cold beverage by the friendly driver. Within minutes of leaving the airport, they were enthralled by the city and then by the lush green hillsides where houses were built seemingly on top of each other.

Sometime later and after leaving the busy freeway, they meandered up the road passing by elegant homes with beautifully landscaped yards. Saying nothing, the women could only stare out the car windows, giving an occasional sigh at what they saw.

"Are you *sure* he's taking us to the right place?" Marie whispered to Ellie who sat across from her.

"I'm quite sure, Auntie," Ellie replied, keeping her eyes welded to the scene passing by outside. "Lucy said it *would* be quite a long ride."

"Do you have any idea what this place is that we're going to?" Rose asked of her daughter. "Didn't she tell you anything?"

"Just that it's a surprise and she has to tell us in person," Ellie answered, realizing the countryside was beginning to look familiar. *Could this be what I'm thinking? But why would they bring us here, so far from Anchorage? They're not extravagant, so why this limousine?* No matter how hard she tried, Ellie could find no feasible explanation to any of this.

Suddenly, Ellie caught her breath at what she saw. "It's true! We *are* in wine country," she blurted, pointing through the window. "Those are grapes over there."

With growing excitement, Ellie told her mother and aunt about her train ride through the area and how she dreamed of living there one day. "It's all so beautiful," she sighed, wondering at the coincidence.

More than an hour later, the driver slowed and entered a driveway. On either side, a red-brick wall marked the entrance; atop the wall were black rot iron lanterns.

The lane seemingly led to a large house some distance away. To the left, behind tall white fences,

Ellie saw pastures where beautiful horses grazed and gangly young colts frolicked in the warm afternoon sun.

"I've never seen anything so lovely," Rose declared, peering through the window. "I had no idea of such places."

"Is that a hotel up ahead?" Marie asked, pointing.

"No, Auntie, that's someone's home," Ellie replied. "Can you imagine living in anything so beautiful?"

"Certainly not," Marie said, shaking her head. "Nor can I imagine cleaning all those windows!"

Sure enough, as they drew near, it was easy to see the many windows spaced across the front of the red-brick, two-story house. Vines of ivy trailed up the fireplace chimney and over the end of the dwelling. Two weeping willow trees cast a cooling shadow over the east and west corner of the elegant looking structure. Throughout the front-yard, flowerbeds held an array of brilliant colors and the well-kept lawn seemed void of even the slightest weed. Huge oak trees towered nearby.

"And, I can't imagine Matt and Lucy splurging on something this lavish," Ellie remarked then. "It's quite mysterious."

Minutes later, having brought the limousine from the lane and up the wide circular driveway, Richard stopped at the front door. Just then it opened and to Ellie's surprise, Matt, Lucy and Chad stepped into view.

With a cry of excitement, Ellie flung open the

car door and jumped out. In an instant she was in Lucy's arms while the men watched and awaited their turn. "Ladies, welcome to Napa Valley," Matt told them.

———————

Having arrived three days prior, Lucy and Matt had finished all the legal matters and could now tell their exciting news to those gathered. Still in awe over the elaborate estate she'd inherited, Lucy reveled in its blessing.

An hour later, after Ellie, Rose and Marie had been shown to their rooms, Matt and Lucy were busy in the kitchen. "This sure looks good, my pet," Matt said, eyeing the freshly made lemonade as well as the platter of sandwiches and homemade pumpkin bread.

"It'll do until supper," Lucy replied, placing napkins on the tray. "I guess that's about it. Oh, Matt, I can't wait to see their faces when they hear what's up," she added excitedly.

"Yes, and I'm very proud of you for keeping it a secret," he replied, pulling Lucy into his arms. "I know it wasn't easy."

"No, it wasn't, especially when I talked to Ellie and her need of some good news was so apparent," Lucy confessed. "What about Chad? Did you really keep it from him too?"

"Of course, I wanted him and Ellie to be excited together," Matt told her. "And now he has his own surprise to tell Ellie."

"That he does," Lucy said. "Now, my darling,

bring the tray along because it's time for our grand announcement." After a quick kiss for his wife, Matt obliged and the two headed outside where their guests sat waiting.

———————————

At seeing Ellie, Chad felt overjoyed. Not only had he missed her terribly since she'd left Anchorage, but knowing her state of mind at that time only fueled his concern. But now seeing her looking so radiant, a month later, he couldn't wait to have some time alone with her. *Do I dare hope she's put her past behind her and will consent to marry me in the near future?* Chad had to wonder. *What will she think about my news when I tell her?*

"Do you know what this is all about?" Ellie asked him as they gathered outside on the veranda. "And, who owns this place?"

"I assure you, Matt wouldn't budge when I asked," Chad had to admit. "As for all this, I have no idea," he sighed, looking around the lavish setting.

———————————

"Here we are," Lucy announced as she and Matt came through the door smiling somewhat mischievously for keeping everyone in suspense. "This is perfectly wonderful, having each of you here to share our celebration," she added, smiling at each one.

"And we're patiently waiting," Chad said,

drumming his fingers on his chair, feigning his agitation.

"Yes, and we've chosen to wait until everything was in place, so there'd be no misinformation," Matt replied, handing each one a glass of lemonade. "Now, if I may offer a toast before we begin," he added, lifting his glass.

"To Rose and Marie: may this day be the beginning of a long and blessed friendship. To Ellie: whom we love as a daughter and has brought immense joy to our lives. To Chad: my brother, whose friendship I'll cherish always," Matt said, looking at each one. "And, last but certainly not least, to Lucy, the love of my life and with whom I long to grow old with. I salute you," he concluded.

"Here … here," everyone said as they lifted their glass toward Matt.

"What a wonderful toast, my darling husband," Lucy whispered when she had reached his side. "When we're using our canes and walkers, will you still say these kind sweet words to me?" she asked, gazing in his eyes.

"You can count on it," he answered with that familiar gleam in his eye.

"Okay you two, let's hear it," Chad spoke up a moment later. "We're all ears and it better be good after coming all this way."

"I assure you, it's worth the trip," Matt told his brother. "Do you want to do the honors, sweetheart?" he then asked Lucy.

"No, you start and I'll finish up if you've left

anything out," Lucy told him, taking a seat next to Rose.

"I'll begin by saying how happy we are that you've come," Matt told them. "No doubt you're wondering about this place and why we've brought you here. Well, here's the reason: everything you see was given to Lucy by a very generous lady named Violet Covington," he informed the others which brought a sudden and unified gasp of disbelief.

"That's amazing," Marie commented.

"*Everything*...even those horses out there?" Ellie blurted, pointing toward the pasture.

"Yes, everything, even the limousine you rode in," Lucy told them. "And, the driver is paid up for a full year!"

"But why and who *is* this wonderful lady?" Chad wanted to know.

"She was once a patient of Lucy's, long ago and far away, in Virginia."

"I was stunned to receive notice that I was named her beneficiary," Lucy said, "and this is part of the estate."

"Only *part* of it?" Chad blurted before letting out a long low whistle.

"Oh Lucy, this is wonderful!" Ellie said jumping to her feet like a schoolgirl. "Are you staying or going back to Anchorage?"

"That's our next big news," Matt continued, taking Lucy's hand. "I think I'll let her tell you what she has planned."

Although a month had elapsed since hearing of her inheritance, Lucy still had trouble containing her emotion when thinking about her dream. Swallowing her tears, she looked up at her husband and then to the others.

"Ellie, remember our talks about helping young girls find a better life? We said we wanted to help them escape from desperate situations? Well, this place *and* the money now make it all possible," Lucy announced.

"Oh, I can't believe it!" Ellie cheered giving Lucy a hug. "It's all so wonderful. You said if God was in it, it would work out, somehow. And just look, it did!" Rose and Marie looked at each other as they sat listening.

"You mean this is going to be a home for wayward girls?" Chad asked, looking somewhat puzzled.

"It'll be a safe haven where they can come and learn basic skills: sewing, cooking, managing money and most importantly, they'll hear about the One who truly loves them," Lucy explained. "That's why I've brought you all here. Rose, I know you sew beautifully. I've seen your handy-work in Ellie's dresses. Would you consider coming here to live so you can teach these young women the art of sewing?" Lucy asked kindly.

"You really...want *me* to do this?" Rose stammered, looking surprised.

"Yes, I really do," Lucy replied. "I want you and Ellie to live here and be my assistants. To do a good job I need people to help me. Marie, I've heard you're a fine cook, so would you consider using your skills here?"

Once again Lucy's words brought a look of surprise from her guests. "Oh my, I've never thought my cooking was anything special," Marie answered, seemingly amazed at such a request. "I'll have to think about this."

"Of course, please. This is a big step so I want you all to think about everything," Lucy told them. "Ellie, you've come so far, I know you could help these young women, too," she said, remembering the horror of Ellie's past.

"You mean we'd live *here* in this beautiful house?" Ellie whispered as her eyes drifted across the large front yard. "Oh, I'd love it!"

"Yes, there's plenty of room for everyone, and up to a dozen young women who might need a place of escape," Lucy remarked. "That's the plan."

For the next few minutes there was silence as everyone seemingly pondered what had just been said. Certainly, this announcement summoned a change in everyone's demeanor.

As Lucy waited, she couldn't help but notice the look on Chad's face. *Will this put a damper on his future with Ellie? God, you've brought us this far, I know you'll work it out no matter what,* Lucy quickly decided.

———

As Ellie let her eyes drift across the landscape, her heart soared with excitement. *Dear Lord, you gave Lucy her dream and mine too. Thank you! And now we can all live and work here together on this beautiful place.*

"I think it's a *splendid* idea," Ellie raved, looking at each one. "What more could we ask? Living and working here together, doing what we love? Mother, just think, you can sew till the cows come home, and teach it, too," she went on. "And Auntie, how often have you wished you had someone to cook and bake for? Well, now you do."

"And, we'll pay all your moving expenses," Matt told the women. "There's room for whatever you might want to bring."

"Well, as for me, I'll *do* it," Rose said, bringing a cheer from the others. "I've never seen anything so lovely and inspiring," she added, looking around.

"What about you, Aunt Marie? You've taught me so much. I know you can help other young women, too," Ellie coaxed. "Besides, what would Mother and I do without you?"

"Well, the warmer winters *would* be nice, and if I can bring my little dog, Sam, then I guess there's nothing holding me in La Junta," Marie said.

With that announcement more cheers erupted. "Well, my pet, it appears you have just hired most of your staff," Matt remarked, putting his arm around Lucy's shoulder.

"Oh, yes! Thank you all. You've saved me many hours of interviews," Lucy told them. "Just as soon as we get moved in we'll let the community know who we are and what we intend to do."

Noticing Chad's silence, Ellie realized he didn't share everyone's enthusiasm. *Chad has his own news to tell me, but whatever it is, it won't top this!* Ellie decided.

"Now, everyone, please sit and enjoy some refreshments while Matt and I make a few phones call," Lucy told them. "Later, we'll take you on a tour around the place." With that the couple went inside, leaving the others seemingly amazed over what they'd learned.

"Let's go take a closer look at those horses, shall we?" Chad told Ellie a few minutes later. "Maybe we'll even take a ride this evening."

"Oh, I'd love to," Ellie said, getting to her feet. "This is the most glorious day I could ever imagine. Didn't I tell you they're great?" she said, looking at her mother and aunt. "And, this wonderful detective is the one who got us all together," Ellie said smiling as she took Chad's arm. "We'll be back."

With Chad's lopsided grin aimed at her, Ellie felt even more elated as they left the veranda and headed for the pasture. Saying nothing, Chad only covered her hand with his as they walked. Closing her eyes, Ellie looked heavenward, letting the afternoon sun drench her face with its warmth.

Slowly, the two meandered in silence. Despite her own happiness, Ellie sensed Chad's news might bring a much different response.

"You're awfully quiet. Is anything wrong?" she finally asked.

"In light of what we just heard, it's somewhat disappointing, but I received a nice promotion last week," Chad replied.

"Oh, that's wonderful!" Ellie blurted. "So how is that disappointing?"

"Because it requires me to move east, to Maryland," Chad told her. "It'll bring a nice bonus and more money every month, but I'll also be farther away from my family, and most importantly, too far from you."

When hearing this, Ellie also felt a sudden wave of disappointment. "But it won't be forever, will it? I mean, you *will* get to move back this way, later?" Ellie asked, knowing she'd miss him terribly.

"It could be years down the road," Chad told her. "The position I've been offered requires security clearance and a certain degree in law enforcement. I studied long and hard for this chance, but now that I have it, I'm not sure I want it."

"Oh, you have to take it, Chad! Don't let all your hard work go down the drain," Ellie told him. "You can come for visits, we can talk on the phone, and besides, it's your chance to have *your* dream."

Just as they reached the fence surrounding the pasture, Chad stopped and looked at Ellie. His face appeared solemn as he seemingly searched for the right words. "My dear, sweet Ellie," he began. "Don't you know by now that *you're* my dream? I love you and I want to spend the rest of my life with you. There is no job or promotion that means as much to me as you do."

Without a doubt, Ellie believed what he said. The look in his eyes revealed his heart. At that moment, she wanted to say yes to his dream. Yet, she knew it wasn't possible—maybe one day, but not anytime soon.

"You know why I can't marry you, Chad. I'm not fit to be a wife to you or anyone," Ellie replied, turning from his gaze. "This is what I'm committed to now, helping Lucy with all this. Since my experience in Homer, I know this place is needed to help young women get a new start."

Making no comment, Chad took hold of the fence railing and pulled himself up. Crawling atop, he braced himself as he looked around. "It's all quite spectacular," he said softly. "I do wish you and Lucy much success."

"Thank you, Chad. And, I hope your new job brings you all the rewards you've worked so hard for," Ellie told him truthfully. Saying nothing, Chad's gaze seemingly swept across the wide pasture while his face grew taut with noticeable emotion.

For Ellie, she wasn't thinking about a future with Chad, instead, she wanted to do the best job she could to help Lucy in this wonderful project God had somehow made possible. Marriage was the farthest thing from Ellie's mind, yet, she loved Chad for his kind and gentle manner. *Lord, you know I want to get married some day, so please, let me get past those horrible memories of abuse,* Ellie prayed as she climbed up the fence and sat down beside Chad. Then, reaching for Ellie's hand, Chad lifted it to his lips and gently kissed it.

CHAPTER SIXTEEN

The next two months were busy for everyone. In La Junta, Colorado, Marie found a renter for her house and she, along with Ellie and Rose, had a huge yard sale. By October fifteenth, the three women were settled in at Covenant House.

Before Lucy could officially open her doors there were several state and county permits to acquire. Plus, she needed to attend classes to update her training as a counselor and move her nursing license to California.

Within days of meeting all requirements, Covenant House had welcomed seven young residents, ranging in age from twelve to sixteen. Each girl had been rescued from the streets where they'd run to escape alcoholic or abusive parents. Covenant House gave each one a second chance for a better life.

Sarah was sixteen; Amy and Ruth were sisters,

ages twelve and thirteen. Kim and Carol were both fourteen; then come Alexandra, thirteen and lastly was Louise, fifteen.

As each one arrived they were greeted by the entire staff of women, and then given a tour of the house and what would be their room if they decided to stay. "This is to be your home, not a jail," Lucy would tell them. "We want to be your family where you are loved and accepted, despite what your past may have been. Living here you will learn a balance for life's journey; skills, accomplishments, self-worth and love."

After hearing Lucy's program and seeing her kind, gentle manner, not one girl had chosen to move on. Instead, they eagerly accepted the rigid curriculum of: Bible study, money management, cooking, sewing and gardening. Each one would also receive extensive counseling.

One day each week they were given a sum of money. The amount they received would depend on their attitude and the effort they put forth in class. No one would receive more than ten dollars per week, nor less than two. They could save it or spend it.

At first they all looked forward to shopping, but after a few sessions on money management, they opted to save it in their 'mock bank.' With eager anticipation each girl worked hard to see who could earn and save the most. Each month there would be a winner who'd receive a bonus from the bank.

With each new arrival, it was Ellie's job to show them around the estate. It was during this casual time of visiting and getting acquainted they would often express to Ellie their feelings and fears. It was evident that each newcomer found her to be a confident and friend, just as Lucy predicted.

With Thanksgiving only a few days away, the house was filled with the tantalizing aroma of fresh baked pies, cinnamon rolls and bread. For Marie, each day was filled with fun and gratification as she taught the young women how to bake and prepare meals. Never before had she felt so worthwhile.

To Rose, Covenant House had opened her eyes to many things. Here, she found a purpose to live and freedom from the guilt that had nearly carried her over the brink of insanity. During their daily Bible Study, Rose learned about that One who is the source of inner peace that Ellie and Lucy enjoyed. Within weeks of moving into Covenant House, Rose, too, stepped out in faith to receive the free gift of salvation, bringing her unimaginable joy.

With Chad flying in from Maryland and Matt arriving from Anchorage the next day, the house was a hubbub of activity. Classes would be suspended for four days, giving everyone a six day break from the routine. After much discussion regarding chaperons and supervision, Lucy finally agreed to let all seven girls go camping with their youth group from church. She decided the two-day outing would be fun and a much deserved reprieve from their studies.

Since opening Covenant House, Lucy had had

little time for her husband. Although Matt commuted between Anchorage and California as often as he could, it was certain to change with the onset of winter. This visit would bring discussion on what changes should be made.

It was Tuesday morning. For everyone in Covenant House the day began early as seven giggling and excited girls prepared to leave for camping.

Now, with their bags packed and breakfast eaten, each nervously glanced out the window, awaiting the arrival of the white church van. "Okay, girls, are you certain you have everything on the list?" Lucy asked when entering the parlor. "Mosquito repellant, extra clothes, Bible, money?" she added kindly.

"Not money," they quickly replied, glancing at each other.

"Well then, I guess I'll need to give you a small sum, in case you stop somewhere," Lucy said, handing them each a five dollar bill.

"Thank you, *thank you*, Lucy," they chimed together as grins appeared on their faces.

"We'll be careful what we buy," Sarah said assuredly, tucking her money in her small handbag. "Thank you for thinking of us."

"You're very welcome, all of you," Lucy replied, looking at each one. "I'm so proud of you all. You've filled this place with happiness because of your sweet spirit and cooperation. We love having you here as part of our family."

Just then a horn sounded outside announcing the van's arrival. Quickly, the girls grabbed their bags and yelled a hurried goodbye as they rushed out the door. From the doorway, Lucy waved and from the kitchen window, Marie and Rose did likewise.

The afternoon sun felt especially warm for November as Ellie headed for the stable. Today she would take a leisurely ride without the girls. Horseback riding was earned by high marks in housekeeping. The girls' rooms had to be neat and clean at all times, even their dresser drawers. Surprisingly, each girl worked hard to attain the privilege of going riding with Ellie.

Soon, she arrived at the stall of her favorite horse, Comet. "Hello, big boy...ready for some fresh air?" she asked, rubbing his head and ears. "Just me this morning, guys," she said, seeing the other horses looking at her. "They'll be back and next time you'll all be going," she said somewhat apologetically, wondering at her explanation to the inquisitive animals.

Minutes later she had Comet ready to go and after leading him outside, Ellie swung atop the Gelded Palomino without using the stirrup.

Whether due to her solitude or because she'd be seeing Chad in a few hours, Ellie felt giddy with happiness. Before long, the trail led into the woods and moments later she saw sunlight filtering through the trees, causing a feeling of wonderment to wash over her.

Dear God, did all that horror really happen to me? How did I get here from there? Ellie wondered, feeling as though it had all been a bad dream. *I can't believe how things have worked out in my life. You've guided my footsteps and brought me to this beautiful place. I have so much already, but Lord, I do want a normal life. Chad loves me and what better man could I find? Lucy said our prayers will be answered and I'll forget all those horrible memories. For now, I guess it doesn't matter since this is where I want to be. Mother and Aunt Marie are ecstatically happy; these girls are being helped and I love being here with Lucy. She says life is full of valleys and mountaintops and we never know when it'll change, so all we can do is keep trusting, no matter what. That's what I'm going to do,* Ellie decided as she nudged Comet into a gallop.

It was nearly two o'clock that afternoon when Chad radioed the tower for clearance to land his Twin Engine Beech Baron. He loved having his own plane and was grateful for the good weather report. This was his first visit to California since taking his new job and he couldn't wait to see Ellie.

Despite the excitement of seeing everyone again, Chad couldn't help but think about the disturbing news he'd heard early that morning. *Barton's still out there and we know he's making inquiries about Ellie. I sure don't like having to tell her, especially when things are going so well for her and Lucy,* Chad thought, recalling the happiness in Ellie's voice each time he called.

As Chad landed his plane and taxied up the runway, he felt excited about the days ahead. Once, he almost decided against the visit, but somehow he felt he had to come. *Perhaps she's missed me enough to accept my engagement ring,* Chad thought, recalling how long he'd shopped for just the right one. *What's the best time? During a romantic dinner, a horseback ride or maybe fly her somewhere special? No matter what, I must convince her…*

After her ride, Ellie enjoyed a hot bath and then spent extra time getting dressed for Chad's arrival. At the thought of seeing him she had to wonder at the feelings stirring inside her. *What is this? I can't marry him,* Ellie decided, running the comb through her still-wet-hair. *Besides, I'm needed here with Lucy, Mother and Aunt Marie. I promised to help so I'll stay,* she vowed.

Thumbing through her closet, Ellie decided on a long navy-blue skirt and white sleeveless-high-necked blouse. When she was dressed, she dabbed some color on her lips, then studied her image in the mirror. "Will you *ever* be ready for marriage?" she muttered softly, realizing Chad wouldn't wait forever. No man would. "Oh, he'll be here any minute," she wailed when seeing the time.

Hurriedly, she left her room and headed downstairs. With the girls gone the house seemed unusually quiet. As she headed for a quick look out the parlor window, Ellie walked by Lucy's office, glancing in. With her back toward the door, Lucy was on the telephone in deep conversation.

"Are you serious? But how can this be, Matt?" she blurted, sounding upset. "Oh yes, of course, the newspaper article."

Although not one to eavesdrop, Ellie froze mid stride. A chill ran up her spine as she listened. *It's Jack Barton! He said he'd never give up,* Ellie decide, remembering his threats.

As she waited, needing to know details, Ellie's anger grew. *He needs to be stopped, once and for all! But how, do we set a trap?*

When Lucy's call had ended, Ellie entered the room. "Lucy? I didn't mean to eavesdrop, but I heard what you said. It's Jack Barton isn't it," she stated. "Has he found us?"

"Oh Ellie, I didn't want to spoil your weekend with Chad, but yes, I'm afraid so. That was Matt. He learned a somewhat *seedy* type was asking about Covenant House," Lucy began. "It seems my leaving Anchorage for California is a well-known fact, and since you lived with us there, all he had to do was make a few inquiries. Apparently, this man has his own connections and they're willing *and* able to give him whatever information he needs," she added, sounding more forlorn than Ellie could remember.

"Don't worry, Lucy. I'm *not* afraid of that man," Ellie said assuredly. "He needs to be stopped and I've no doubt Chad will know just the right plan."

Saying nothing, Lucy reached out and hugged

Ellie to her. "Oh sweetie, I couldn't bare it if anything happened to you," she whispered. "I don't know what we'll do, but we *must* do something."

A sinister grin appeared on Jack Barton's face as he looked up from the paper he'd been reading. "We got her!" he blurted. "Here's *proof* she's there in that fancy dump with nothin' but females. How hard can *that* be? We'll find a nice cozy spot to just sit and wait. When she shows, we got her," he sneered, kissing the barrel of his stub-nose 38.

"Are you *sure* of this, Boss?" Bumps asked. "Sure that it's all women?"

"So what *if* a man or two shows up? That's what I got you for," Jack fired back. "You've my bodyguard, ain't ya? Besides, who'd mess with a three-hundred-pound ugly monster like you?" he said, laughing.

For Jack, he felt sure no one would mess with the likes of Bumps Shay. Due to the deformities on his face, the man looked more like a circus sideshow than a body guard. Large bumps covered his face, chin and forehead. Not only was the man big, mean and ugly, he was tough.

"So, we're doing this soon?" Bumps questioned as he interlaced his fingers and bent them back, causing a popping sound. "I'm ready."

"Me too, it's been too long comin'," Jack said, nodding his head. "We'll take a leisurely drive to scope out the place and find our spot. Then, when

no one's around, we'll sneak in and plant ourselves.
We might just get lucky."

CHAPTER SEVENTEEN

When Chad stepped from the limousine, Ellie felt her heart leap inside her chest. Dressed in dark trousers and an emerald green shirt, he looked more handsome than she remembered. His hair was neatly trimmed and its shiny blondness glistened in the afternoon sun.

"Hello, Ellie," he said softly, giving her that familiar grin.

"Hello, Chad," Ellie replied, giving him a smile. Suddenly, she realized how much she'd missed him and that smile he so easily aimed at her. "Welcome to Covenant House."

"It's good to be here... I've missed you," he said taking hold of her hand. "You're looking lovely as ever," he added as his eyes scanned her face and hair.

"I've missed you, too," she answered, throwing her arms around his neck. "Oh Chad, what are we going to do?" she wailed unashamedly. "That horrible man knows where I am!"

"Marry me and let me protect you, my sweet Ellie," Chad whispered in her ear. "I love you now more than ever."

When she heard Chad's words, Ellie closed her eyes to bask in the sound of his voice and the feeling of being in his arms. For that moment she wanted to believe it was possible; she wanted nothing more than to say yes to Chad.

"Oh, if only it was that easy," she said, fighting her tears. "He'd find us no matter where we go. We can't live in fear, not knowing when he'd show up. Isn't there *some way* we can stop him?" Ellie asked, ending the embrace.

"Are you saying you'd marry me if Barton was no longer a threat?" Chad asked then, studying her face. "Please, Ellie, *is* that what you're saying?"

Stepping back, Ellie looked in Chad's eyes, seeing his desperate need to know the truth. Suddenly she, too, needed to know if anything had changed.

For months she and Lucy had prayed for a miracle from God. They believed together that Jesus would heal Ellie's mind of the abusive memories that haunted her. Surely, without a miracle, Ellie would *never* marry. This was the day of truth. Today she'd know if those prayers had been answered.

"Hold me, Chad," Ellie requested, stepping up to him. "Take me in your arms and hold me. I need to know if I *can* accept your proposal."

Saying nothing, Chad gently reached for Ellie. As though she were a delicate porcelain doll, he took her in his arms. Tenderly, he pulled her to his chest, resting his head against her hair. Holding her breath, Ellie felt herself being cradled in Chad's arms.

Next, she felt his hand slowly caressing her face. She felt his hand on her back. She waited for memories to bombard her mind, reminding her of other hands, indecent and vile. None came. Instead, tears of joy erupted when she felt only love and protection radiating from Chad's touch.

"I love you, Ellie," he whispered. "And, I'll wait for you no matter how long it takes."

"It's okay, it's *really* okay!" Ellie blurted, pushing herself free of his arms. "It's you I feel, not him!"

"But you're crying."

"These are tears of celebration, Chad. I'm *free!* Thank you, God!" For a moment Chad only stared at her, seemingly in shock.

"Do you…are you…*sure?*" he stammered.

"I'm *very* sure," Ellie replied, covering her cheeks with her hands. "It worked. Our prayers *really* worked! We have to tell Lucy." Reaching out for Chad's hand, Ellie pulled him toward the front door. "Oh, *she'll* be surprised!"

———————

Chad felt ten-feet tall. Suddenly, his life had changed—for the better. Indeed, when they found Lucy she was thrilled to hear Ellie's good news. "There's no limit to what God will do for us," she told Ellie, giving her a hug. "Well Chad, what better welcome could there be for you?" Lucy teased a moment later, giving him a hug.

"None that I can think of," he said, looking at Ellie. *Thank God I made this trip after all. If only we didn't have Barton to worry about,* Chad reasoned, knowing he'd protect Ellie with his life.

Since his arrival, Chad had spent much of his time on the telephone talking to local FBI agents, regarding Jack Barton. Although he was no longer on the case, Chad was determined to do all he could to protect Ellie, and those living at Covenant House.

It was late afternoon by the time Matt arrived from Anchorage. Within an hour of his arrival, everyone was enjoying one of Marie's delicious dinners. "This is wonderful. Certainly better than *my* cooking," Matt remarked, dishing another helping of roast beef on his plate.

"You could stay and have this everyday," Ellie coaxed.

"Well, we might work something out," Matt commented, looking at Lucy who sat next to him. "Now, that we have a certain problem to solve."

"Yes, until Jack Barton is caught, we'll need all the help we can get around here," Lucy remarked, looking at those at the table. "But, thanks to Chad, we will have round-the-clock police protection."

"Well, he *is* wanted by federal agents since he killed two deputies," Chad told the others. "We all want to get this killer. Unfortunately, we have a lot of innocent people living here."

"Won't this man know they're cops, if he sees them?" Rose then asked.

"They'll be disguised as yardmen and stable boys. Certainly, they won't look like federal agents," Chad assured everyone. "But, given Barton's past history we know he's slick and covers all his bases."

"What about the girls? We can't expect them to stay in seclusion until you catch him, can we?" Marie spoke up. "They're outside much of the time, gardening, riding horses. This all sounds pretty risky to me."

"Yes, yes it is," Matt replied, sighing. "So we have a plan. We can't put these young girls in harms way. Not only could they get hurt, but if the news media gets wind of all this, we're ruined. I can see it now: *Covenant House Loses Credibility as Feds Look for Killer*. And, we'd never forgive ourselves if any-one got hurt in all this," he concluded.

"So, what *can* we do?" Marie asked, looking puzzled.

"We're going to rent another house some dis-tance from here. It'll be large enough for everyone and Barton won't make the connection. Besides, the bait will still be here," Matt announced solemnly.

"*Bait*, you mean Ellie?" Rose blurted, obviously shocked at such news.

"Yes, Mother. I *have* to stay here. It's me he wants and none of us can live normal lives until he's caught. I'm willing to do whatever it takes," Ellie told the others. "Besides, I won't be alone, you heard what Chad said."

As he listened, Chad knew she was right. Yet,

he hated to think of his sweet Ellie being used for such a purpose. *This has to be solved somehow,* he reasoned, wishing he could marry Ellie today and take her away with him.

"Tomorrow, we'll find a house where you'll all be safe. And Ellie, my dear girl, we'll make sure you're well protected. Right, Chad?" Matt concluded, looking concerned.

"I'm going to insist on it. If I have to quit my job to do it, I will," Chad said, looking in Ellie's eyes.

———————

It was late when Chad coaxed Ellie outside. "I think it'd be a shame to miss that night sky. Let's see if you agree," he said, leading her through the door.

Sure enough, the sky sparkled as though a million diamonds had been flung across its vastness; the full moon looked like a giant silver ball, bringing a gasp of excitement from Ellie. "Oh Chad, you're right. It's beautiful!"

"You must enjoy this sight every night here in California," Chad remarked as they both looked heavenward.

"Actually, we aren't allowed outside after dark— house rules," Ellie replied. "But, no one seems to mind. We're usually busy playing games or just talking about different experiences. Now however, I just *might* slip out to see all this," she admitted.

"Not until Barton's behind bars," Chad cautioned, looking at her. "Please, stay inside as much as possible. Promise me you will." As he stood beside Ellie, Chad wondered if this was the right time. During the day his thoughts were often on her and the ring he carried. "I'd go crazy, Ellie, if anything happened to you," he whispered, reaching for her hand.

"I just want this over with. He's disrupted all our lives, from the very beginning," Ellie lamented, turning to look at Chad.

"Yet, if he hadn't been on that ferry, we never would have met," Chad reasoned, lifting his hand to caress Ellie's cheek. "Isn't that right?"

"I believe God brings people into our lives at the right time, using any means necessary," Ellie said. "So, if we're meant to be together, Chad, God would have worked it out somehow, without Jack Barton."

"How did you get to be so smart?" Chad asked, realizing she was right. "I know there's a special purpose for all of us, and a certain someone we're meant to be with. I believe we *are* meant for each other, Ellie. Do you?"

Saying nothing, Ellie turned away. Then, with a gasp, she suddenly yelled. "There's someone out there!" Just then two loud pops were heard.

Instantly, Chad was in a nightmare as he saw Ellie's body go limp. "No!" he cried, reaching out to catch her. The scene felt surreal as he looked at his beloved Ellie, lying motionless. In the moonlight he saw two men running. He heard Lucy's cry of agony as she and Matt rushed outside. Instinctively, Chad reached for his gun. "Call an ambulance!" he ordered.

With his heart pounding, Chad left Ellie's side

and started after the assailants. "Police! Stop or I'll shoot!" he yelled, closing in on them. There was no regard for the warning. Stopping, Chad took aim at the shadowy figures and then fired. In the dark a cry of pain was heard. *I hope that's you, Barton!* Chad thought as he cautiously continued on.

———————

Unable to speak, Rose and Marie watched in horror as Matt and Lucy hurriedly worked on Ellie. In stunned silence, they watched as Ellie's bloodied white blouse was torn, revealing a gunshot wound. A bloody gash was seen on her head. *My little girl, please, God, don't take my little girl. We've only begun to live,* Rose pleaded as she and Marie clung to each other.

In surprising calm, Lucy relayed information over the phone to the hospital, her words becoming lost to Rose amid the carnage she saw. There was no response from Ellie, instead, she lay silent and unmoving...

———————

Adrenalin surged through Chad's veins as he reached the man on the ground. Visions of Ellie tore at his heart. *I hope you're dead, Barton! At least you aren't going anywhere,* he decided, seeing a dark stain on the back of the man's jacket.

Just then he heard a noise behind him. Turning, he had no time to avoid the massive figure that suddenly lunged at him, knocking him to the ground; the gun flew from Chad's hand.

From years of training, Chad knew what to do, yet, it was soon obvious his opponent was no novice in the art of combat. Not only that, he was monstrous in size.

Over and over they rolled atop each other, breaking each hold the other tried. Then, in the moonlight, Chad saw the shiny edge of a knife being raised over him. At that moment, he felt the hard steel of his own weapon lying on the ground beside him.

Seemingly in slow motion, Chad wrapped his fingers around the grip and lifted his gun. Just as he pulled the trigger, the knife plunged downward...

CHAPTER EIGHTEEN

For Lucy, the events of the past few hours seemed a blur as she stared out the window. She felt disconnected, finding no reason to hope. Her mind was numb with disbelief as she watched the ambulance, then the hearse slowly drive away. Somewhere, in the deepest part of her being, she knew there was a reason for everything; some reason why God allowed such events to happen.

In the background she heard voices, people saying polite phrases, their comments laced with sadness. Policemen wandered across the front yard; one held a camera while others talked on two-way radios.

"Let's go, darling," Matt whispered, draping a jacket around Lucy's shoulders. "I've given Rose and Marie a sedative. They'll be okay until we get back."

In robot-like-fashion, Lucy only nodded as Matt

led her from the room and outside to the limousine that sat waiting. Richard stood solemnly nearby and then closed the door after they were seated inside.

It's all a bad dream, surely I'll awake any minute, Lucy thought, feeling Matt's arms around her. Cradled against her husband, she closed her eyes, but there it was, that horrible scene of Ellie lying, perhaps mortally wounded.

Softly, the tears ran down her cheeks as she fought to dispel the scream that threatened to erupt. Somehow, she needed to jar herself from this nightmare. Only when she felt the soft crying of her husband did Lucy realize his sorrow; the torture of knowing his human limitations as a doctor.

"We have to keep trusting," Matt barely whispered. "It's in God's hands now." Being a nurse, Lucy knew such wounds were often fatal. Too much blood had been lost; too much trauma had assaulted their young bodies.

"Chad did his job. It might well cost him his life, but he's a hero," Matt went on, choking back his tears. "We must believe for *two* miracles."

Overwhelming despair shoved its way into Lucy's whole being. No matter how much she believed in miracles, somehow her reasoning left her wanting. *Oh God, I can't even pray. It's just too much!*

At that moment, from the depths of her spirit, Lucy heard the soothing comfort of her God. *I will carry this burden for you, my child; just trust and believe in me...*

Once more hot tears spilled down Lucy's face, yet, this time they were tears of relief, for surely she had heard from on High. God himself had given her hope and she could ask for no better guarantee...

Silently, they rode past the elite homes of Napa Valley. Due to the late hour, only a scattering of lighted windows were seen. The full moon that earlier had brought sighs of delight now hung on the distant horizon.

In a few hours, the small towns they traveled through would be filled with people rushing to prepare for Thanksgiving. For Lucy and Matt, their destination was the trauma center in San Francisco where Ellie and then Chad, had been flown earlier...

For those at Covenant House, Thanksgiving this year was far more than the usual festive gathering. It was a celebration of miracles. Although Chad and Ellie were still critical, they had survived against impossible odds and had gotten through those first crucial twenty-four to thirty-six hours.

Upon her arrival at the trauma center, Ellie was pronounced dead on arrival. Had it not been for a very astute young intern who rechecked her vital signs one final time, the young gunshot victim would have been moved to the hospital morgue.

Instead, when seeing a slight flutter on the heart monitor, the young man alerted the trauma team into action. There was no doubt in anyone's mind: their patient had a guardian angel on duty. Not only did a bullet graze the side of her head, but another one entered her chest below the right shoulder. Miraculously, it passed through without shattering bone. Yet, Ellie's blood loss was extreme, causing even the most seasoned doctor to shake his head in disbelief. Eleanor Cooper was heralded as a 'most memorable miracle patient.'

For Chad, surgery was required to repair the knife wound to his chest and right lung. He too, had lost a critical amount of blood. To his credit, he had brought an end to the long and arduous manhunt for Jack Barton and one of his most violent cohorts, Bumps Shay. Both had been taken to the county morgue where their bodies would await burial in a pauper's cemetery.

For December, it was an exceptionally warm day, even for California. Everyone was excited as they awaited Ellie's arrival. Since his release from the hospital, five days prior, Chad had been recuperating at Covenant House and was being pampered by everyone, especially Rose and Marie.

"Are you sure you'll want to leave all this?" Matt asked his brother as he joined him on the veranda. "It's pretty hard to give up, I'd say."

"Yeah, you're right. What about you, are you going to stay for good this time?" Chad wanted to know. "After all, this is where your wife is and I'd say you could help plenty around here."

"Well, I'm being coaxed and I have to admit, this *is* my kind of weather. By the way, Chad, I got a call from the police department. They want to do something special for you," Matt revealed. "They feel somewhat responsible for what happened, especially since you had already asked for men to be posted."

"That all takes time. If anyone's responsible, it's me," Chad replied. "I'm the one who brought Ellie outside that night. I knew Barton was closing in, but wanting to spend time with her, I got careless. If we had lost her I couldn't have lived with myself—it would have been too much."

"No one blames *you*, Chad. Your life was on the line, but you did your job and brought an end to this nightmare, for all of us, especially Ellie. I know she's grateful," Matt said, patting Chad's leg. "It's finally all behind us. Now, I'm supposed to help Lucy with some things before Ellie arrives, so I better get moving," he said, glancing at his watch.

When Matt left, Chad replayed that night over in his mind for the hundredth time. Again, he came to the same conclusion: he was at fault. *I never wanted to hurt you, Ellie. I said I never would, but I almost got you killed,* Chad lamented, wondering how she felt about him now.

Once more he gazed toward the road, looking for that long shiny car that would be arriving any minute. His heart began pounding when he thought about seeing Ellie for the first time since it all happened.

———————

The ride from the hospital was a bit tiring for Ellie, but she was grateful for Aunt Marie's company. It was obvious the woman didn't plan to talk about that horrible night, yet Ellie felt led to.

"It was quite miraculous, Auntie," Ellie began. "In that instant, before I lost consciousness, I knew I'd been shot but I wasn't afraid. I felt complete peace and somehow I knew I'd be all right, regardless of whether I lived or died."

"You mean you weren't afraid to die?" Marie asked in shock. "But, I thought everyone was scared of dying."

"Not when we know Jesus, Auntie," Ellie replied, gazing out the window. "We have his promise that he's preparing a far better place for us than we could ever imagine, and oh, it's true!"

For Ellie, life was far sweeter now since she had been privileged to see heaven's glory; that place of constant joy and breathless beauty. Yet, she had told no one what she had seen or experienced. For now it would remain her private adventure, but, it had taught her so much. No longer would she fear the future; she knew life here was in preparation for the life to come.

"Oh, Auntie, you just *have* to be ready because life is so uncertain," Ellie said, reaching for Marie's hand. "It's so easy—we just trust in faith believing."

"Well, to be honest, dear, I've heard what you've all been saying, and have noticed the changed lives and attitudes, and lately I feel I need this, too," Marie told her. "Is it *really* as easy as you say?"

"Oh yes, you can pray anywhere and ask Jesus

in your heart," Ellie proclaimed excitedly. "Right here, right now!"

"Well then, I want to," Marie announced boldly. "Will you help me?"

"Yes!" Ellie blurted excitedly. So, there in the back of the limousine, Ellie led Aunt Marie in a prayer of repentance that brought tears of joy moments later. "What a homecoming this has turned out to be!"

"Yes, *indeed*," Marie answered while wiping her tears. "I feel wonderfully refreshed and lighter somehow."

"Isn't it marvelous?" Ellie raved, giving her aunt a big hug.

With this exciting news, they couldn't wait to get home. Minutes later, they saw the familiar red-brick fence marking the lane to Covenant House. Although she faced days of recuperation, Ellie knew coming home would help immensely, and she couldn't wait to see everyone, especially Chad.

It had been a night of horror for everyone, but for Ellie, the thought of Jack Barton being gone for good somehow made it all worthwhile. *Thank God, I can finally get on with my life,* Ellie thought, feeling excited about the future.

Soon, Richard was opening her car door and helping her out, into the loving arms of those who had eagerly waited. The afternoon sun was no match for the warmth Ellie felt as each one welcomed her home. Words of love and thanksgiving for her survival were given by all.

In the background, she saw Chad. Looking somewhat thinner, he gave her that familiar grin as he walked toward her. Magically, all else faded from view as Chad remained her focus.

"Hello, Ellie, welcome home," he said softly, taking her hand.

"Hello, Chad. Thanks for staying alive," she replied, smiling at him. "Can we get married now? I think we've wasted enough time."

At that, Chad wrapped his arms around Ellie and next to her ear he whispered, "I thought you'd never ask."

"Hey everyone, we have a wedding to plan!" Ellie announced as she lingered in Chad's embrace. Cheers erupted and in their weakened conditions, Ellie and Chad turned and walked hand in hand to the veranda.

This had been a glorious day and Ellie couldn't wait to see what the future had in store...

Nearly six months had elapsed since that horrible night everyone still remembered, but no longer talked about. Instead, there were happy occasions.

Due to the many at Covenant House whose hearts and lives had been changed by their newfound faith, a baptismal service was planned at church. This marked a milestone in everyone's life and following the service, the front lawn at Covenant House was the site of a great celebration.

In April, Ellie and Chad both celebrated their birthdays just eight days apart. Now, with May flowers in abundance, they would be married in the garden at Covenant House. No one was excluded from having part in the much anticipated event. The date: May 9, 1961.

It was Rose's ultimate joy to have whatever material and accessories she needed for Ellie's wedding dress and those of her attendants. Lucy was determined to give Ellie the wedding of her dreams, so plans proceeded.

Marie, having help from Amy and Louise, her prize students, had worked long and hard to get just the right taste and texture for the wedding cake. Now, much like guards at Buckingham Palace, the three allowed no one inside the large pantry where it sat waiting.

At precisely two o'clock on this warm sunny afternoon, with a hundred or so guests in place on the spacious lawn, the orchestra struck the cords that began the wedding precession.

From the side, Chad, his best man and four groomsmen entered. Each one handsomely dressed in gray tuxedoes, turned to face the guests. Then, the bridesmaids slowly started down the grassy carpet toward a white arch bedecked with beautiful flowers.

Wearing soft pink to lavender shade dresses and perfectly matched shoes, the four carried baskets of spring flowers. Then, it was Lucy, the Maid of Honor, in her dress of deepest lilac.

Next, a murmur of excitement swept through the crowd and everyone stood to their feet as the Wedding March began. The bride was on her way...

For Chad, every fiber of his being was wrapped in excitement and thanksgiving. He had *never* felt this happy. Today, his deepest desire would become a reality as he and Ellie vowed their love to each other.

Just then he saw her. Despite his manly composure, Chad's eyes welled with tears. Never before had he seen a more beautiful sight than his bride walking toward him.

Ellie's long white dress, with fitted bodice and long tapered sleeves, billowed out around her. On a white Bible she carried a bouquet of pink and purple flowers, with trailing ivy.

With majestic poise she drew near and Chad saw her smile radiating from behind her veil. Then, with a broad grin, Matt placed Ellie's hand in his as the moment finally arrived.

Although it was hard to say goodbye to everyone at Covenant House, Ellie looked forward to life as Mrs. Chad Ryan. Following their honeymoon to Hawaii, they were soon settled in their spacious apartment in Maryland.

Because of his continued dedication to his job and law enforcement in general, Chad was again promoted. This time it was to a federal bureau office in San Francisco. Everyone was thrilled to have them back in California just six months after their wedding.

For Ellie and Chad, life had continued as it started that May afternoon. Seemingly, nothing could mar their happiness or dampen their enthusiasm. Life was good and each day they thanked God for their endless blessings.

Both felt overjoyed to again be living in California, and being close to Napa Valley allowed Ellie time to spend many hours a week at Covenant House. She was thrilled to get reacquainted with the older resident girls and to meet each new arrival. As before, she became their confidant and friend.

For Ellie, life was far beyond anything she could have imagined…

CHAPTER NINETEEN

TWO AND A HALF YEARS LATER

With the success of Covenant House and following Ellie's marriage, Lucy moved her mother from Virginia to enjoy the warmer weather and happy surroundings. Mona soon became close friends with Rose and Marie, *and* her loving grandmotherly ways were readily accepted by each of the girls.

When Covenant House reached full capacity, Matt decided to close his medical practice in Anchorage, at least temporarily, to help Lucy full time. He'd miss flying and helping the Alaskan people he'd come to know and love, yet, with each arrival of another hurting and confused young woman, Matt sensed a far greater challenge. Each one needed an abundance of love and direction.

For everyone, Covenant House had become their

safe haven where seemingly nothing could harm or destroy them. Yet, as time wore on, it became apparent that nowhere on earth could boast such a claim, not even this elegant home where happiness dwelled and lives were changed for the better. For here, within these walls, a silent enemy had subtlety gained access.

It was late December, nineteen sixty-three. Although the looming changes in everyone's lives had dampened the holiday spirit, Lucy and Matt had determined Covenant House would ring with song and merriment one last time. To their credit and hard work, the festive activities of Christmas did indeed lift the gloom that had shrouded everyone in recent weeks.

Today, a cold wind blew through the door each time it opened. Somehow, it matched the chill Lucy felt deep within her soul as she watched men load the moving van. *It's been wonderful living here, working together as a team, helping each other. But, now we have other challenges to face,* she thought, remembering the news she'd received weeks earlier.

Although Mona lived with her, Lucy had paid little mind to her mother's sagging memory. Instead, they had often joked about the way names slipped away or Mona forgot details of past events. Then, one day, Lucy realized it was no laughing matter. Suddenly, there were surprising mood swings and times of great agitation, both so unlike the mild-mannered woman. After a hurried appointment with a Neurologist to have her mother tested, Lucy's fears were confirmed: mental illness was now their reality.

Immediately, Lucy began searching for the best doctors and facilities to help her mother. Her search ended in Phoenix, Arizona. Again, Lucy was grateful for her inheritance which helped provide the best medical care.

It was also apparent, living in Covenant House with so many around, only added to Mona's confusion. Therefore, Lucy made the decision to close and devote however much time was left, to her mother.

As she thought about the future and the past years at Covenant House, Lucy was overcome with emotion as memories paraded through her mind. Memories of those unforgettable moments; Ellie's and Chad's brush with death, then, their wedding six months later that somehow erased the horror of that night.

She thought about each girl they had rescued. Here, they had blossomed into beautiful young women. Each one had graciously accepted the rules and training required of them. Some had reconciled with their parents. In faith, all had reconciled with their Heavenly Father through their trust in Jesus.

Yes, for Lucy, memories of this place would live on as would the extreme gratitude to God for allowing it to happen, if only for a season.

It was raining as Matt and Lucy prepared to leave

that morning. The van with their belongings left two days earlier and now, Matt's small plane would take them to Arizona.

As they hugged everyone goodbye, Lucy tried to forget about the days ahead and the sadness of seeing her mother fade even more from reality.

"Oh Lucy, this isn't goodbye," Ellie whispered as they embraced. "Thank you just isn't enough for all you've done for me. And, if you ever need me, just call, I'll come running."

"I know, sweetie," Lucy replied. "Thank you. I wish you'd reconsider and take my offer," she added. "I know you love it here."

"Oh, I *do* love it here, we all do, but it's time to move on," Ellie replied. "We have plenty of room in our home for Mother and Aunt Marie. Besides, they'll be great help when the baby comes," she announced softly after tugging Lucy to the far side of the room.

"Oh Ellie, that's *wonderful*," Lucy cheered, feeling grateful for this bit of good news. "When, how long must we wait?"

"It's not until late July. I haven't even told Chad," Ellie confessed. "But, I wanted to tell you before you left."

"Thank you, *thank you* for that," Lucy whispered, giving Ellie another hug. "You know I love you like a daughter and I expect to be Grandma, too, you know." At that, Ellie smiled.

"Okay, my dear, it's that time," Matt coaxed, giving Ellie his fatherly hug. "We expect to see you all very often, so get that husband of yours to fly you down whenever possible."

"I'm sure we'll be coming often enough, since you're there in all that sunshine," Chad teased as Ellie stepped from Matt's embrace.

One by one, Ellie, Rose and Marie gave Mona a hug and said their goodbyes. Barely a smile came in response.

Although the New Year was about to begin, Lucy knew it was sure to hold many challenges, yet, she was ready. Just as she impressed upon each girl she had rescued: God's mercy is new every morning.

———————

It was decided Ellie would stay with Rose and Marie at Covenant House, until it was sold. Chad would come after work on Friday afternoon and stay the weekend.

By now, everyone knew about the baby. Already, Rose was sewing and knitting baby clothes; Marie was pampering Ellie as though she were the first woman to give birth; Chad was thrilled beyond words.

Since closing Covenant House, Lucy had hired a neighbor to board all the horses. Although Ellie missed Comet immensely, Chad preferred his pregnant wife take walks for her exercise, instead of going riding.

It was January twentieth and so far the month was especially cold. A full week of rain had just ended and Ellie was eager to be outside.

"The sun is out, at least for now," Ellie cheered

looking out the window. "Time for my walk," she told Marie and Rose who sat in the parlor, reading.

"Okay dear, but *be* careful," Rose said, looking up from her magazine. "It's bound to be muddy *and* slippery in places."

"I will, Mother, and if a realtor should call, tell them anytime is fine to show the house. I won't be long," Ellie replied, zipping up her jacket.

The air felt brisk when she stepped outside causing her to reach for the earmuffs she'd stuffed in her pocket, just in case. To avoid the obvious mud, Ellie decided on the paved lane instead of the dirt path she normally used.

Stepping from the veranda she took a deep breath, filling her lungs with the clean fresh air. *Oh, this is wonderful, but better yet if Chad were here,* Ellie thought, anticipating the weekend.

As she walked, her mind filled with random thoughts of Lucy and Matt being so far away and the heartache they faced everyday. She thought about the happiness she and Chad enjoyed, not just the baby, but his great job, their own lovely home and having family with them to share it all. *Dear God, we're so blessed and I'm thankful for everything. No matter what happens in the future, our trust is in you,* Ellie prayed as she headed toward the road.

She had just reached the gate and was about to head back toward the house when she noticed a car slowing. *Perhaps it's someone looking to buy a place,* she thought, deciding to wait. As she did, the shiny red Cadillac stopped beside her. By this time the driver's window was rolled down.

"Excuse me, miss, could you tell me how to find Covenant House?" the man asked. "I know it's along this road somewhere."

"Well, you've found it; at least it used to be," Ellie said. "Now it's for sale."

"Oh, I'm sorry to hear that," he remarked solemnly. "Are you the owner, if I may ask?"

"No, but I'm watching over things until it's sold. How do *you* know about Covenant House?" Ellie asked, thinking the man looked familiar and wondered if she'd met him somewhere before.

"My daughter came here and it helped her immensely," he replied, glancing away momentarily. "I wanted to see this place and thank the people who helped her."

"I met every girl who came here. What's your daughter's name?" Ellie asked eagerly.

"Louise McGuire, but she might have used Louise Browning," he offered somewhat sadly. "She loved it here so much."

Quickly, Ellie's mind darted through the names and faces of the many girls who had lived at Covenant House, searching for one named Louise. "Oh yes, Louise, I remember her," Ellie said as the pretty-faced-redhead came to mind. "She *did* love it here and told me many times. Sweet girl…we all loved her and that beautiful auburn hair. How's she doing?"

Making no reply, the man shook his head and then lowered it against the car's steering wheel, surprising Ellie. "Are you all right?" she asked when seeing his obvious emotion. Getting no reply, she then stepped up to the car and reaching through the window she rested her hand on his shoulder. "Please, what is it?" she asked, fearing bad news.

"I'm sorry, miss, forgive me. I guess I shouldn't have come," he finally said. "We buried Louise this morning and I just wanted to see the place where she'd been the happiest," the man said in noticeable anguish.

Feeling stunned, Ellie could only watch as this father mourned for his child, the beautiful young woman whom she remembered so well. "I'm *sorry*," Ellie gasped. "Please, I'd be honored to show you Covenant House. If not today, then whenever you'd like," she added.

"You wouldn't mind, really?" the man asked, regaining his composure. "I'd like to see it now, if that's okay. I wouldn't want to impose—"

"Right now is fine. I was just taking a walk and about to head back," Ellie said. "It's that house at the end of this lane," she said, nodding that direction.

"Please, let me drive you," the man offered kindly. With that he quickly got out and opened the passenger side door for Ellie. "This means so much to me, especially now. By the way, miss, my name is Craig McGuire," he added, helping Ellie inside his car. "I didn't get your name."

For the second time Ellie was stunned and was grateful she had just sat down. "I'm Ellie Ryan, Mrs. Chad Ryan," she said, looking up at him.

As Craig closed her door and again got in the driver's seat, Ellie's mind darted back in time. *He doesn't recognize me. But, how could he? I was a scared young girl. Now, I'm married and totally changed*, Ellie thought, remembering the kind, handsome man who had once befriended her.

As they headed down the lane toward the house, Ellie glanced at Craig as he drove. He gazed intently at the place where his daughter spent a year of her young and troubled life. *Should I tell him? Would he even remember that particular train ride or how he lied to protect me?* Ellie wondered, still in shock at seeing the man again and how much he'd changed.

When they arrived at the house and exited the vehicle, Craig said nothing, but rather he stood seemingly in quiet reverence, letting his eyes drift across the estate. Unashamedly, tears again rolled down his face as he gazed across the lawn toward the stables. "She loved everything about this place," he finally said. "I can see why; it's peaceful here. My girl needed that in her life. God knows she didn't get it out there," he went on, lifting his hand toward some unseen enemy. "It was my fault, at least a lot of it, but she forgave me. She learned how to do that here, and so much more."

"You can spend however long you'd like, Mr. McGuire," Ellie told him. "Louise loved to ride. The horses are gone now, but you can see the stables and the woods where she rode if you'd like. After that I'll show you her room and where she spent much of her time."

"Thank you, that's very nice of you," Craig responded as a soft smile touched his face for the first time. "I'll see you a little later then."

Heading for the front door, Ellie stopped for a

moment and watched as Craig started down the path toward the barns. *He looks different; thinner and much older, but still quite handsome,* she decided, recalling the strikingly handsome man who had once offered her a job.

It was nearly an hour later when Ellie finished showing Craig through the house and particularly his daughter's room. "Mr. McGuire, I'd like you to meet my mother, Rose Cooper and my aunt, Marie Fuller," Ellie began when they had entered the parlor. "Louise spent many hours with both of them."

"What a pleasure to meet you," Craig said, shaking hands with each one. "And thank you, too, for helping my daughter. When she left here, it was apparent she was not the same girl," he told the three women. "This place gave her mother and me a second chance with Louise. I'm so grateful."

When Ellie had told her and Rose about their surprising visitor and of Louise's death, they felt shock and deep sadness. Now, upon meeting the girl's father, Marie hoped he'd stay a little while longer.

"Mr. McGuire, you and your wife have our deepest sympathy," Marie said, feeling heartsick that their darling Louise had died.

"Thank you very much," Craig replied. "But, her mother and I aren't married. That's only one of the mistakes I made for which Louise forgave me."

"Will you please stay and have some coffee with us?" Marie coaxed sensing he wanted to talk about

Louise. "And, I have some freshly baked cinnamon rolls just out of the oven."

"Oh, well, if I'm not keeping you lovely ladies from anything," he replied kindly. "That would be very nice."

With a smile, Marie left the others and hurried to the kitchen, wishing they could somehow ease the heartache of their unexpected guest.

As they had coffee and enjoyed Marie's cinnamon rolls, Craig talked nonstop about Louise. It was obvious he needed to share those months of her life after leaving Covenant House. "She seemed so content, so at peace," he said shaking his head. "I couldn't believe the transformation that took place. Then, when I got the call about the accident, I rushed to the hospital. It was like she waited for me to get there," Craig said, choking back his tears.

"So you did get to see her?" Marie asked, moving to the edge of her seat.

"Yes … for a moment … before the end," he whispered staring at the cup he held. "'I'm not afraid, Dad. I can see the angels,' she told me. She smiled and that was it. It was a very sad moment for me."

"I'm glad you made it there in time," Ellie told him. "I'm sure God allowed you that precious moment for a reason."

"What reason? I had to see my daughter take her last breath," Craig lamented, shaking his head in rebuttal. "It tore my heart out."

"I'm *sure* it did, but what comfort to know she

wasn't afraid and that she saw angels at her bed-side," Ellie told him.

"In all your conversations with her, before that day, did Louise tell you *what* had made the difference in her life?" Rose then asked.

"Yes, many times. She told me God had changed her and she felt a love she couldn't explain. She said it was being born-again, like starting over brand new with a new life, new direction," Craig went on. "I thought it was just a fad, like other things she'd tried, but this was different."

"You're right, it's no fad," Marie commented. "It's a miracle and each one of us here has experienced that same *tremendous* feeling. It's like walking out of a dark cave into sunlight."

Before Ellie could say what she intended, the telephone rang. "Please, excuse me. I'll take that in the kitchen," she said, leaving her chair.

Although Chad called everyday after work, Ellie knew it was too early when seeing the time. "Good afternoon, this is Ellie," she greeted.

"How's my best girl?" she heard, bringing a smile to her face.

"Hi honey, I'm doing great. How are you?" she asked in return.

"I was fantastic until about ten minutes ago. It seems I'm needed on a special assignment and it's urgent that I leave this afternoon," Chad told her.

"Where and for how long?" Ellie asked, feeling sudden disappointment.

"All I can say is back east and I'm not sure *how* long it'll take. I'll call you when I can, sweetheart.

Right now I have to run home and pack a bag," he told her. "Ellie, I love you. Take good care of yourself and our baby, okay?" Chad hurriedly added.

"I will and you too, *please*, stay safe. I love you, Chad," Ellie replied as the call ended.

Hanging up the phone, Ellie felt a sudden wave of uneasiness. *He's never had to go on special assignment before, not since our wedding. Yet, he's one of the best, so it's understandable I guess, but I don't feel good about this,* Ellie reasoned as she rejoined the others.

"I really must be going," Craig was saying as he got to his feet. "Meeting you and being here has helped me through a very difficult day. Thank you all."

"We're glad we could help," Marie told him. "Our dear Ellie here was such a comfort to every girl that came to Covenant House. Her own life had its trials so the girls could relate," she added, taking hold of Ellie's hand. "Just like your precious Louise, Ellie's *our* butterfly that shed her cocoon. When she came home from Alaska we couldn't believe our eyes! What a change we saw."

As he listened, Craig's eyes were on Ellie. She could feel his scrutinizing stare as she looked away. When looking back she realized, he knew.

"A *butterfly*, yes indeed," he said softly, nodding his head. "Ladies, it's been most enlightening and I thank you again," Craig remarked as he kissed the back of Rose's then Marie's hand before releasing them. "And now, Ellie, if you'd please walk me out," he said, motioning her to lead the way.

As requested, Ellie accompanied Craig outside. *Is he upset that I didn't tell him? Why didn't I? After all, he helped me a great deal,* Ellie reasoned.

When they had reached his car, Craig took hold of her arm. "Ellie, I've thought about you so often," he said, releasing his hold on her. "You *have* changed. I felt sure behind those glasses and loose-fitting clothes there was hiding a lovely young woman. I was right. So, what happened in Alaska? Did you marry your intended?" Craig asked.

"No, and it's a long story. But, thank you for being so kind in light of my dishonesty in not telling you who I was," Ellie replied, feeling somewhat embarrassed. "It's good to see you and thank you properly for what you did for me on the train. You saved me hours of questioning and I'm indebted to you, Craig. Mother and Aunt Marie have no idea of what happened," she confessed.

"Oh Ellie, your debt to me is nothing compared to what I owe you and everyone here for helping my daughter," he replied. "Perhaps one day I can meet this Lucy I've heard so much about. I should kiss the ground she walks on," Craig proclaimed as his eyes drifted across the yard.

"She *is* an exceptional woman and I'm sure she'd be delighted to meet you as well," Ellie told him. "By the way, I have a question, if you don't mind," she added, feeling inquisitive.

"Certainly, what might that be?"

"On the train you said you weren't married and had no family. How is it that you had lovely Louise?" Ellie wanted to know. With a frown, Craig looked away and for a moment Ellie felt she had stepped beyond good taste in asking such a personal question.

"I *wasn't* married nor did I know about my daughter, at least for several years," Craig finally admitted. "I never wanted the responsibility of a family, but I did like the women and had one in most big towns I traveled through. One day, when Louise was about eleven, Mary, her mother, wanted to see me. She had this young girl with her and when I saw Louise, I knew she was mine. Louise was the exact replica of my sister at that age," he said, nodding his head. "From then on I tried to be a father, but Mary found a hundred ways to keep us apart. Finally, when Mary's husband beat Louise during one of his drunken rages, she ran away from home. Thankfully she came to me, but I wasn't ready for a teenager. That's when we heard about Covenant House and the rest you know," Craig concluded.

"I'm afraid that story is quite typical of the girls that came here," Ellie told him. "But, I'm happy to report they all left a far different person than when they arrived. By the way, do you have a business card, just in case?"

"Certainly," he replied, taking one from the visor of his car. "Ellie, if you ever need me for anything, please call and I'll be there no matter where it is," he said assuredly.

Reaching for Ellie's hand, he gently squeezed it. "Take care of yourself and that husband of yours. He's a very lucky man," Craig said as he opened his car door. "I hope one day I can find whatever you all seem to enjoy."

"It's very simple. We're all stumbling through life trying to find peace, but the only true path to get there is Jesus," Ellie said in haste.

With a wave of his hand, Craig started his car and slowly headed down the lane. *Help him reach out to you, Lord, just as his daughter did.*

As she watched him drive away, Ellie wondered if she'd seen the last of Craig McGuire.

CHAPTER TWENTY

It was dark and gloomy when Ellie crawled out of bed the next morning. Rain soon splattered against her windowpane. *Another wet day,* she sighed, feeling the affects of her sleepless night.

Rarely did she have insomnia, yet, last night proved otherwise. Somehow, the thought of Chad leaving so suddenly had left her uneasy.

Over and over her mind echoed his words as she tossed and turned. *Something was different in his voice. Was he apprehensive about going or just disappointed?* Ellie wondered, realizing both could be true.

Yawning, she thumbed through her closet and found a pair of warm pants and a comfortable sweater. "It could be a long day," she muttered as she dressed in the matching blue garb. *It must be the hormones; the doctor said they bring mood swings during pregnancy,* Ellie thought as she then combed her recently trimmed hair.

Just then, she felt the tiniest flutter and she quickly placed her hand on her belly, hoping to feel it again. "Oh, you're really there, little one," she whispered, reveling in the new life she carried. "We can't wait to hold you." Quickly, Ellie calculated the months and wished for summer to arrive. For that moment Ellie's gloom lifted. Minutes later, she headed downstairs.

"Just in time," Marie said, removing two blueberry pancakes from the griddle. "That little fellow should like this just fine," she added, handing Ellie the plate.

"I'm *really* not hungry," Ellie told her, "at least not for all this."

"You're eating for two now and that baby needs nourishment," Marie told her.

"Yes, and if I keep eating like this, I'll weigh as *much* as two people," Ellie protested somewhat sternly.

With that, Marie looked at her. "You do look a little pale, dear, aren't you feeling well?" she asked, studying her niece's face.

"I'm just tired, Auntie. Don't mind me," Ellie apologized, smearing butter on the pancakes. "I wish Chad would call; it's been eighteen hours."

"You know he's probably very busy and I'm sure he'll call the first chance he gets," Marie assured her niece. "I know it hasn't been easy living here away from your husband all week. But, Covenant House should sell before long."

"All in God's timing, isn't that what Lucy always says?" Rose remarked upon entering the kitchen. "I do believe she's right."

"Yes, Mother, she *is* right. I guess we all get too impatient at times," Ellie said, remembering the events in her own life. "Who can know tomorrow? We have no guarantee of it so we must live today and make it the best we can. Chad says that all the time," she concluded, desperately missing her husband.

With each passing hour Ellie became more alarmed at not getting the call she waited for. It was just after one o'clock when the telephone rang. "That's got to be him now," Ellie announced, racing to answer. "Hello, Chad?" she blurted excitedly.

"No, Ellie, this is Matt," she heard instead. "How are you?"

"Oh Matt, I'm worried sick about Chad. He's gone off on some special assignment and hasn't called like he promised. I'm getting concerned."

"I'm sure, but listen: Lucy and I are on our way there. We might have a buyer for Covenant House," Matt told her somewhat hurriedly. "We'll be there in two hours. Please, tell Richard to pick us up at the usual place, okay?"

"I will. And Matt, this is *great* news. Can't wait to see you two," Ellie replied as the call ended. "Matt and Lucy are flying in. They might have a buyer," she told Rose and Marie who sat folding laundry

In the next moment, Ellie had more questions.

Matt sounded different, not his usual self. No comforting words or reassurance about Chad, Ellie reasoned. *Oh these hormones! Everything seems strange to me these days. Yet, not hearing from Chad isn't just that,* she had to admit, feeling sick to her stomach. "I'm going upstairs to lie down. Please, tell Richard to pick Matt and Lucy up in two hours," she said before leaving the room.

"Feel better, dear," Rose told her daughter. "And, try not to worry."

Don't worry, Mother? You might as well tell me not to breathe, Ellie thought as her eyes welled with tears.

Within a few minutes Richard arrived. "May I be of service?" he asked from the doorway. With his living quarters on the estate, the middle-aged chauffer was always nearby if needed.

"Yes, Matt and Lucy are flying in and they'd like you to be at the airport in two hours," Marie told him. "Before you go, would you care for a piece of fresh apple pie?"

"You know I'd *never* turn down one of your delicacies, Marie," Richard replied with a boyish grin, following her to the kitchen. "I'll truly miss you and your wonderful cooking when I'm no longer needed," he was heard saying.

Smiling to herself, Rose continued folding laundry. *Marie has no idea how smitten that man is over her. Should I tell her or just play dumb like always? Yet, if Covenant House is sold, they may never see each other again,* Rose thought, deciding what she must do.

It wasn't long before Marie returned to the parlor. "Has Richard gone?" Rose asked, retrieving the last towel from the laundry basket.

"Yes, after he gobbled down that pie," Marie laughed. "He *is* an easy man to cook for and always very pleasant."

"I think he likes you. In fact, I think he's quite gaga over you," Rose said, finally expressing her insight to her sister.

"Do you really think so?" Marie asked, looking surprised *and* quite pleased.

"Yes, he's *always* ready to help and hangs out in the kitchen more and more," Rose remarked. "And it's *not* just your cooking."

"I've never been interested in any man, not since my sweet Russ was killed. It'd take a mighty special guy to change my mind," Marie replied, retying her apron around her waist. "Oh, I nearly forgot, this came in the mail today," she told Rose, pulling an envelope from her pocket. "The oven timer was going off just as it came so I stuffed it in my apron."

"Whoever is it from?" Rose asked, seeing no return address. In scrawled handwriting, it was addressed to her at Covenant House.

Opening the rather wrinkled envelope, Rose then unfolded the single piece of lined paper. Its writing matched the scribbled penmanship; in pencil the words appeared childlike.

Dear Rose Cooper,

You don't know me, but I am Morton Cooper's son, Henry. My ma says you killed him and I'm glad. We never saw him much, but yet he was still mean to Ma and me when he came to town.

Ma told me I have a sister, but would never get to meet her. She said you sold the farm and are rich now. I'm happy for you as I'm sure he was also mean to you. Ma took to drinking and spends her days in bed. I am sixteen and had to quit school to work. The lady at the post office gave me your address. I hope you don't mind.

I'm not expecting anything, but wanted you to know about me. I sure would like to hear about my sister. If she wants to write here's my address: Henry Ivan Mackie ... Syracuse, Kansas. Ma and my dad were never married, but I guess you know that.

Sincerely,

Henry Ivan Mackie

In silence, Rose folded the letter and tucked it in her pocket. *It seems my suspicions were right after all,* she sighed, thinking of Morton's extended trips to town. *Two more lives ruined because of his evil ways. Indeed, I will tell Ellie about her half-brother, but not until she's heard from Chad,* Rose decided, knowing Ellie's state of mind at the moment.

It was nearly dark by the time the limousine entered the lane leading to Covenant House. Silently, Matt and Lucy rode, bearing each others pain and knowing the heartache to come. "Lord, give us strength to get through this," Lucy whispered as they arrived at the front door.

"He will," Matt said softly, gently squeezing his wife's hand. Fighting her tears, Lucy nodded her head letting Matt know she was ready. When Richard opened their door, there stood Ellie waiting to greet them.

A cold blast of air swirled around them and as Lucy stepped from the car, Ellie flew into her arms. "Oh, I've missed you so much!" she blurted.

"We've missed you too, sweetie," Lucy said, fighting her emotion. Then it was Matt's turn and Lucy couldn't help noticing how he held Ellie just a little longer, but could say nothing.

"This is *wonderful*! I can't wait to hear all about Arizona," Ellie told them, taking hold of Lucy's hand. "Maybe it'll get my mind off Chad."

Minutes later, after Matt and Lucy had greeted Rose and Marie and Richard had retrieved their luggage, it was time. "We have some news," Matt stated after they'd all found a seat in the parlor.

"Have you sold Covenant House?" Ellie asked, sitting beside Lucy.

"That's not certain as yet, but this news isn't about Covenant House, I'm afraid," Matt replied as he looked at Ellie. "I got a call this morning, from one of Chad's supervisors."

When hearing this Ellie's hand flew to her

mouth. "He's hurt isn't he? I *knew* it when he didn't call. How bad is it? Please, tell me," she pleaded.

With noticeable anguish Matt shook his head. "Sweetheart, the plane he and the other men were on apparently went down during a storm. They haven't found the wreckage as yet, but they feel it might have gone down in Lake Michigan."

"No! This can't be!" Ellie gasped. "Surely, *some-one* must have heard their call on the radio. Chad assured me they send distress signals when a plane is in trouble. They give their exact location so they can be rescued. Matt, you *know* this is true! *Please,* tell me this is true!"

"Yes, normally it is. Unless the radio's been knocked out by the storm, in which case they have no way to notify anyone," Matt said solemnly.

Saying nothing, Ellie turned and looked at Lucy, her face filled with sudden anguish. "What am I going to do without him?" she whispered a moment later. "My baby won't have his father. Oh, Dear God, how can this be?" she cried, falling into Lucy's outstretched arms.

Suddenly, this place where laughter and happy conversation often echoed through its rooms had become a place of unmatched sorrow.

Across the room, Marie sat staring in silence, seemingly too stunned to speak. Rose closed her eyes against threatening tears as she slowly shook her head. Leaning forward in his chair, Matt rested his head in his hands. Outside the wind moaned its own sounds of despair.

For Ellie, nothing could have prepared her for the devastation she felt. Unrelenting waves of grief washed over her, bringing sobs of disbelief.

"Ellie, please, for the baby's sake, this will help you rest," Matt coaxed, giving her a sedative.

Like a child, Ellie did as she was told. Then, closing her eyes, she saw Chad's face; she heard his voice reassuring her. *You'll always be my best girl, Ellie. No matter if I die tomorrow, you've made me the happiest man alive and I'll love you for always, my darling…*

As she teetered between sleep and awareness, Ellie remembered how Chad cradled her at night. Wrapped in his arms she felt loved and protected. *Dear God, what will I do now without my Chad?* Before the sedative would calm her, all Ellie could do was sob against her pillow.

The persistent winter rains continued; their unrelenting gloom matched the pain felt at Covenant House. Without Chad's body there could be no funeral; without the wreckage, the myriad of questions would go unanswered.

"It could be spring before they find the crash-sight and if the plane *did* go down in Lake Michigan, well, it may never be recovered," Matt told Lucy one afternoon. "Perhaps we should start thinking about a memorial service."

"Oh Matt, are you sure? It's only been a week,

isn't that too soon to give up?" Lucy asked, wondering how Ellie would accept the idea.

"They'll call off the search in a few days," Matt replied. "As it is, they're risking even more lives looking for the downed plane in bad weather."

In practical terms, Lucy knew Matt was right, yet, somehow, she felt certain Ellie hadn't given up hope that some miracle would bring Chad home. Surely, they needed a reprieve from the uncertainties surrounding them.

Although it was hard leaving her mother in a nursing home for the time being, Lucy knew this was where she needed to be. *Dear God, I won't ask why this happened, but I'm asking for your Comfort. Ease our sorrow and bring peace to Ellie's troubled soul,* Lucy prayed.

Each day Matt received the daily telephone call regarding the search and the news was always the same: no sign of the downed plane.

Two weeks had elapsed since the plane carrying six federal agents had disappeared and still no sign of the wreckage. Because of the continuing harsh weather the search was called off. For the families, there'd be no answers. For Ellie, life hung in limbo as all hope faded.

"I feel as though I'm falling, Lucy. Free-falling through space without a parachute and not knowing where the ground is or when I'll finally hit bottom," Ellie said, turning from her bedroom window. "I have control over *nothing*."

Leaving her seat, Lucy walked to Ellie and wrapped her arms around her. Quietly, they stood, sharing their grief. "Life is hard to understand sometimes," Lucy whispered a moment later. "Yet, we can be assured of those Everlasting Arms to rest in. I don't know what you're feeling, Ellie, but God does."

Returning to the window, Ellie looked out at the persistent storm. As she gazed across the landscape she couldn't help noticing the trees. The giant oaks stood seemingly untouched by the strong gale, while the smaller, younger trees were yanked and pulled as the wind tore at their branches.

"I'm like those young willows out there," she said softly. "The first real storm that comes along, I'm fighting to stay put and not fly off into oblivion. And, you're like those oak trees, Lucy, strong and sure of everything."

"No, sweetie, there are *many* things I'm unsure of," Lucy replied. "But, like those oaks, I'm older and my roots have grown deeper. Deeper in my faith and anchored in God's Abiding Love that I've learned to lean on. Your faith is new, yet, it's been tested in more ways than most. You're a strong woman, Ellie, stronger than you know."

"Thank you for that, but right now I'm just trying to get through the day, minute by minute. Chad's words, I keep hearing them, Lucy. He wasn't afraid to die and he talked about it often. Maybe he was trying to prepare me," Ellie said as she began pacing the floor. "I keep remembering how happy we were and I'm clinging to those memories. It's *all* I have left."

Often during the day, waves of anguish would bring Ellie to tears when thinking of life without Chad. At those times she would get spasm-like pains low in her belly that lasted only briefly. But now, they were there, deep and piecing, ripping through her body. "Oh, Lucy something's wrong!" she wailed, bending over in pain.

In haste, Lucy helped her to the bed. "Lie here, I'll call your doctor." As Lucy rushed from the room, Ellie feared for her baby. Over and over she heard Chad's last words. *You told me to take care of our baby, but I haven't. I'm not sleeping or eating right. What have I done?* Ellie cried against her pillow.

————————

More disappointing gloom settled over Covenant House. For Ellie, the loss of her baby had taken her to a new level of despair. Despite the doctor telling her it was nothing she had done, it made no difference. *'This is nature's way when it isn't quite right. You're a healthy young woman, Ellie, you'll have plenty more children,'* he told her.

But, to Ellie, those words sounded empty, for without Chad she'd have no such family. "I know it isn't right to question God, Lucy, but I am. How much more will there be?" Ellie asked a few days later.

"God understands your pain, sweetheart. He knows your heart and how much it's breaking right now," Lucy said, taking her hand. "I don't have all the answers—I only know we'll have trials and heartaches in this life. Some more than others, yet, in our sorrow we learn to trust more," Lucy explained. "In our weakness we find his strength."

Deep down, Ellie knew Lucy was right. Sorrows come to everyone and yet, life goes on. "I'm so glad you're here with me," she cried, throwing her arms around Lucy's neck. "I haven't even asked about Mona," she said then. "I'm sorry you had to leave her to come here."

"I had to come. Mother's in good hands and I wanted to be here for you *and* Matt. He's trying to be strong, but I know this has devastated him, too," Lucy admitted. "He was so proud of Chad and loved him very much."

"Yes, and Chad talked often about Matt and what a great brother he was. He loved you both and bragged about your marriage. Our goal was having a successful one just like you two," Ellie said choking back her tears. "You were always good role models and you still are."

As tears glistened in Lucy's eyes, she said nothing as she looked at Ellie. Sometimes, words just weren't needed.

With each passing day Ellie worked hard to accept reality. Chad was not coming home and now there'd be no baby, nothing of Chad was left.

The days that followed brought even more bad news. 'I'm sorry Mrs. Ryan...without a body the insurance carrier will pay no benefits.' *No insurance money? What do I do now?* Ellie wondered.

As she lay on her bed, Ellie closed her eyes trying to forget the world that was crumbling around her. *Dear God, how will I cope without Chad? He was my life. Trust me, Ellie.* So distinct were those words that Ellie sat straight up in bed. For the first time since losing Chad and her baby, she sensed a calm presence settle over her. *Okay, Lord, I'm going to keep trusting, no matter what.*

Decisions had to be made. Without insurance money, Ellie had to sell her and Chad's home in San Francisco. After much coaxing from Matt and Lucy, she accepted their generous offer to live at Covenant House indefinitely, along with Rose and Marie. Richard, too, would stay for the time being.

Within days of its listing, the house sold and a moving company was hired. Now, she would pack all of Chad's clothes along with hers. *How will I ever discard these? It's just impossible to imagine,* Ellie thought, hugging one of Chad's favorite shirts.

When everything had been packed and moved, the time had come for Ellie to lock the door and turn over the key. Yet, she needed to take one final walk through each room, remembering the happiness she and Chad shared.

I'll never say goodbye to you, Chad. You'll always be with me. Your smile, your laughter, your whispers in the dark as you held me. No one will ever take your place, sweetheart, Ellie vowed, secretly hanging onto a wisp of hope for his return.

CHAPTER TWENTY-ONE

The small-framed woman stood quietly in front of the woodstove stirring the kettle of cabbage soup. Outside, another winter storm bombarded the old farmhouse, pulling at the now unhinged shutters. Inside, the kitchen's wood floor creaked and the fire crackled with intensity. At hearing footsteps behind her, she turned, studying the face of her husband. "Is he—"

"He's still alive, Wilma," the man told his wife, handing her the basin filled with blood stained water. Saying nothing, Wilma took the pan and emptied it down the drain.

Days before, Roy Murphy, an Amish farmer and his wife had found a plane crash in their cornfield. Cautiously, they looked over the tangled mass of metal, finding bodies and ripped luggage strewn across the area. With no apparent survivors, the two began covering the remains with tarps, marking each location in the snow.

Just as they were about to cover the last victim, they were startled to hear a distinct moan. Surprised, they looked down at the bloodied body of a man. Having no telephone and being miles from town and the nearest hospital, they had to do their best to care for the unfortunate fellow until he succumbed to his extensive injuries. Using a horse-drawn sleigh, the middle-aged couple transported the crash victim to their farmhouse.

Winter's fury battered much of Wisconsin for days, bringing all travel to a standstill. And, despite his lack of medical experience on humans, Roy used what skills he had used on his animals to disinfect and bandage the man's injuries.

At times, in feverish delirium, his patient uttered the same undistinguishable words over and over. However, most of the time, the man lay unmoving, yet continued to live.

———

When a break in the frigid weather occurred, Roy traveled by horse and sleigh to the nearest telephone. There, the store clerk called for an ambulance and directed them to the Murphy Farm. Barely alive, the man was taken to the nearest hospital, a small under-equipped facility.

After their assessment of the unidentified, comatose victim, the doctors felt little could be done to save his life. Yet, they would do what they could while trying to discover his identity and next of kin.

Dehydration, lacerations and the broken arm were treated, but the mangled right leg and any internal injuries would have to wait. If he survived through the latest storm, the patient would be moved to a larger city hospital.

The small community was still talking about their major event—the plane crash that had narrowly missed farmhouses and barns.

Adding to that was the shock of hearing the lone survivor was clinging to life due to the aid of Roy Murphy and his wife. Everyone knew a miracle had occurred in their midst since Roy was 'slow' and had never gone to school. Certainly, he and his wife knew nothing about doctoring a dying man.

In and out of consciousness the man known as John Doe defied reason. By mid-February, he was moved to a larger hospital where doctors accepted the challenge of doing all they could to save his life. Despite their best efforts, they agreed amputation of the leg was their only recourse. Without identification, no relative could be found.

It was March twentieth. Two months had inched by since Chad's apparent death. Now, settled in at Covenant House, Ellie tried to stay busy to keep her mind occupied. Yet, in the still of night the tears fell and loneliness hovered over her like a dark cloud.

When sleep finally came she dreamt of Chad. It

was always the same. Some distance away he waved at her as he casually leaned against a fence. He wore his familiar grin. *You're my best girl, Ellie,* he called out to her. Each time she awoke with a weight of sadness at never hearing those words again

After the memorial service for Chad, Matt and Lucy returned to Arizona. Days later, Matt received a generous offer for his practice in Anchorage. It was a hard decision, but after deliberation he and Lucy decided it was best. He would make one last trip to Alaska to complete the deal the last week of March.

Spring would soon arrive, but for Ellie, the changing season meant nothing. *No husband, no baby to plan for, now what do I do?* She wanted to find something worthwhile to occupy her time. Two days later, she had her answer.

Due to the tragedy of Chad's death and Ellie's miscarriage, Rose hadn't told anyone about the letter from Kansas or the confirmation from the lawyer. Having debated as to the right time to tell Ellie about her half-brother, Rose decided it was time. Perhaps it would help take her mind off her sorrows.

"Will you two join me for tea on the veranda?" she asked Ellie and Marie that afternoon. "I have something to tell you," she added when seeing the reluctant look on her daughter's face.

"I was going to lie down for a nap," Ellie replied. "Can it wait?"

"It's waited long enough, dear, and it won't take

long," Rose answered. Soon, the three were on the veranda, commenting about the beautiful day.

After everyone was given their cup of hot tea, Marie took her seat. "Well, let's have it," she urged her sister.

"You remember the letter that came for me some time ago?" Rose asked, retrieving the crumpled envelope from here pocket. "It was from Kansas and quite shocking, I must say."

"Who found you way out here?" Ellie asked, taking a sip of tea.

"A young man named Henry Mackie, your half-brother," Rose replied. Noticeably stunned, Ellie's expression froze as she peered over the rim of her teacup at her mother. Slowly, she then placed it on the table, saying nothing.

"*What...* are you *sure* of this?" Marie gasped.

"I have the letter right here," Rose said, handing it to her sister.

Hurriedly, Marie opened the letter and read it aloud. As she listened, Ellie shook her head in disbelief.

When Marie had finished reading, no one spoke. "I believe him," Ellie said a moment later. "He's another victim of Morton Cooper."

"It seems he only wants to know you, Lizzie," Marie remarked. "If this is true, he has quite a load for a young man of sixteen. Yet, he could be lying."

"No, he isn't lying. I had a lawyer check his birth certificate in Kansas. He's Morton's son all right," Rose confessed nodding her head. "And, now that I know for sure, I'll be writing to him. It's obvious he needs someone who cares."

"I'll write to him, too, Mother," Ellie said. "I always *did* want a brother."

———————————

When first arriving in Arizona, Lucy and Matt had set a daily routine for Mona's sake. She seemed less confused when following a schedule. After breakfast, Lucy would take her mother for a stroll in her wheelchair; a long afternoon nap became routine. Recently, Lucy realized the walks were causing more irritation than pleasure for Mona so they stopped going. Lately, she seemed most content to lie on her bed and listen to soft music.

Every afternoon Matt and Lucy would sit on their patio to enjoy a glass of iced tea and talk. It was here they discussed concerns and future plans.

"I'll be flying out tomorrow. Are you sure you won't come with me?" Matt asked, savoring the warm afternoon sun. "Mona did okay in the care center while we were in California."

"Yes, she did. But, this time I feel I shouldn't go," Lucy replied. "You won't be in Anchorage long and besides, why would I want to leave this lovely weather?" she said grinning.

With a smile, Matt looked at his wife and then reached for her hand. "Have I told you lately how much I cherish you?" he whispered as his eyes held hers. "I can't imagine my life without you."

"I'm the blessed one, sweetheart," Lucy replied softly. "You're such a generous and loving man, and one day perhaps we'll expand our dream and start helping both troubled girls *and* boys. You have such a wonderful way with them."

"We've discussed an ideal place, yet, we never know what tomorrow may bring. I can't help but think about Chad and Ellie," Matt admitted, his gaze drifting across the yard. "Who would think their life together would end so tragically, or so quickly."

"It's been over two months since Chad's death, but it still seems unreal, like some nightmare," Lucy remarked, wishing she could somehow snap her fingers and turn back the clock. "My heart aches for Ellie. Losing her baby, just two weeks later, has overwhelmed her with grief."

"Yes, it's hard to understand, yet, we know God gives us strength to get through anything, if we trust him," Matt said softly. "We all miss Chad and that baby was part of him."

The lump in Lucy's throat kept her from speaking. All she could do was nod her agreement.

The morning was filled with preparations for Matt to leave for Anchorage; his trip to finalize the sale of his practice. Lucy's decision was firm: she would not be going with him. Instead, she would look after her mother and answer letters she'd received in recent days.

"Barring bad weather or any trouble, I should be back in three days," Matt said, closing his briefcase. "I'll miss you." Saying nothing Lucy wrapped her arms around her husband's neck and looked in his eyes.

A sudden chill washed over her. "I wish you weren't going," she blurted. "Isn't there *some* way you can close this deal without flying up there?"

"Afraid not, besides I'll be back before you know it," Matt replied, giving Lucy a quick kiss on her nose. "What is it, sweetheart? You sound worried."

"I am," Lucy admitted, releasing her embrace. "I don't feel right about you going, perhaps it's due to us losing Chad so recently or because it's dangerous to fly this time of year. I'm not sure *why* I feel this way."

"Sweetheart, my plane is in good condition, the weather is clear and you know if it changes I'll put down somewhere till it blows over," Matt assured his wife. "As for Chad's accident, they had orders for an urgent assignment. They knew a storm was facing them, but their supervisor insisted they proceed as ordered. Needless to say, that person was fired and a lawsuit has been filed against the agency on behalf of the families."

"Do you suppose *Chad* knew about the storm?" Lucy asked, feeling sick that the whole tragedy might have been avoided.

"I've no doubt. Regardless, whether he was piloting the plane or not, he would have checked weather conditions on his own," Matt assured Lucy. "It was a horrible mistake in judgment and six good men paid the price."

For the next while Matt and Lucy silently held

each other. "I love you *so* much," Lucy whispered then as the ominous feeling remained.

"And I adore you, my pet," Matt replied, looking in Lucy's eyes. "Our lives are in God's hands. Please, don't worry, darling." For a moment longer, Lucy snuggled against Matt's chest, feeling his arms around her. "I'll call you tomorrow evening, after I meet with the buyer, okay?"

"Please do," Lucy told him. "I'll be waiting." Then, she remembered the phone call Ellie had waited for, but never received. Pushing aside her feeling of concern, Lucy hugged and then gave her husband a lingering kiss.

A restless night had Lucy up early. Throwing on her robe, she headed for the kitchen to make coffee, but as she passed her mother's room, she quietly opened the door. "Good morning, Mother," Lucy greeted, seeing Mona sitting on her bed. There was only a blank stare in response.

Lovingly, Lucy helped her mother with her robe and slippers and walked with her to the kitchen. There, Mona sat while her breakfast was prepared. In recent weeks, the challenge of getting Mona to eat a sufficient amount of food and drink liquids had become a daily battle, a battle Lucy was losing.

Each visit to the doctor revealed weight loss, bringing more suggestions to admit Mona to the hospital and place a feeding tube. So far Lucy had refused, but this morning with her mother refusing to eat even a few bites of breakfast, Lucy was ready to give up. Starvation was not what she wanted for her mother.

As she studied the face looking back at her, Lucy saw eyes that appeared empty and vacant of feeling. The once vibrant and happy woman who would care and comfort a lost animal or offer assistance to any stranger was now unaware of her own world. "Oh, Mother, I miss you *so* much," Lucy whispered as tears blurred her eyes.

"Can I go now?" Mona asked softly, staring at her daughter.

"Go? Where do you want to go, Mother?" Lucy asked, feeling surprised at the question and the clarity of words.

"Home ... home," she stated, pounding her small fist against the tabletop. For a moment Lucy had to wonder at her response. Certainly, home had been with her for over three years. Finally, she realized what she meant.

"You mean home to heaven, Mother? Is that what you want?" Saying nothing, Mona looked back at her. Then, closing her eyes, she slowly nodded her head. Once more Lucy was stunned. Suddenly, after months with little or no rational communication, Mona had made her wishes known.

"Yes, Mother. You can go home," Lucy answered, fighting her tears.

Looking back at her Mona made no reply. Seconds later, a faint smile touched her face as she slowly stood to her feet. Quickly, Lucy left her chair and took her mother's hand. With a slow unsteady gait, Mona led Lucy from the kitchen, back down the hall to her bedroom.

Then, sitting on the edge of her bed, Mona looked up at her daughter. Slowly, she lifted her hand and touched Lucy's face. "Good girl," she whispered. A moment later the frail woman leaned back against her pillow and with a sigh, closed her eyes.

A range of emotion swept over Lucy as she looked down at her mother, the one who gave her life and taught her well. *You suffered too, when Kate died, but your faith never faltered. Still you glorified God just as you taught me to do,* Lucy thought, remembering the many lessons she'd learned at her mother's knee. "You've finished your race, Mom, and Heaven is waiting," Lucy whispered, bending down to kiss the soft wrinkled cheek.

Taking a quilt, Lucy lovingly covered the fragile form of her mother. In quiet reverence she then sat in the nearby chair. Closing her eyes, she laid her head back, hearing the shallow unsteady breaths.

In her mind's eye, Lucy imagined the life beyond where no pain or sorrow could exist. That place of boundless joy and endless praise that only God inspired. That was Home, the place reserved for those who had reached out in faith and received the free gift offered to all, but refused by most.

Amid her confusion, Mona remembered such a place and knew it was her promised destiny. How could any daughter forbid her mother's parting for such a place? For Lucy, there'd be no goodbye, but rather, a brief farewell.

The day wore on and still Lucy sat at her mother's bedside. Memories tumbled through her mind as her heart longed for those days filled with fun and conversation. Now and then she would leave her chair to quietly stand by the bed. Looking down at her mother, Lucy saw past the withered shell of flesh to the woman once filled with love and vitality.

Oh, Mother, how blessed I've been to be your daughter. No matter what came your way you pressed on without complaining. Always keep the faith, for behind every dark cloud the sun is shining. How often you've told me that, and you were so right, Mom.

Dear God, if this is Mother's time then please take her. If it isn't, then let her wake up hungry so she'll eat. You know her suffering, her longing to be with you, so please, Lord, Lucy tearfully prayed.

Before she sat back down, Lucy pushed the 8-track tape in the stereo that sat nearby. Soon, the room filled with the soft, soothing sound of Mona's favorite hymns.

Again, sitting at her mother's bedside, Lucy leaned back and closed her eyes, listening to the lyrics about that heavenly abode, that glorious residence that waits beyond the stars. For Lucy, she, too, longed for that grand reunion.

Sleepily, Lucy looked at the bedside clock before answering the ringing telephone. *Eight-fifteen, it must be Matt,* she decided, putting the receiver to her ear. "Hello, sweetheart," she greeted, still half asleep.

"Hello, Lucy, this is Ellie," she heard. "I know Matt was going to Anchorage, is he okay?"

"Yes, he left yesterday. Why are you wondering if he's okay?" Lucy asked, sitting up on her bed.

"Haven't you heard about the earthquake in Alaska?" Ellie asked.

"What, Ellie, did you say *earthquake!*" Lucy wailed in shock.

"Yes, it happened around five-thirty. It's been on the news, but few details. Oh, Lucy, it even caused a tidal wave. Is there *any* way you can reach Matt?" Ellie blurted.

In that instant, Lucy remembered how she felt before Matt left. *This is why I didn't want him to go. Dear God, please take care of him,* Lucy quickly prayed. "No, I'm afraid not. He said he'd call me this evening."

"Oh, Lucy, Chad was supposed to call, too. I felt he was going to come home to me, but he didn't," Ellie wailed in tears. "How can this happen … again?"

"Ellie, we don't know that it has. We *can't* give up and think the worst," Lucy said, fighting the fear gnawing at her. "I won't let fear overtake me and you mustn't either. We need to pray instead, for all those poor people up there. Perhaps Matt is helping," Lucy said, knowing he would be if at all possible.

For a moment there was only silence on the line. A million thoughts raced through Lucy's mind. "This is one of those times, Ellie, when we have to keep trusting, no matter how bad things appear to be," she added softly. "We have to believe Matt is okay and that he's safe."

"You're right," Ellie replied. "Please, let us know when you hear from him, okay?"

"I will, as soon as I have any word," Lucy promised at goodbye. With the phone still in her hands, Lucy fell to her knees beside the bed. "Dear God, please be with Matt, keep him safe and give us strength."

Trembling, Lucy got to her feet a moment later and headed for her mother's bedroom. Quietly, she opened the door and stepped inside. The room was still; no sound came from the small form lying on the bed. Slowly, Lucy approached and looked down at her mother, seeing the calm, peaceful look on the face that in years past was rarely without a smile.

Once more Lucy was on her knees. Gently, she then laid her hand on a cold, lifeless cheek. "Precious Mother," she whispered as tears burned her eyes. "I *will* miss you, but oh, what glorious beauty you must be seeing right now. And, so much more I can't even imagine."

With tears streaming, Lucy wrapped her arms around her mother and cradled her, weeping for lost years and for the unknown still to come. *Have I lost you both today? Dear God, what more can there be?*

CHAPTER TWENTY-TWO

As the hours passed details of the massive Alaskan earthquake trickled in over the airwaves. Those at Covenant House kept a keen ear trying to learn anything they could. Still no word regarding Matt and now Ellie, Rose and Marie held their breath as they listened:

"The number of victims from the 9.2 earthquake won't be known for days, perhaps week's authorities are saying. Centered near Prince William Sound, between Anchorage and Valdez, the quake caused a giant tsunami which extended to the coast of Oregon and California. Casualties are expected to be in the hundreds. Keep it here for the latest news and updates..."

In stunned silence Ellie slowly left her seat and went to the window. The weight of sorrow felt heavier with each passing hour, knowing Matt might well be one of those many victims.

Dear God, help us! Right then that was all Ellie could pray.

In Arizona, Lucy tried to stay focused on the task at hand, laying her mother's body to rest. Knowing the inevitable, she and Matt had already purchased a plot and arranged a quiet graveside service. Today, she'd be attending that simple ceremony without the strong support of her husband.

The kindly neighbors and minister were all that stood with Lucy at the gravesite on this beautiful March morning.

"For those who know the Lord, death is not the end. We read this promise in God's Word: *Therefore, we are always confident, knowing that, whilst we are at home in the body we are absent from the Lord … and willing rather, to be absent from the body and present with the Lord,*" the elderly pastor said assuredly.

These words Lucy knew so well and once more they assured her of that blessed hope. *Yes, Mother, you're free of those shackles that held you prisoner and now you're more alive than you've ever been,* Lucy reasoned, visualizing that land of endless days. *Your body is here but your spirit is soaring!*

Then, for the millionth time, she wondered about her husband. *I've committed him to you, Lord. No matter what, Matt is in your Care. I know you'll see us through whatever lies ahead,* Lucy prayed, wiping a tear from her cheek.

Carnage was everywhere. Dark, gapping crevices split the earth; the few paved roads were now impassable mounds of buckled blacktop; piles of rubble marked where buildings once stood.

No one here had ever witnessed such a disaster, including Dr. Matthew Ryan. Beyond any doubt, he knew he was here for a purpose and his survival was only by God's grace and protection.

Due to a thunderstorm, Matt had put down in Seattle which delayed his arrival in Anchorage. Seconds after his plane touched down, the earth-quake hit. Like a giant zipper the earth opened up, leaving an unavoidable chasm in the runway.

"Jesus, help me!" Matt yelled as his aircraft plunged nose first into the mammoth hole. With a jolt the plane stopped, stunning its occupant.

Amid an eerie blackness the earth rumbled and shook, inching Matt and his plane downward, deeper into the abyss. In shocking disbelief he worked to dispel this sudden nightmare; trying to grasp what had happened, yet, sensing some unseen force directing him, helping him escape certain death.

In a daze, Matt climbed out of his plane and began clawing his way upward, toward daylight. Blood ran down his face from a gash over his eye. His hands were soon raw from climbing out of the gigantic pit.

When finally reaching the surface, Matt was on his knees, giving thanks for his life. Certainly, he might have been buried alive with his plane.

Moments later he stood to his feet, seeing dozens of people. Some searched for loved ones or co-workers. Others cried in anguish after finding those who died from fallen debris. Still others screamed in horror as the earth again shook beneath their feet.

"Dear God in heaven, help us!" Matt wailed as he saw the devastation. Then, his instinct urged him into action as he began helping the injured. Looking for a safe place, he decided on a nearby hanger which appeared undamaged. "Move everyone in there," Matt shouted, pointing toward the huge gray building.

Tired and hungry, the handful of people had worked feverishly for hours, helping the growing number of injured brought to the makeshift hospital. The airport, too, had suffered major damage when its sixty-eight-foot concrete tower toppled, killing the air traffic controller. Wrecked airplanes were scattered across the mangled tarmac; some still smoldered from earlier fires.

Amid the earlier confusion, someone realized the National Guard stored their supplies in a nearby warehouse. Soon, they had blankets, first aid kits and bottled water. "Thank God!" Matt cheered over and over.

Occasionally, the ground rumbled from aftershocks. Momentarily, the frantic hubbub was stilled as everyone waited. A collective sigh of relief swept through those gathered when the shaking stopped.

"Over here!" someone yelled. "I found a survivor." Two men ran to assist in digging the victim out.

In a dimly lit corner, a woman's cry of despair was heard as she helplessly watched her husband die in her arms.

Utilities would be out of service for days, perhaps weeks. Contacting loved ones was impossible and for Matt, that brought renewed anguish.

Lucy will think I'm dead, my poor darling. She wanted me to stay home, no doubt this is why. Was it a Divine warning or a woman's intuition? Matt wondered, realizing there'd been other such times in past years.

No matter how desperate the situation, Matt felt blessed to be alive. Now, seeing the injured and dying, he knew this was where God wanted him to be.

Time passed slowly for Lucy in Arizona and those at Covenant House. With every phone call good news was anticipated, yet, still no word from Matt.

Everyday, Lucy and others would meet at church to pray, not only for Matt's safe return, but for the many others whose lives had been changed forever in the wake of the devastating earthquake.

After each prayer session, Lucy felt renewed optimism that Matt was alive despite news reports filled with grim statistics. The death toll was mounting and still the outer regions had yet to be combed for victims. Utilities were slowly being restored, but for emergencies only. The tragedy had touched hearts and lives thousands of miles away.

Relief efforts were in progress as communities joined together to send needed supplies. Construction companies offered men and equipment to clear debris and help repair structural damage.

If you're able to help those people, Matt, I'm thankful you're there, Lucy thought, knowing he would have gone to help if not already there. Her heart swelled with love for the generous man she knew her husband to be.

"Ten days," Lucy muttered to herself as she marked another day off the calendar. *April sixth. How much longer, Lord, until I hear something?*

Having finished lunch, Lucy was ready to leave for the short walk to her church when the telephone rang. Due to past disappointments she no longer raced to answer. "Hello, this is Lucy," she greeted kindly.

"Oh, sweetheart, it's so *good* to hear your voice," she heard Matt say.

Sudden tears of joy erupted as Lucy fell to her knees in thanksgiving. Words caught in her throat as excited relief washed over her. "Matt...*Thank God* you're alive!" she gasped. "How are you...*where* are you?"

"I'm in Anchorage, tired, but doing okay. It's a mess here, Lucy, but we're saving lives. Keep praying, my darling. I'll call you again, but right now I have to go. I love you," Matt hurriedly concluded.

"I love *you* and we'll keep praying," Lucy replied

in haste. When the line went dead, Lucy lifted her eyes heavenward. Despite the hurried call, she felt grateful. *Thank you for keeping him safe,* she sighed with relief. *I got my awaited call, unlike dear Ellie,* Lucy thought sadly. Suddenly, she realized she hadn't had time to tell Matt of her mother's passing.

Upon hearing Matt was alive and well, Lucy started making plans.

Nearly three months had passed since Chad's death. "I want to do something really special for Ellie's birthday this year," Lucy told Rose during a phone call. "Do you have any thoughts or ideas about what she'd like?"

"Well, perhaps, if it isn't too expensive," Rose replied.

"Expense doesn't matter. What is it?" Lucy asked excitedly.

"Ellie has always dreamed of playing the piano, so perhaps a piano and some lessons would lift her spirits," Rose concluded.

"I had no idea she had such a dream," Lucy said, feeling grateful at such news. "What a wonderful idea! I'll do it!"

"I hear Ellie coming now. I know she'll want to talk to you," Rose said in haste, ending their conversation.

"Hello, Lucy," Ellie greeted a moment later. "We miss you. Can you come for a visit?"

"As a matter of fact I'll see you next week," Lucy told her. "We'll have time for a nice long visit."

"I'm so happy to hear that," Ellie replied, sounding somewhat cheerful for the first time since
Chad's death. "I can't wait to see you."

At this moment it seemed Ellie was getting past
her sorrow. Yet, as a counselor, Lucy knew mourn-
ing brought different responses. Certainly, Ellie had
grieved and with God's help, it appeared she was
looking to the future...

With warmer weather, Roy Murphy would check
every few days on the condition of the snow-cov-
ered wreckage in his corn field. Slowly, the wings
and fuselage were becoming visible.

One sunny morning, he spotted a brown case
and carried it to the house, hoping his wife could
read the papers contained inside.

Silently, she read the water soaked documents
as Roy eagerly looked on. "These are important
papers, Roy," Wilma told her husband. "They say:
important and confidential with names, dates and
lots of numbers. Roy, what did the sheriff say when
you told him about the crash?"

"He said he'd go talk to the man we found, when
he had time," Roy replied. "I didn't tell him there
are dead people out there. Maybe he thinks there's
only this one man. Do you think I should tell him
there are more, now that the snow is melting?"

"I believe you should, Roy. Maybe he'd come
and look after those poor souls so they'd have a
decent burial," Wilma said, closing the briefcase.

"Take this to the sheriff, too. I think today would be a good day to go."

Heeding her advice, Roy headed to town with his horse and buggy that same afternoon. *I sure need to get that pile of metal out of my cornfield, and maybe the sheriff will see to it when he sees these papers,* Mr. Murphy decided on his way to town.

In the distance, a faint beeping sound was heard. In his drugged state, Chad found it impossible to open his eyes, yet, he had to fight...he couldn't let go and give in to that place that beckoned. Somehow, he knew he had to stay...someone needed him.

Desperately, he tried to remember what happened. Where was he? Why did he hurt so badly? Soon, the pain and drugs won the battle and he again slipped into that peaceful black void.

CHAPTER TWENTY-THREE

For Ellie and Lucy it was nearly like old times. Talking and laughing, they meandered across the spacious front yard, enjoying the warm April sun. "Will you reopen Covenant House?" Ellie asked as they reached the gazebo.

"Since it didn't sell, I believe the Good Lord wants me to," Lucy replied, "but with all we've been through the past few months, I'm going to wait until fall. We need some time to relax and I'm thinking a vacation would be nice."

"Where do you think you'll go?" Ellie asked, knowing Lucy more than anyone deserved to have some fun.

"That's something we will *all* decide on," Lucy answered, patting Ellie's hand. "Since we're all going."

"Oh, Lucy, are you sure?" Ellie wailed in surprise. "You and Matt deserve some peace and quiet—something you haven't had since I've known you."

"Vacations are for families to enjoy, and you're all family," Lucy explained kindly. "Besides, it wouldn't be nearly as much fun without you."

"Speaking of family, we've learned I have a half-brother," Ellie remarked. "He wrote to mother some time ago, but she wanted to make sure it was true before saying anything. We're both corresponding with him now."

"What a surprise! How old is he and where does he live?" Lucy asked.

For the next while Ellie revealed what she knew about Henry, her newfound sibling. "I'm so glad he was determined to find us," Ellie admitted. "One day we're going to meet in person, but that won't be for awhile. When's Matt coming home?" Ellie then asked, changing the subject.

"As soon as he can," Lucy said. "He's worked hard to do all he can, but he admits he's nearing exhaustion—not just physically, but emotionally, too."

"He loves those people up there, and it must be devastating for him to see what's happened to them," Ellie remarked sadly.

"Yes, but despite everything, he said they've seen miracles and one day he wants to write a book about the whole experience," Lucy revealed for the first time. "I mentioned he could maybe hire you to type it for him."

"Oh, I'd love to help with it," Ellie replied. "It would help pass the time."

At that, Lucy looked at her. "Sweetheart, is it getting *any* easier?"

"Sometimes I think the worst is behind me … then, I hear a song or see something that reminds me of Chad and I lose it," Ellie admitted with a sigh. "I just can't *imagine* my life without him, Lucy. My head is rational, at times, but my heart isn't … it still acts as though Chad is alive somewhere."

"Oh, Ellie, I'd give anything if I could bring Chad back to you," Lucy moaned. "It was such a *senseless* trip, knowing bad weather was ahead."

"What … *what* do you mean?" Ellie stammered in surprise. "They *knew* there was a storm?"

"Yes, they knew, but unfortunately they were ordered to carry on with their assignment."

"*That's* why Chad sounded like he did!" Ellie blurted. "He knew! But why … *why* didn't he refuse to go?"

"Because Chad was dedicated; he'd never be insubordinate to his boss," Lucy explained, "regardless the risk."

"Yes, I know, I know," Ellie said, choking back her tears. "Chad did his job, no matter the danger. We all know that."

"Ellie, I'm sorry, perhaps I shouldn't have said anything," Lucy lamented.

"No, I'm glad you told me. I've thought often about Chad's last words and why he sounded like he did. Now I know."

For the first time, Ellie understood the disappointment in Chad's voice. In his own way he was saying goodbye. It was obvious he knew he may never see her again. Sudden tears filled Ellie's eyes as she realized how hard it must have been for Chad to get on that plane that fateful day.

Seeing the sad look on Ellie's face, Lucy was grateful that her special gift would be arriving this afternoon, two days before her birthday.

Quietly, they sat. Around them were signs of new life. Tulips and daffodils bloomed in nearby flowerbeds. Tiny birds darted among the newly leafed shrubs. Life was bursting forth in abundance, and yet, life had also ended far too soon and abruptly for Chad and their unborn child.

For the next while, Lucy tried to keep the conversation light and free of sadness. She asked about Henry Mackie, but that soon revealed heartache, too, as she learned of his abuse. "Henry was treated like the rest of us," Ellie revealed. "At least I had Aunt Marie helping me, but there's been no one for Henry. He's all alone but for his sick mother. He doesn't have a place like Covenant House to go to," she concluded with a sigh.

When hearing this, Lucy remembered what she and Matt had discussed many times in recent months. "It appears we need a place where boys and girls can *both* get help," Lucy said, wishing she could say more.

"You're right, Lucy. Could it be here?" Ellie asked of her, sounding hopeful for the first time since they'd sat down.

"When hearing Ellie's question and seeing her

concern, Lucy hated to disappoint her. "I'm afraid we're not set up for the opposite sex," she replied. "We'd need much more room to spread out. Boys have much different interests than what we have going on here."

"I guess you're right," Ellie answered, again sounding disappointed. Just then a delivery truck was noticed arriving at the front door. "Boy, I'd say those men are lost."

"Well, perhaps we'd better go see if we can help them," Lucy told her, getting to her feet.

Minutes later, Ellie appeared in shock when seeing her beautiful birthday gift…a shiny solid oak upright piano. "Oh! Oh, I can't *believe* this!" she stammered with tear filled eyes. "I've always wanted to play, but how did you know?"

"I heard it from a good source and it comes with a year's worth of lessons," Lucy said, handing her a coupon book. "If you want another year, it's on me."

"Oh *Lucy*, how can I ever thank you?" Ellie wailed with glee before giving her a hug

"By giving us a recital in six months or so," Lucy said with a smile, hugging her back.

"That's a deal, and if I need more lessons, I'll pay for them. I made a good profit from the house sale, if you remember?" Ellie quickly replied.

A frenzy of excitement filled the office of Sheriff Whitaker. Upon reading the documents that had arrived that afternoon, the sheriff and his deputy realized their small town would soon receive nationwide notoriety.

"Federal agents crashed in our own backyard?" the young deputy blurted in disbelief. "Didn't you *know* such a plane was missing? And, where did you think that dying man came from?"

"I don't recall hearing *any* report of a plane missing," Sheriff Whitaker replied, shaking his head. "Besides, that old farmer is half-baked and everyone knows it. If he told *anyone* he had a dying man at his house, they'd never believe him. But, I guess these documents are proof we found what was missing!"

Throwing a frowning glance at his new boss, Deputy White cringed at the remark. "I'd say Roy Murphy *found* it. And, folks might be asking why you didn't investigate when you first heard about it," he fired back, realizing the sheriff's reputation of being lax was obviously true. "Mr. Murphy acted like you knew about the survivor he found, but since I wasn't here at the time, maybe you should fill me in."

"Well, I'm just *too* busy to go chasing after some cockamamie story, especially when I heard *nothing* about a missing plane!" he said, glaring at the younger man.

"Well, Sheriff, this is one time you might wish you had," Deputy White remarked solemnly.

With noticeable irritation, the portly sheriff took the seat behind his desk and lifted the telephone to his ear. "Operator, I need the FBI office in San Francisco," he said gruffly.

It was Friday morning and due to Matt's surprising phone call, stating he'd be arriving later today, the women of Covenant House now faced a full and hectic day.

The dinner menu was hurriedly planned which included most of Matt's favorites. They would have prime rib, seasoned red potatoes, baked squash, spinach salad and homemade bread. For dessert, Marie would make his favorite pie, sour cream raisin.

While Marie worked feverishly in the kitchen, Lucy and Ellie made sure the house was spotless. On the veranda, Rose arranged two lovely bouquets of spring flowers in a matching pair of crystal vases.

For Lucy, knowing her husband was safe, after such a terrible disaster, brought renewed thanksgiving. Yet, her excitement of seeing Matt again was bittersweet knowing the pain Ellie was suffering. *If only we could be celebrating Chad's return, too,* Lucy thought as she dusted the parlor.

By three o'clock that afternoon everything was in place for Matt's arrival. From the kitchen the delicious smell of dinner drifted through the house. The afternoon sun filtered through the parlor windows, bringing a soft glow to the spacious room. On the stereo, Guy Lombardo's orchestra played a soothing instrumental. Outside, Lucy and Ellie relaxed with a glass of iced tea.

"Are you expecting anyone else today?" Ellie asked when seeing a dark sedan approaching. "I'm sure it's no one for me," she added.

"Can't imagine who it could be," Lucy replied as they watched from the veranda. Slowly, the car made its way up the lane and was soon stopping at the front door. "I'll go see who it is," she told Ellie, leaving her seat.

Now alone, Ellie took a sip of her tea and then rested her head back and closed her eyes. Like so often in days past, she rested her hand on her belly, remembering the baby that was no longer there. Hot tears stung her eyes and her throat tightened with emotion. *Dear God, help me get past this pain,* Ellie prayed. Just then, she sensed someone nearby and opened her eyes.

"Sweetheart, this is Agent Curtis. He'd like a word with you," Lucy told Ellie as she and the man arrived on the veranda. "Agent, this is Ellie Ryan."

"Mrs. Ryan, I'm sorry to disturb you, but I felt you'd want to know the latest on your husband's accident," the young man said, offering his hand.

In that second, Ellie felt she was dreaming as she shook the man's hand, but could say nothing. "Please, have a seat," Lucy offered.

With a nod of thanks the man seated himself and then looked at Ellie. "Mrs. Ryan, the wreckage of the plane has finally been located, in Wisconsin," he began solemnly. "As we speak, the agency's investigators are on their way."

As she listened, Ellie felt renewed despair. Somehow this made Chad's death final. No more dreams of his safe return and no more chance of it being a big mistake. Now, it seemed certain.

"Surely, *someone* had to know about the crash before now," Lucy remarked. "Why is it just now being reported?"

"It appears there was a break-down in communications in the small Amish town where it happened," the agent replied. "I'm told telephones are pretty scarce around there, plus the bad weather played a major role in taking so long."

"It's hard to imagine such a thing," Lucy said, shaking her head.

"As soon as possible, the victim's remains will arrive for burial. I am *very* sorry for your loss, Mrs. Ryan," Agent Curtis said kindly. "I had often worked with your husband and knew him to be one of the finest men I know," he added, getting to his feet. "Please, let me know if there's *anything* I can do."

"Thank you," Ellie could only whisper. With that, Lucy and Agent Curtis left the veranda and immediate tears ran freely down Ellie's face.

By the next day, the small town of Mayville, Wisconsin was swirling with activity. News media of all kinds clamored for information regarding the search and ultimate discovery of the missing plane. Much to their dismay, the eager newsmen weren't allowed at the crash site until all remains could be removed. Never known to pass up free publicity, Sheriff Whitaker volunteered to avail himself to those wanting exclusive insight to the discovery.

However, upon hearing the sheriff's fabricated account of the event, Deputy White decided to give his own interview, telling the real story so those truly responsible for the find could be rightly acknowledged.

"Undoubtedly, we'd still be unaware of this tragedy if it weren't for Roy Murphy," the deputy admitted to those listening. "He's the Amish farmer who found the wreckage in his corn field. Since I'm fairly new here, I'm only aware of the briefcase he brought to our office. I'd say, Mr. Murphy is the one who can tell you what you need to know," he concluded.

With their notepads and cameras in hand, the dozen or so reporters raced from the small room to find Mr. Murphy, the man who truly knew the facts. To his chagrin, the sheriff was quickly deserted amid a flurry of discarded notes from his interview. Red-faced, he reached in his desk drawer and pulled out a cigar. In obvious ire he bit off the end and spit it on the floor. Watching from the next room, Deputy White turned his back and smiled…

―――――――――

With Matt's arrival, Covenant House was filled with praise and shouts of thanksgiving for his safe return. He looked thinner than Lucy could remember; deep new creases were on his face; his eyes were bloodshot from too little sleep.

"It's good to be home again," he whispered, tugging Lucy into his arms. "God is so faithful and I witnessed it more during this time than ever before," Matt admitted. "I'm so sorry about Mona, my darling. I'm sorry I wasn't there with you."

"You were where God wanted you to be; where you were needed more," Lucy assured her husband. "Our lives have been a whirlwind of events these past few months, and today was no exception," she remarked, leading Matt to the sofa. "Ellie had a visitor. An agent came by. They found the crash site."

Laying his head back, Matt closed his eyes and let out a deep sigh. "Where did they find it?" he finally asked.

"Somewhere in northern Wisconsin; the investigators are already there. This news has obviously upset Ellie all over again," Lucy concluded, studying Matt's face as a sudden, deeper frown creased his forehead.

"No doubt, the poor dear," he again sighed, shaking his head. "And now she'll have to endure another goodbye, with a funeral." It was evident to Lucy the sorrow Matt felt over his brother, hadn't lessened either

---

As soon as she could excuse herself after dinner, Ellie retreated to her room where she crawled atop her bed. Against her pillow she cried for Chad. The news she heard today had reopened wounds not yet healed. The grief of losing her husband was again there, causing a physical ache in her heart. *I need help, Lord!* Ellie pleaded.

A moment later she remembered Lucy's advice about writing down her feelings. She knew it worked. The letter she'd written to Morton Cooper two years before had ended the hatred she felt. It healed the hurt so she could finally forgive the unforgivable. Perhaps writing to Chad would help, too.

Going to her desk, Ellie retrieved pen and paper. In the lamp's soft glow she sat quietly gathering her thoughts about her one true love. *There's so much that I love about you, how do I start?* Ellie wondered. As though guided by an unseen hand, she began...

> Grow old with me...it's what we said...but now my life is filled with dread.
>
> In saddest gloom my heart now breaks...in loneliness each day I wake.
>
> Yet, somewhere on that distant shore...you dwell with God forever more.
>
> Now, I'll live out my destiny...in God's Love I've been set free...
>
> So, my love, I'll do my best...to finish my course with zeal and zest...
>
> Until our meeting on distant shore...where sorrows cease, forever more...

I commit Chad to your care, Lord. I trust you, Ellie prayed as she laid aside her pen.

Lifting her face heavenward, she closed her eyes. Just then, a sense of peace washed over her. Nothing of this magnitude had before enveloped her with such love. At that moment, Ellie knew she had begun her climb from her valley of despair.

Finally, she had let go...

CHAPTER TWENTY-FOUR

Despite his extreme lack of sleep during the past several weeks, Matt was up early the next morning. The house was quiet and after making coffee, he poured a cup and headed for the veranda. The sun felt warm as he walked to the front lawn to get the morning paper. "Oh, it's good to be home," he uttered softly, letting his gaze drift across the yard.

When he was seated in his favorite chair, Matt took a sip of his coffee and then opened the newspaper.

Missing Plane Discovered in Wisconsin

Rumors of lone survivor being investigated

A shockwave surged through Matt as his eyes lingered on the headlines. Then a feeling of hope welled up as he hurriedly read the following:

Authorities have arrived in the small town of Mayville, Wisconsin to investigate a plane crash that was discovered in a farmer's corn-field. Although some doubted this was in fact the missing government plane, newly recovered documents have proven otherwise. The flight was more than one hundred miles off course when it apparently went down in bad weather. It is suspected that the plane suffered navigational difficulties as well as radio failure during the winter storm.

An immediate search began for the Twin Engine Beach Craft when it was reported missing on January 20th. However, due to bad weather, the search ended ten days later without success. The plane carrying six federal agents was headed for an undisclosed destination when it lost radio contact.

Yesterday, it was learned the Amish farmer who discovered the wreckage weeks before, had also found a lone survivor. However, due to severe weather the farmer, Roy Murphy and his wife, Wilma, could only move the critically injured man to their farmhouse until the storm cleared. It was there the couple did what they could until medical help was summoned days later.

At this time the whereabouts of the crash victim is unknown. A state wide search is currently underway to find him and to determine, if he is in fact, still alive.

When Matt had finished reading the article he felt overwhelming disgust at such incompetence.

How can they lose a patient? Fuming, he threw down the paper. *Dear God, could this be Chad?*

Without more information, Matt and Lucy decided to keep this latest news from Ellie. Certainly, there was only one chance in six that this survivor *was* Chad and even less chance that he was still alive, given the lack of medical care. Yet, they couldn't deny the fact it *could* be Chad. What's *your* intuition saying?" he asked Lucy later that morning.

"I feel we *have* to make sure one way or the other," Lucy replied. "But, how do we do it without knowing where to start?"

"Hire a private investigator; I already have one in mind," Matt admitted. "And, he's only a phone call away." With that, he left his seat and headed inside. "Good morning, Miss Ellie," he greeted kindly, meeting her in the doorway. "Please, join Lucy and I'll be back shortly."

"Good morning and thank you, I will," Ellie answered with a smile. "He seems to have rested well," she remarked, taking a seat at the patio table.

"Yes he did," Lucy said, "and now he's eager to get busy."

"What about the vacation you mentioned?" Ellie asked, pouring coffee from the carafe.

"We haven't had a chance to talk about it," Lucy confessed, wishing she could tell Ellie this latest news. Yet, there was no use getting her hopes up, at least, not before they had more to go on. "Home may be the best place for a vacation after all," she told Ellie, trying hard to keep her mind on their conversation and not on this shocking information.

For a moment there was silence, and then Lucy noticed the newspaper lying on the chair next to Ellie. In haste, she reached for it just as Ellie had the same idea. "Oh, I'm sorry," Ellie said. "You go first. I'll see it later."

With a smile, Lucy took the publication and while making sure Ellie didn't see the headlines, she nonchalantly opened it to the sales page. However, on this particular day, the sales were sure to go unnoticed.

"If you ladies would like to spoil me this evening, I have a suggestion," Matt told Lucy and Ellie at breakfast later that morning.

"Of course, what would that be?" Lucy asked, winking at Ellie.

"I've been hungry for some good Mexican food. Enchiladas, tacos … or anything else you can think of," he told them.

"We can do that. Want to go shopping for ingredients?" Lucy asked Ellie.

"Sure, and I need to get a few things in town myself," Ellie replied. At that, Matt grinned at his wife, knowing he could now make some phone calls, and also inform Rose and Marie of this latest news they were keeping from Ellie. Certainly, the radio and television had news and right now they had to keep Ellie from hearing any of it.

A somber cloud hung over the investigators as they gathered information and placed the victim's remains in body bags. Because of the frigid temperatures and mounds of snow covering them since the crash, each body was preserved enough for easy identification.

Using fingerprints, the authorities would have positive proof of their name and next of kin. Finally, the long ordeal would be over for those who had waited so long to bury their loved ones.

As news of the discovered plane crash was released, every newspaper in Wisconsin carried a full page story regarding the missing survivor. "This is *our* John Doe...I'd bet money!" nurse Marilyn blurted as she read the article. "We have to let someone know about him."

"Wow...just imagine if he *is* that poor guy!" her friend Mary remarked, filling her coffee cup. "We might be interviewed on TV!"

"Let's go show this to Eva...*she's* got the last word around here," Marilyn replied as the two hurriedly headed for the nurse's station.

Within minutes every staff member was talking about their patient...the man who not only had survived his major injuries, but was actually improving. Certainly, this would bring their facility some favorable publicity, *and* give credit to those who had worked hard to keep their John Doe alive.

As she stood in line at the drug store, Ellie's eyes drifted across the various magazines and gossip tabloids nearby. "Isn't that *something* about a survivor of that horrible plane crash?" the clerk commented to her customer. "Hard to imagine anyone living through such an ordeal," she added.

"Yes, and now they can't find what hospital he's in. I sure hope this isn't just some hoax," the customers replied, handing the clerk her money.

Feeling stunned, Ellie's mind darted back over the past few hours. *The newspaper … is this why Lucy didn't want me to read it?* "Excuse me please … are you talking about the plane they just found in Wisconsin?" Ellie asked, interrupting the women.

"Yes, it's all over the news this morning," the clerk told her. "They say a farmer and his wife took care of the poor man until they could get him some medical help. And now they don't know where he's been taken. It's all *quite* bizarre if you ask me," she concluded.

An unexplained jolt shot through Ellie and in her heart she knew it was Chad. "He's alive! My Chad is alive! I *know* it's him!" she blurted as those around her looked on. "Thank you!" she cheered as she hurriedly placed her few items on the counter. "Please excuse me," she said in haste.

Rushing from the store, Ellie arrived at the news stand outside and deposited the required coins. Trembling, she quickly read the article. Seconds later her eyes welled with tears, thinking of Chad suffering in such a manner. *Dear Father in Heaven, please, let them find Chad still alive,* Ellie pleaded as she sought the stability of a nearby bench.

————————

Now that Ellie was privy to this shocking news, she was informed of the man Matt hired to discover whether this mysterious survivor was in fact Chad.

"We should be hearing something soon," Matt told Ellie. "I am sorry we didn't tell you, but we didn't want to subject you to more disappointment."

"I appreciate that, but I *know* its Chad," Ellie said assuredly. "Don't ask me how I know, I just do. My heart has known it all along."

"Sweetheart, if this *is* Chad, he may have suffered extensive injuries, so it's hard to know what condition he'll be in," Lucy explained. "If he had head trauma there may be complications, so we have to prepare for anything."

"I know, but *whatever* his condition, he'll be here, with us," Ellie replied in earnest. "God works miracles, isn't that what you've always told me? Well then, whatever we're facing, we'll get through it."

Nodding, Lucy reveled in the innocent and unyielding faith of this young woman. In the past months since the plane crash, Ellie's optimism of Chad's return may have faltered, but Lucy knew it had never died. No matter the evidence, God had kept that flicker of hope alive within Ellie's heart for a very good reason.

————————

Everyone at Covenant House was a bundle of nerves as they awaited word from the private investigator. Each time the phone rang Ellie's heart quickened with excitement. Thirty hours had gone by.

It was early afternoon when Matt answered yet another call. Saying nothing, he listened intently as he glanced at the others nearby.

"How long will that take?" Matt was heard saying. "We'll be waiting." As he ended the call he then faced the four women. "He found the survivor, but it'll take fingerprints for positive identification. They're doing that now."

"This man doesn't know what Chad looks like?" Ellie hurriedly asked.

"Yes, he's seen Chad in the past, but they'll use fingerprints to be sure," Matt informed them. "It won't be long now."

"Did he say anything else…about his condition?" Ellie prodded.

"Only that everyone's saying it's a miracle that he's alive," Matt told her. "His injuries are *quite* extensive."

With that came silence. For Ellie, it didn't matter what challenges they faced, she only wanted to have Chad home again. *It can't be any harder than what we've already been through,* she decided, thinking of her abuse and then how she and Chad were nearly killed by Jack Barton.

———

It was late morning when the call came. "There's *no* doubt?" Matt asked, looking heavenward as he listened. "Thanks a million, Pete. Great news!" he said at goodbye.

"Well, I guess we'll be flying to Wisconsin," he told Ellie, grinning ear to ear.

The kitchen was immediately filled with shouts of thanksgiving and tears of joy. For Ellie, the shackles of doubt and despair had fallen away, leaving a newfound hope for a future she once feared would never be. And right now, she couldn't wait to see her husband.

The next twenty-four hours were a maze of excitement. With the news of Chad's identification and the whereabouts of his family, news reporters hounded Covenant House. It was decided Matt would give one major interview, hoping to dispel any further questions by the news hungry media.

"Ladies and gentleman, we understand the interest you all have in such an event as this, but, I do hope after today you'll respect our privacy. I'm sure you can understand also, there will be a time of adjustment and healing for my brother when he returns home. Right now I'll be happy to answer your questions," Matt told the rather large gathering on the front lawn.

For the next ten minutes, he gave respectful answers but refused to divulge anything of the personal nature. When asked about Chad's injuries, Matt's answers were vague since he'd had no communication with the doctors.

Seemingly satisfied, the reporters gave a kind

word of appreciation as they loaded up their cameras and microphones after their barrage of questions.

That same afternoon Matt and Ellie left for Wisconsin to be with Chad until he was ready to come home.

Upon their arrival at the hospital and immediate conversation with the doctors, Matt and Ellie heard the unvarnished truth about Chad's injuries. Yet, when learning the circumstances of his rescue and delay in receiving medical care, they realized Divine intervention was the only explanation.

It was late evening by the time they were directed to Chad's room. "Are you sure you're up for this?" Matt whispered to Ellie, taking her hand.

"Yes, but I know it won't be easy," she told him as they reached the door. Taking a deep breath to calm her nerves, Ellie nodded. "I'm ready." Slowly, Matt opened the door to his brother's room.

As they entered Ellie felt weak and feared she'd collapse, if not for Matt's steady arm. Slowly, they moved closer and looked down on the frail body of a man said to be her beloved Chad.

In the dimly lit room she saw a marred and discolored face that held dozens of sutures. Bandages covered the right side of his head; his broken left arm was immobilized in some strange looking apparatus. Beneath the blankets, an empty space marked his missing right leg.

Beside the bed were machines attached to tubes,

IV needles and monitors, each one chanting its own minuteness rhythm.

"Chad, can you hear me? It's Ellie," she whispered past the lump in her throat. Suddenly, a horde of memories paraded through her mind. She thought of all the changes in her life and knew Chad was responsible for most. The way he smiled at her; the loving gleam in his eyes; his laughter so easily shared, had all helped to ensnare her heart completely. The man responsible for who she was today had beat impossible odds to stay alive. Now, it was her turn to be there for him, no matter what.

In this small hospital room, far from home, Matt knew he'd been blessed beyond measure. Not only had his own life been recently spared, but under more grave conditions, Chad had also survived. *You've kept us alive for a special purpose, Lord, and I believe that reason will soon be underway,* Matt thought, feeling excited about the future.

"We are truly blessed, little brother," Matt whispered as he leaned close. "We'll get through this, so hang on," he added softly, gently taking hold of Chad's hand.

Just then, Matt felt the slightest response. "Good Chad, I felt that," Matt said. "Now, can you open your eyes?"

The seconds seemed like hours until they saw what seemingly took great effort for Chad to do—he opened his eyes enough to look at them.

"Hello, sweetheart, it's so good to see you," Ellie

said through her tears as she leaned down. "I love you, Chad, with all my heart."

"You hang on, little brother," Matt said then. "Ellie and I are right here with you and we're staying until you can come home." As he looked on, Matt saw the tiniest movement as Chad tried to nod his head; at the corner of his eye, a tear gathered.

CHAPTER TWENTY-FIVE

The day had finally arrived, Chad could go home. It was obvious, having Ellie and Matt nearby during the past several weeks had helped with Chad's recovery. Each milestone was reason to celebrate; the hardest day was when Chad asked about the baby. Together, he and Ellie mourned their loss.

The best day for Ellie was when Chad could return her kiss, and give her his lopsided grin. It was then she knew her husband had really returned.

It was May fifteenth, and for Ellie, the day couldn't have been happier. As they rode toward home, she reveled in the feel of Chad's arms around her. Certainly, after this long ordeal, their love felt fresh and rekindled, and had grown deeper still.

Fading pink scars were reminders of Chad's numerous lacerations; a small piece of his right ear was missing; his broken left arm had healed without any lingering effects.

"I'm so blessed," Chad said as they rode. "I might have been a helpless invalid, but here I am. The doctors tell me I'll likely have some post traumatic problems, but I believe God will heal me of all that, too," he added.

"I *know* he will," Ellie said snuggling close. "We have our lives to live, so there'll be no such thing," she added smiling. "Right, Matt?"

"That's right, and I can't wait to get started," Matt answered. "We've had enough valleys to last us a lifetime, so now it's time for those *mountain-tops*," he said quite emphatically.

At that, Chad looked at his brother. "I think you're up to something, but you know *I* won't be climbing mountains anytime soon," he remarked, patting the stump of his leg. Matt only looked at him and grinned.

For Matt, he couldn't wait to reveal the exciting plans to everyone. Of course, Lucy was privy from day one and was thrilled with the idea. Again, this would be their secret until everyone could gather for the big announcement.

In the weeks following their decision, Matt and Lucy had worked hard on their project, yet, still more work was needed to see it completed. Nonetheless, the pieces were all in place and it was sure to bring joy to many.

Everyone waited to welcome them home and as the limousine stopped at the front door, cheers of jubilation and hugs of welcome were given all around. For Chad, he knew more than anyone, what a miracle this day really was. For him, life would never be the same. No longer would he do the job he loved, but rather, he'd be tethered to a prosthetic leg. Yet, he knew things were allowed to happen for a reason, and somehow, the reason for this would be revealed in due season. Whatever it was, he was grateful to have Ellie beside him.

Until his prosthesis was ready, Chad would use a wheelchair to get around. Soon after their arrival, he and Ellie took a walk to enjoy their time alone where three years earlier they had vowed their love. "It's the same kind of lovely day as our wedding," Ellie sighed when they had reached the garden. "What a *glorious* day that was."

"Yes, and here we are again, making another new start," Chad said, taking hold of her hand. "To think, I almost missed it."

"Oh, Chad, I can't tell you how horrible it was, thinking I'd never see you again; to never feel your arms around me," Ellie said as she knelt down beside him. "I never knew anyone could hurt so badly and still live."

"Me either," he said, making them both laugh at the irony. "My dear, sweet Ellie, what peril you've gone through in your young life. I'm sorry to have caused you more agony. But, I promise to make it up to you somehow."

"Nonsense, it wasn't you," Ellie blurted. "You

had a job to do, but not with the storm coming. That plane should *never* have taken off."

When hearing that, Chad tried to remember that day. Somewhere in the far recesses of his mind there were faint images, visions he couldn't quite see as they lingered just beyond reach. One day perhaps he'd remember it all, but for now, he was grateful to be alive.

"Before we go back, I have something for you," Ellie said, retrieving something from her skirt pocket. "I've learned to put my thoughts down on paper and it helps somehow," she admitted, handing Chad a note.

Opening it, he saw Ellie's neatly written words as he began reading.

> In eagerness I waited, my love, to see your gentle smile … to hear your voice … to feel your touch … it's been such a long, long while.
>
> My heart was torn with unmatched grief … to live my life without you here. But, in His wisdom and answered prayer … God has wiped away my tears.

The lump in his throat kept Chad from speaking. Instead, he stared at the words that revealed some of what Ellie had suffered. Then, reaching out for her hand, Chad lifted it to his lips and gently kissed it.

During supper, everyone at the table was giving Marie her usual accolades for another delicious meal, including Richard who had joined them at Matt's request. Richard's presence brought an obvious smile to Marie's face.

Hours before, Ellie had inquired of the latest news and was surprised when Rose revealed Marie and Richard had become quite close. Seeing them now, it was apparent the couple had made great strides in their relationship. For this, Ellie was thrilled.

"Well, I guess it's time for that announcement," Matt said as they enjoyed dessert. "I'm excited about it and I believe you will be too. As you all know, Chad and I grew up in Wyoming, in the shadows of the Teton Mountains. In the summer, we'd hurry to finish our chores and then we'd grab our fishing poles, our can of worms and we'd hike across the field to the river to catch some trout for supper," he explained as everyone listened. "In the winter, we'd go ice skating, take sleigh rides and go ice fishing with Dad. What a paradise for kids to grow up in."

"It sounds like you're planning a vacation to Wyoming," Ellie remarked. "You've always talked about going back there."

"You're half right, Ellie," Matt replied, nodding his head. "But, this isn't just a vacation; it's to live there permanently and help troubled kids. I guess you can say we're moving Covenant House to the country."

"Are you serious?" Chad blurted, looking at Matt. "How are kids going to live there on that old rundown homestead?"

"It's not rundown anymore," Lucy spoke up.

"We've been busy with architects, building contractors, plumbers, electricians, and they've sent some pictures so we could see what they've done. I've got them right here."

From under her chair, Lucy retrieved a folder which held several pictures of the renovations being done. "Not long ago, I'm sure you remember, Ellie, we talked about wanting to help troubled boys as well as girls, which we couldn't do here. I knew about our plans then, but it was too early to say anything," Lucy confessed as she handed the photos to Rose who sat nearby. "As you can see we're well underway. We hired reliable people to start working although we hadn't sold Covenant House as yet. But, I'm happy to report, yesterday, God opened the doors and sent us a buyer and we'll be moving in six weeks."

With that announcement everyone looked stunned; a moment later they cheered the good news. "Oh Lucy, this is wonderful!" Ellie blurted.

"I can't believe this," Chad said, studying the pictures. "Just look at this place! How long have you been doing this?"

"Well, Lucy and I've talked about it for months, ever since I closed my practice. We started talking to people back then, but after Mona passed away, the earthquake happened *and* I sold my practice, it was full steam ahead," Matt explained. "I guess we needed to get our minds off our tragedies and do something important."

"Now, the question is: how many of you will join us on this new venture?" Lucy asked, looking at each one. "We'll still need a cook or two; we'll need a seamstress to keep those jeans patched up; we'll need a good driver to haul kids around to field trips and whatnot; plus, we'll be hiring house-keepers, counselors and more as time goes by," she concluded.

"I'm in," Rose said. "It sounds like fun to me." As for Marie, she looked at Richard and smiled.

"Well, I do believe we need to make our own announcement," Richard spoke up for the first time, reaching for Marie's hand. "I've asked this lady to marry me, and she's accepted. So, if she's ready to try ranch life, I'd like to accept the offer for both of us," he said, gazing at his intended.

"My, oh my, things *sure* do change when one leaves for a while," Chad commented, bringing a round of laughter. Then, it was congratulations for the newly engaged couple and wanting to know how soon they'd be tying the knot.

"I guess it better be quick, if we're all heading to Wyoming soon," Marie said with a grin. "After all, I hear they have some mighty cold nights there and I'll need a husband to cuddle up with," she added as Richard smiled, somewhat red-faced.

Although the news media had kept their distance, Chad's recovery and discharge from the hospital was front-page news. With that came a barrage of well wishes from the White House on down.

Telegrams, cards, letters and bouquets of flowers were now arriving at Covenant House for Agent Chad Ryan, the 'iron man.'

Requests for interviews were a daily occurrence the first week Chad arrived home, which he declined. Yet, as bits and pieces of false information appeared in newspaper articles, he decided one interview would help set things straight.

The day and time was set and once again the front lawn of Covenant House was the gathering place for the news media. With microphones, television cameras and news-hungry reporters clamoring for the best position, Chad read his statement:

"I'm grateful to be alive," he began. *"Only by Divine intervention did I survive a plane crash that killed five of my fellow agents. Each one was a husband, father, son and brother and each one was my friend. They deserve the greatest tribute this nation can bestow. These men died doing their job to protect fellow citizens.*

I owe a great debt of gratitude to many people. First and foremost, I hope to one day meet Roy Murphy and his wife, Wilma, who no doubt were the greatest link to my survival. To the doctors, nurses and others who worked hard to keep me alive, I say thank you.

To my wife, Ellie, whose prayers and unwavering love somehow gave her strength to keep hope alive for my return. To all my family who will continue to stand by me, and lastly, to God, who is the Sustainer of all life, I give each one my deepest gratitude," Chad concluded to a scattering of applause.

For the next few minutes, Chad answered an array of questions about that fateful day and his months in the hospital. Some he could answer, but for many, he had no recollection of the events.

"I'm afraid I've run out of answers," he finally told the sea of faces. "Thank you for coming." Despite being disappointed at not hearing more, many offered a word of thanks and well wishes for Chad's complete recovery.

"You did wonderful, sweetheart," Ellie told Chad when he had finished.

"I hope that's the last of it," he replied. "Now, I'm ready to hear you play your new piano, and if I had two legs, I'd race you to the door." Chad teased, as he started rolling his wheelchair. For Ellie, she could only smile when seeing that sense of humor she always admired in her husband.

CHAPTER TWENTY-SIX

Ten days after he arrived home from the hospital, Chad received a check from the government. It was his share of the lawsuit against the agency for its negligence. After a thorough investigation, it was decided the agency and two of its supervisors were responsible for the deaths of five men, and Chad's near fatal injuries. Therefore, the families of the deceased and Chad each received a check in the amount of one million dollars.

Although stunned at such an amount, Chad suddenly knew what he wanted to do with some of this money. Since he wanted to surprise Ellie, he needed a cohort and Matt was eager to help. Every minute counted if they wanted to complete the surprise before their move to the ranch.

Also on Chad's list of things to do was getting his prosthesis. After all, living on a ranch required two legs and he wasn't about to sit around in a wheelchair. He wanted to be involved and there'd be those leisurely horseback rides with Ellie, too, so he had much to learn about that new leg he'd be using.

It was mid July. The move from California was nearing completion and everyone looked forward to getting settled in at "Ryan's Roost…the Ranch of New Beginnings." Here the incorrigible would have their attitudes adjusted, and the bullies would meet their match. Already the word was out and applications were pouring in.

"I have a surprise for you," Chad told Ellie as they drove. "It's something special I wanted to do for you. I hope you'll like it."

"Where is it, at the ranch?" Ellie asked excitedly, seeing the smile on Chad's face as he glanced at her.

"Yes, but if you don't like it we can make other arrangement," he quickly informed her, taking her hand. "I want you to be happy, Ellie."

"Oh Chad, don't you know how happy I am already?" she replied, leaning against his shoulder. "I've *never* been this happy and content in my life, nor did I ever dream I *could* be. And you're the reason."

For the next while, Ellie rested her head against Chad's shoulder as he drove their new truck. Behind was a trailer full of their belongings Ellie had saved from their home in San Francisco, and her piano.

Traveling had been an adventure. Following

behind Chad and Ellie, were the newlyweds, Richard and Marie. It was decided Rose would be more comfortable flying and she was waiting at the ranch with Matt and Lucy.

"It won't be long now, sweetheart," Chad told Ellie as they crossed the Wyoming border. "Getting tired of traveling?"

"Oh no, this is exciting, seeing all these new places," Ellie assured him. "I must admit though, I'm eager to see the ranch." As she looked out the window, Ellie was in awe of the bright blue sky. Here, away from the city, everything looked fresh and clean—the colors were vibrant and distinct.

On the flatlands of Kansas even a small hill is rare, but here even the prairie had hills and rim rocks that Ellie found beautiful. "I'm going to love it here," she boasted, feeling overjoyed as she snuggled close to Chad.

———————

An hour later, Chad smiled as he slowly brushed Ellie's cheek with the back of his hand. Now sleeping on the seat, she rested her head on his leg as he drove. "We're here, Sleeping Beauty," he said softly, hating to disturb her.

A moment later Ellie yawned and then sat up. "Oh Chad, I've never seen *anything* so majestic!" she wailed seconds later, seeing the Teton Mountains just ahead. "I can't imagine living here amid such beauty."

"They *are* something all right," Chad replied,

remembering the many times he and Matt had climbed their rocky slopes.

Within minutes they saw Matt, Lucy and Rose on the front porch of the ranch house, waving. "Here we are, sweetheart. Welcome home," Chad said, leaning forward for a kiss.

"It's breathtakingly beautiful!" Ellie gasped a moment later. "I *never* would have imagined anything like this." Leaving their vehicle, they were soon given hugs from those waiting. By now, Richard and Marie had also arrived and were expressing their amazement at what they saw.

"This is for you," Chad said then, handing Ellie a key. "Shall we go see what it opens?" Seeing the key, Ellie then looked at those who stood around smiling at her.

"Do *all* of you know about this?" Ellie asked, looking at the others.

"Just recently for me," Rose told her daughter. "But, I'm sure some had to know a while back. It's a mighty fine surprise, if you ask me."

"Well then … I'm ready to go," Ellie said, taking Chad's arm.

"We'll be back," he told the others smiling as they headed for the woods.

Hand in hand, Ellie and Chad walked, leaving the others behind. "This is glorious!" she remarked, taking a deep breath. "Smell that fresh air! Feel that sun!" she boasted joyfully, tilting her face heavenward. Neither one spoke as they walked. Ellie wallowed in the day's delightful pleasantries.

Nearing the wooded area, she noticed a somewhat spicy smell. "Okay, my sweet, close your eyes and give me your hand," Chad told her. "We're almost there."

Doing as she was told, Ellie couldn't imagine Chad hiding anything in the woods. *It wouldn't be a car, would it, or some other kind of vehicle?* Suddenly, she felt gravel beneath her feet and heard what sounded like running water.

"Now, don't open your eyes until I tell you, okay?" Chad told her. "Just stand here for a minute and I'll tell you when."

Trying hard to be patient, Ellie lowered her head and kept her eyes shut while trying to identify the sounds around here. *Birds, water bubbling, smell of pine and something sweet, like Aunt Marie's cedar chest,* Ellie decided. Nearby she heard noises. "Is that you, Chad?"

"It's me, sweetheart. Okay, you can look now," he told her. Lifting her head, Ellie slowly opened her eyes.

She caught her breath, but no words would come for what she saw was beyond description. Somehow, she'd been magically transported to a land of fairytales. A beautiful log cottage sat among the trees, bedecked with window boxes filled with flowers; a tiny redwood bridge spanned a narrow stream. Flowerbeds and shrubs adorned the patch of green lawn. Two cedar benches now sat in the shade beside a pool of clear water.

"Shall we look inside?" Chad whispered as he now stood next to her. In a daze, Ellie felt Chad take her hand and lead her across the bridge, up the path to the front door. Still she found no words to express her transformation into a fairy princess. Certainly, Chad was her prince and here, in this enchanted setting, she felt nothing could harm them.

Inside was no less charming, yet, the kitchen appliances were missing and the rooms sat vacant of furnishings. Picture windows looked out to the peaceful surroundings that reminded Ellie of a beautiful park.

"Do you like it?" Chad asked, gently wiping Ellie's cheek. "I hope these are happy tears."

"Surely I must be dreaming," Ellie whispered, finding her voice. "I love it, Chad. I can't describe how I feel. *Are* we still in Wyoming?"

"Yes, but I wanted our own special place, apart from the world. This is our hideaway, darling, and it's off limits to anyone not personally invited," he assured her. "Behind us is a mountain and in front are trees, to keep us secluded. Tonight we'll camp out in our sleeping bags, and tomorrow we'll go buy whatever appliances and furniture you want," Chad told her. "Now, I guess we'd better join the others and then get unloaded."

"Thank you, my dear, sweet husband," Ellie said, throwing her arms around Chad's neck. "This is the most spectacular surprise ever!"

The two-hundred-acre ranch far surpassed everyone's expectation. Not only was the construction completed as promised, but the workmanship was superb. The landscaping, too, brought a sigh of delight from everyone.

The old farmhouse had been torn down and a spacious modern one stood in its place. A new barn, corrals, and two bunk houses were built; one for boys and one for the girls. Each one could house eleven residents and one adult counselor and contained two bathrooms with walk-in showers.

For Richard and Marie, their private dwelling was a new doublewide mobile home. Rose had a large comfortable bedroom and sewing room on the main floor of the ranch house, while Matt and Lucy had the upper level.

The house had three bathrooms, a large dining room where each meal would be served, a sitting room and a kitchen to delight any chef. Refrigerators, freezers, stove and ovens were all commercial size and the cooking island was well stocked with a vast array of utensils and small appliances. Nothing was overlooked.

For Marie and Richard, a Caribbean honeymoon was planned once they were settled in their new home. They would leave in five days.

"This will feel like vacation instead of work," Marie commented, when seeing the elaborate kitchen and dining area. "When do we get started?"

"Matt and Chad will review the applicants and they'll decide who we accept," Lucy told her. "I'd say by the time you get back from your cruise, we should have our first arrivals."

"Who'll cook till I get back?" Marie wanted to know.

"We'll manage. Of course, it won't be anything like we're used to, but I guess we'll rough it till you get back," Lucy said with a smile.

Early the next morning, Chad and Ellie drove to Jackson Hole to see what the small town offered in furniture and appliances. Although the store carried little of what was needed, the owner assured them all items could be ordered and delivered within days. "This is life in the country," Chad said teasingly when they had finished their business.

"It's a small price to pay for all this," Ellie said, feeling excited about their new life in this beautiful setting.

That afternoon Ellie finished unpacking. She loved everything about her new home that Chad had built especially for them. Her heart overflowed with love for her husband and nothing could ever change that.

Sitting at her piano, Ellie thought of a song and played it in her head as she touched the keys. Instinctively, she picked out the melody in no time. "I love it!" she blurted, feeling overjoyed. *I need those lessons so I can really play!*

Slowly then, Ellie wandered through the house, envisioning how she'd decorate. *I'll get frilly kitchen curtains, matching dishtowels, tablecloths and beau-*

tiful cookware for making Chad delicious meals. Oh, I can't wait to get started! Ellie thought excitedly, remembering some of her favorite recipes.

Just then she heard someone. "Come along, my sweet," Chad called out, sticking his head in the door. "Someone has arrived that I'm sure you'll be thrilled to see." Hurriedly, Ellie ran to see who it might be.

As they cleared the woods, Ellie was thrilled to see Comet being unloaded from the large horse trailer, along with six other equine. "Oh Chad, you're right! This is wonderful and I can't wait to go riding!" she blurted. After supper, they did just that and Chad showed Ellie where he and Matt had made many childhood memories.

———————

Each day was filled with fun and new surprises. The local newspaper sent a reporter to do a story on the ranch and its intended purpose. Neighbors dropped by to welcome everyone to the area; some came seeking a job at Ryan's Roost. Within the first week it appeared everyone knew the Ryan brothers had returned to the place of their birth.

———————

It was August first when Ellie received a long awaited letter from Henry. Eagerly, she opened the envelope with its familiar scribble.

> *Dear Ellie,*
>
> *Sorry I haven't written lately as I'm sure you've*

been wondering about me. Ma died some time back and I'm working extra to pay for her funeral. Mr. Roth says I can make payments, but still it's hard to pay the ten dollars a week.

I hope you are happy in Wyoming. It must be very pretty there. Once, I saw a magazine showing Wyoming and I read about all the elk and deer that are there.

Someday I sure hope we can meet, but it won't be for awhile now. I'm working long hours at the grain elevator and I might get a job for weekends too.

I hope to hear from you, Ellie, and I will try to do better next time.

Your brother,

Henry

When she'd finished reading, Ellie folded up the letter and stuffed it in the pocket of her jeans. *He's only a boy, yet, he has adult responsibilities,* she thought sadly. "Well, it's time Henry had some help!"

As she hurriedly headed for the ranch house, Ellie's mind was full of plans. *He can come here…Mother and I will pay off the funeral so he can finally have a real life! Surely, he can help out around here. Chad can show him how to fish, hunt, ride; all those things I doubt he knows anything about,* she eagerly planned.

"Mother, are you here?" Ellie called out as she entered the house.

"We're in here, dear," Rose answered from the sitting room. As she reached the spacious room where residents would visit family members, or the group would socialize, Ellie was quite surprised to see a rather lovely blond haired woman sitting with her mother.

"Pardon me for interrupting," Ellie quickly said, not wanting to barge in.

"Oh, it's quite all right. I was about to leave. My name is Belladonna. Belle for short," she told Ellie, getting up from her chair. "I'm your neighbor. I have a ranch over yonder," she said, lifting a well-manicured hand and pointing east. "I've known Chad and Matthew since school days," she added, tossing her mane of long hair over her shoulder.

"And I'm Ellie. Pleased to meet you, Belle," she said, offering her hand. At seeing the woman's hesitation, it was obvious she wasn't the cordial type.

"Yes, quite," Belle replied, barely taking hold of Ellie's finger tips. "So *you're* Chad's wife," she added somewhat disdainfully.

"Yes I am and *very* happy to be, I might add," Ellie replied. "He's the *most* wonderful man I've ever met, and he showers me with love and gifts at *every* turn. Right, Mother?" she boasted.

From the way Belle tightened her lips and glared at her, Ellie knew the woman was not pleased at hearing such news. "*Do* come again. We'll have tea and by then I'm sure I'll have *lots* more wonderful surprises from my husband to talk about," Ellie said, taking Belle's arm and guiding her to the front door.

Somewhat in a huff, the woman hurried to her shiny red truck and climbed inside. Only then did Ellie rejoin Rose in the sitting room. "Why dear, is that *any* way to treat a neighbor?" Rose asked, grinning.

"Mother, it's obvious *she* has eyes for my husband! I'm afraid it'll take lots of prayer before I can love that neighbor as I should," Ellie replied, trying to calm her sudden agitation.

"Well, I'm very glad you arrived when you did," Rose went on. "She *was* beginning to ask lots of personal questions."

"What nerve!" Ellie blared, shaking her head with disgust. "Oh, I almost forgot why I came. I heard from Henry and he said his ma died. Now he's working hard to pay funeral expenses, so I really think we should help him out, Mother," she went on in haste, still feeling perturbed over what just happened. "What do you think?"

"That poor young man," Rose lamented, shaking her head. "Yes, dear, of course we need to help him. He's a victim of circumstance and we can't let him fall by the wayside. Hard telling *what* he might end up doing if he gets desperate enough," she concluded.

"I think he should come here, to the ranch," Ellie said then. "After all, this is a place for troubled boys. I'll talk to Chad about it. By the way...where *is* everybody?"

"Lucy and Matt went to the airport to get Richard and Marie. They should be back before too long,"

Rose informed her daughter. "The ranch hands are out putting up hay. I guess that's everyone."

"And Chad is checking the fence line. He noticed some loose wires the other night when we were out riding," Ellie explained. "I have bread to go in the oven so I better get back over there. See you later, Mom," she said, giving a hurried kiss on the cheek. "I'll write Henry regarding how much money he owes."

"No dear, I'll just call the funeral home and tell Mr. Roth what we want to do. I'll write a check to cover that, and then we'll decide how much we want to send Henry," Rose told Ellie.

"That's great, Mother. He'll be so surprised." With a wave, Ellie left Rose and headed back to her cottage in the woods. Although she felt excited about helping Henry, Ellie's thoughts were soon on Belle. *I wonder: just what does that woman have up her sleeve?*

CHAPTER TWENTY-SEVEN

That evening, everyone gathered to hear Marie and Richard talk about their exciting cruise. It was obvious the couple had a great time and would soon have dozens of pictures to share. "So warm and lovely, we *almost* decided to stay. Didn't we, dear?" Marie said jokingly, nudging Richard's shoulder.

"Yes, but then she thought about this lovely kitchen and decided it was just too much to give up," Richard teased in return, bringing a round of laughter from those gathered.

"We're happy to hear that!" Lucy stated as everyone agreed.

"Yes, especially since our first group arrives tomorrow. There'll be three boys and one counselor so I guess we're underway," Matt informed them.

As for Ellie, she hadn't had a chance to talk to Chad about Henry, but now seemed like a good time. "I have a request," she began, sliding to the edge of her seat. "You all know about Henry, my sixteen year old half-brother? Well, I truly believe *he* belongs here, too. His mom recently died so he has *no* one. He had to quit school to take care of her and now he's paying her funeral expenses. It seems so unfair and Mother and I want to help him."

"If this is all true, then the boy *does* need help," Matt replied. "What about it, Chad? Since he knows how to work, maybe he could be a positive influence on some of these rowdy kids we're about to see."

"I think you're right," Chad said, taking hold of Ellie's hand as she sat beside him. "We *are* here to help kids and Henry's had a hard life."

"Okay, Miss Ellie, I'd say you're about to meet your brother. Write or give him a call and we'll get him here," Matt said with a smile.

"Thank you both," Ellie cheered, giving Chad a hug. From across the room Rose grinned and gave thumbs up to her daughter.

By the time Ellie and Chad walked back to their cottage, the sky held lingering shades of purple as the sun was setting. "Oh Chad, this is *beyond* splendor," Ellie sighed, looking heavenward. "It's just wonderful!"

"And you're wonderful," Chad said, pulling her next to him for a quick kiss. "It *is* good to be back here, after all these years. The best part is having you here, too."

"After all our sorrows... God has given us wonderful blessings," Ellie said, feeling happier than she thought possible. And, she'd soon be meeting Henry. "Thank you, sweetheart, for bringing my brother here. I'm sure you two will be great friends."

"I've no doubt if he's anything like you," Chad replied. "But, we must remember, he's Morton's son, not Rose's."

"I know, I've thought about that. Still, after reading his letters I feel sure he's nothing like our dad," Ellie said assuredly. "He deserves a chance in life."

Then, for the hundredth time since meeting Belle, Ellie's thoughts were on her and decided to tell Chad. "I met one of our neighbors today," she began. "She said she went to school with you and Matt. Somehow, I felt she *might* have been more than just a friend," Ellie concluded as the arrived home.

Making no reply, Chad opened the door for her and let her enter first. It seemed strange that he hadn't asked who the neighbor was, yet, Ellie waited as Chad closed the door behind them. "Do you know who it was?" she then asked.

"Yeah, I know," Chad finally said, taking hold of Ellie's hand. "I'll start the fireplace and then we'll talk. It's time you know about Belle."

For Chad, the time had come to reveal a past he'd buried eleven years ago; yet, he *had* to tell Ellie; it was certain Belle *would* at the first opportunity. It was also certain her version would be far from the truth.

Soon, the fire's orange glow flickered inside the living room. As Chad gathered his thoughts, he sat down beside Ellie on their new sofa and gently pulled her in his arms. "I love you, my sweet Ellie, more than I ever thought I'd love any woman," he told her, feeling her warmth next to him.

"And I love you, Chad. *Nothing* will ever change that," Ellie said softly. Those words brought a measure of comfort to Chad for what he was about to say. Taking a deep breath, he knew the time had come...

"Yes, Belle and I *were* more than just friends," he began as those long ago memories filled his mind. "I was rowdy back then, and she was the new girl in school. Her dad bought the ranch next to ours and it was soon obvious he was rich, *and* his daughter was spoiled rotten. Belle got anything she wanted...clothes, cars, trips, it didn't matter. Her mother died when she was eight, so it was just Belle and her dad. She was his whole life and I took advantage of that situation," Chad said with a sigh. "My folks didn't have much, just this homestead where they barely made a living, and I wanted more."

"How old were you?" Ellie asked as she left his embrace.

"We were both seventeen when we met, but we soon had adult problems," he went on. "Belle wanted to get married. I told her I couldn't support her, but she said it didn't matter, her dad had plenty of money and he'd take care of us. I wasn't much in favor of that, but I finally agreed and we decided to run away and find a Justice of the Peace when we turned eighteen."

"You were *married* to her?" Ellie shrieked in dismay.

"No, my darling, we never got married and for that I'm forever thankful," Chad assured her. "A tragedy prevented that horrible mistake from happening. Belle's dad was found murdered that very week and we were both suspects. She'd been bragging to her friends what we planned, and her dad found out. For the first time ever, Belle was denied something she wanted and she had a major blowup with her dad. Someone heard them fighting and when her dad ended up with his skull caved in, we were arrested," Chad admitted, recalling how scared he was.

"That must have been *horrible* for you and your family," Ellie gasped. "Did they ever find who did it?"

"No one was ever charged. Thanks to Matt, I had an alibi," Chad said. "When they determined the time of death, they knew I couldn't have done it. I was with Matt visiting my dad in the hospital. I had numerous witnesses as to the time I was there and how long we stayed."

"So, what happened with you and Belle?" Ellie wanted to know.

"It was over for me. I'd had enough and to tell you the truth, sweetheart, I never quite believed her story of what happened. She said she was asleep and someone must have broken in and forced her dad to open the safe and then killed him, since a large amount of money was taken," Chad went on. "After that, Belle went back east to live with an aunt and I never heard from her again. I was really surprised to learn she was back here."

"You mean she never tried to see you before she left here?"

"Oh yeah, she tried, but Matt made it clear she wasn't welcome here and our relationship was over. And, that's when I finally got it through my thick skull that I needed the Lord in my life," Chad confessed. "Being accused of murder at eighteen gets your attention, and besides, I finally realized I was headed for disaster in many ways."

"Why do you suppose Belle came back, after all this time?" Ellie asked. "Could she *possibly* think you'd still have feelings for her?"

"I didn't love her back then. It was lust and excitement, not love," Chad admitted. "I was young, rebellious and nothing my family said mattered. I was going to do as I pleased, and if I hadn't been with Matt that day, there's no doubt they'd have pinned Mr. Johnson's murder on me."

"I think Belle is still hoping to rekindle that lost romance," Ellie said, leaving the sofa. "Have you seen her since we arrived?" she then asked, standing in front of the fire. "What will you say to her when that time comes?"

"I have *nothing* to say," Chad assured Ellie. "She's a part of my very foolish past and our lives now have no connection. I hope she stays away."

"I hope so, too, but from the way she looked at me, she'd *love* for me to drop dead," Ellie told Chad, rejoining him on the sofa.

At hearing those words a jolt of fear shot through Chad. "Sweetheart, *promise* me you won't let her near you," Chad cautioned. "If she killed her own dad, then she's capable of doing most anything."

"Do you really think *she* murdered her father?" Ellie wailed.

"Yes, truthfully, I think she did. That event in my life was the driving force of why I became a detective," he admitted for the first time. "When I finally got my life on the straight and narrow, I knew I wanted to help find the ones responsible for such crimes. So often the guilty ones go free and they do it again," Chad explained, feeling sure Belle would never be proven guilty.

"Thank you for telling me all this," Ellie said, snuggling close. "I will stay away from Belle, but I won't run from her."

"Then you'll learn to shoot a gun," Chad announced. "Out here there are many reasons to carry a gun, and Belle might be one of them."

The next morning, Chad helped Matt welcome the new residence to the ranch and gave the orientation. The rules and boundaries were clearly set, including no admittance to the area of his and Ellie's cottage. Anyone breaking the rules would be disciplined by losing their privileges. Three such actions would mean dismissal from the program.

For some, this was their last chance before reform school. "We're here to help you," Chad told them. "This is your chance for positive changes in your life; to do something you can be proud of. I know how you think, because I was young and foolish once too. But thank God, I finally saw the light before it was too late. And now, we want to do the same for you," he concluded, barely seeing a response from the three boys.

"It's a challenge," he told Matt later. "Yet, we know it can be done. By the way, have you seen Belle hanging around here?"

"No, but I heard she dropped by," Matt replied. "I hope she won't make that mistake again. Rose told Lucy she was very inquisitive about where you and Ellie live; if Ellie could ride and many other things."

"I never *dreamed* she'd be back here or we might have scrubbed this whole idea," Chad replied, shaking his head. "See you later. I'm taking my wife target practicing."

True to his word, that afternoon Chad took Ellie out for her first lesson in how to handle a gun. Before he'd be satisfied, his wife *would* know how to shoot a rifle and a handgun. *And,* she'd know some defensive moves, too. There was no way his precious Ellie would be helpless against Belle Johnson.

It was late August. Although the days were still quite pleasant, the nights were cold and the trees were beginning to show off their vibrant autumn hues.

"Life is glorious. Thank you, Lord," Ellie sang out, looking out her kitchen window. "Henry will be here in a few hours and I can't wait to see him!"

After finishing the breakfast dishes and tidying up, Ellie grabbed her jacket and headed for the ranch house. Everyone eagerly waited for Chad and Matt to arrive with Henry. "Good morning," she greeted, opening the door.

"Good morning, Ellie. Come in and have some coffee," Lucy called out from the dining room. "It won't be long now," she added with a smile when seeing Ellie.

After setting a mug of coffee in front of Ellie, Marie joined them at the table. "Did you hear the commotion last night?" she asked, looking at Ellie. "It was quite something."

"No, I heard nothing," Ellie replied. "What kind of commotion?"

"Firecrackers, gunshots—we aren't quite sure," Marie answered. "But, it sure had the horses in an uproar. Matt will check it out when he gets back."

"Comet, I need to go see if he's okay!" Ellie said, bolting from her seat. In seconds, Ellie was running for the corral, praying the horses were all right. Relief swept over her when she saw all of them standing near their feeding box eating. Just then, she noticed holes in the side of the new barn.

"Well, it wasn't firecrackers!" she muttered, seeing the now splintered boards. "Who'd do a foolish thing like this with animals and humans right here?"

Then, Chad's words about Belle came to mind.

Surely, she wouldn't stoop to such childish pranks would she? Well, I'm sure Chad and Matt will get to the bottom of this! Ellie decided, heading back to the house.

Ellie's heart was pounding as she waited for Matt to park his truck. *He's here! Henry's finally here!* Ellie's thoughts raved as she watched the men exit the vehicle.

Within seconds, Henry stood in front of her. For a brief moment they said nothing, instead, they only looked at each other. Instantly, Ellie noticed her half-brother looked nothing like Morton Cooper, except for his build. Tall and slender, Henry's muscular arms were easily noticed under his denim shirt. His face was quite handsome even with a day's worth of whiskers. Certainly, he looked older than sixteen.

"Hello, Ellie," Henry finally said, his voice sounding mature yet soft.

"Hello, Henry. I'm so happy to finally meet you," Ellie replied. "May I hug you?" she then asked. A broad smile appeared as he held out his arms.

"I have a sister and I'm *so* happy!" Henry said next to her ear.

Lord, you've taken Morton's despicable actions and made something good come of it, Ellie thought, feeling her brother's arms around her.

When everyone had welcomed Henry, it was time for lunch. As usual, Marie had outdone herself by preparing a delicious meal for the dozen who now resided at Ryan's Roost...

When Ellie informed Matt and Chad about the bullet holes in the barn, they were more than a little irate. "Well, little brother, I guess its time for your investigative expertise to take over," Matt said as he eyed the damage. "Next time, it might be one of the horses *or* one of us."

Although Chad was silent, his face wore a look of disgust and ire. At no time had Ellie ever seen her husband so mad. "I guess this means we'll have to pay our *neighbor* a little visit," he finally said. "Let's go, Matt."

As she watched the men walk away, Ellie still felt amazed at Chad's complete recovery from the plane crash seven months earlier. His gait was nearly normal despite the prosthetic leg he used. The lacerations on his face had faded into tiny lines that added a handsome ruggedness to his features.

Dear God, don't let Belle get away with this. If she is a murderer, then it's time she's found out. Perhaps this is the beginning of her end, an inner voice softly whispered.

For Chad, seeing Belle again was worse than a beating. Not only did it dredge up old memories of his rebellious youth, but it reminded him of how he'd talked back to his parents, saying horrible things he'd always regret. *At least Mom lived long enough to know I'd changed my ways, but Dad died thinking I was an ungrateful rebel,* Chad lamented, heading for Belle's ranch.

"I doubt she knows what your job was," Matt commented. "In that case, she'll probably say something incriminating and you'll catch it right off."

"Maybe, but Belle always *was* a good liar," Chad responded, thinking of all the schemes she planned *and* got away with. "I'm not sure what she'll do."

"It's a sure fact she *won't* be glad to see me," Matt chuckled as he turned down her lane. "She must still have money, to keep this spread going."

Sure enough, the ranch did look well-kept. Black Angus cattle grazed in the pasture and the outbuildings appeared freshly painted. The yard was well-maintained with flowers and a well-manicured lawn.

As his eyes scanned the property, Chad said nothing while trying to curb his anger before seeing the woman. *Lord, don't let me do something stupid and please forgive me, too, because right now I could choke her!*

By the time they reached her door it opened. "Hello, strangers," Belle greeted wearing a tight red sweater and jeans. "It's time you came calling."

"This *isn't* a social call, Belle," Chad told her. "It's about some damage to our barn and I have a strong suspicion it was some of your late night pranks. So, why did you do it?"

"Oh Chad, you know I'd *never* go shooting up

anyone's barn," she said, using the husky tone he still remembered.

At hearing that, Chad quickly glanced at Matt who was grinning. "Well then, you wouldn't mind letting us see your rifle," he replied.

"Whatever for, I *told* you I didn't do it," Belle answered as her mood suddenly changed. "What gives you the right to question me like this?"

"It's either us or the sheriff," Chad told her. "The best way to get us out of your hair is to come clean."

"Oh, I wasn't going to *hurt* anyone," she blurted defiantly. "It was just, well, a little welcome back celebration."

"If that's your idea of a celebration, then I guess the sheriff needs to know about this!" Matt blared. "You might have killed someone!"

"I'm a better shot than that! When I mean to hurt someone, they're dead!" Belle snapped, glaring at Matt. "So my advice: stay your distance."

When hearing Belle's remark, Chad's instincts processed her every word. Knowing her personality like he did, he realized she was bragging about what she'd done in the past, namely, murdering her own father.

"And, there's no reason for *you* to come to Ryan's Roost," Chad told her. "We'll let last night go. But I promise you, if you cause *any* more problems, you're going to jail," Chad warned, glaring at her. With that, he and Matt turned and headed for the truck.

"There's a lot of open range out there," Belle

yelled after them. "And you don't control it all so you might want to watch that little wife of yours!"

"Let it go," Matt said, grabbing Chad's arm as he was about to turn back. "We'll give her just a little more rope and she'll hang herself."

It wasn't long until Henry was acquainted with everyone on the ranch. Just as Matt hoped, the young man was having a positive influence on the resident boys. His maturity was far beyond his age, so it was decided he deserved a salary. It was accepted with overwhelming gratitude by him and his sister.

Most evenings, Ellie would invite Henry over to have supper with her and Chad. As they shared their past, Ellie realized she and Henry bore many of the same childhood scars. In telling him how God's love and forgiveness had transformed her life, Henry wanted it too. With elation and tears of joy, Ellie led her brother in that all important prayer, on his seventeenth birthday.

Autumn arrived and so did hunting season. Nothing more was heard from Belle since Chad had issued his warning. Everyone seemed more at ease having had no further problems or contact with the woman.

"You have a wonderful time and don't worry about me," Ellie told Chad. "It'll be good for you. Besides, those boys *did* earn the privilege of going."

"Maybe Henry should come and stay with you," Chad suggested. "I'd feel better about leaving you if he did."

"I'm not afraid. You taught me how to protect myself, remember? So go and find those elk," Ellie told her husband.

Later that morning, Chad, Matt and the three resident boys left the ranch for their three-day hunting trip. They would camp midway up the mountain where elk still grazed before winter set in.

The next day dawned clear and bright. The forecast was for sixty-eight degrees. It was mid-morning when Ellie headed for the barn to find Henry.

"Let's go riding," she suggested when she'd found him. "It's a lovely Indian Summer day and too nice to pass up," Ellie added enthusiastically.

"What's Indian Summer?" Henry asked, looking puzzled.

"Well, it means an above average day. Warm, sunny and spring-like, although it's really autumn and should be much cooler. I learned *that* since coming to Wyoming," she boasted teasingly, reaching to remove a piece of straw from Henry's hair. "I'll pack a lunch and take you to see some of our beautiful country."

"Sounds like fun. Okay, give me twenty minutes. I'll saddle the horses when I'm through here," Henry said with a broad grin.

With a nod, Ellie raced home to make sandwiches and put on her riding boots. Within twenty minutes she was ready to go. As she was about to head back to the barn, Ellie heard Chad's words of warning. *Never go riding without a gun, there are too many predators out there.* Quickly, she retrieved the rifle from its place over the fireplace and grabbed a box of ammunition. With her thoughts on the day's adventure, she hurried out the door.

"I see you're ready," Ellie called out, noticing Comet and Max saddled and waiting. Getting no response, she placed the rifle in its sling and stored the ammunition in Comet's saddle bag. "Henry, are you here?"

Just then, he rounded the corner. "I couldn't forget these," he remarked, wrapping the strap of his binoculars around the saddle horn. I'm ready now."

The warm sun and fresh air felt invigorating to Henry. Closing his eyes, he lifted his face heavenward. "Ellie, I never imagined my life could be like this," he told her as they rode side by side. "All my life I wondered how *some* folks got so lucky, to have a nice family and a decent place to live. And now *I've* got all that," he said, letting his eyes gaze across the meadow they rode through.

"I feel the same way," Ellie admitted. "My life held no hope of anything, not until I met Chad. We've had sorrows, but so many blessings, too."

For the next while the two rode and talked,

enjoying the day and each other's company. There was no doubt, a strong bond was set and despite their sad beginnings, they had survived and now had these happy times to enjoy.

Before long, they found a shady spot to have their lunch. While they ate, Henry used his binoculars to look around. "It's really beautiful here and I for one will *never* go back to Kansas," he vowed, remembering his dismal life there.

Ellie felt elated to be having this time with Henry. The day was perfect and she was eager to show her brother all the places Chad had shown her. After lunch, they again mounted their horses and headed for the river to find Chad's favorite fishing spot.

Before long, they reached the narrow path leading down to the river. Here it was necessary for them to ride single file. On the right was a steep embankment and on their left was a grove of trees. "I'll go first," she told Henry, nudging Comet in front.

Just then, a horse and rider came barreling toward them from the trees. With no time to react, they were helpless to avoid impending disaster. As the powerful black horse charged past them, its rider reined in sharply, driving it into Comet's side.

Amid a sudden nightmare, Ellie heard only the cry of distress from her horse as Comet lost his footing. Seemingly in slow motion, they fell sideways into mid air. In that split second, Ellie somehow knew she must free her feet of the stirrups to be thrown, instead of being crushed beneath Comet's weight. *Help us, God!* That was her last thought before they were slammed against the embankment.

In horror, Henry could only watch as Ellie and Comet tumbled down the steep incline. On the first roll, Ellie was thrown free of the saddle, yet, the momentum carried her downward, toward the river.

Jumping off his horse and having no thought for his own safety, Henry headed after Ellie. Bushes and weeds hindered his descent, but soon he was at his sister's side. Sprawled out, Ellie was unmoving, nearby Comet lay, his sides heaving from his ordeal. In that moment, Henry felt hate for the one responsible for this senseless act of cruelty.

"Ellie, please wake up," he begged, feeling helpless as he saw blood on her face and hands. "Don't leave me, please." Finally, a moan was heard and then Ellie opened her eyes, but only for a moment.

Pulling his handkerchief from his back pocket, Henry raced to the river where he quickly dunked it in the cold water. Seconds later, he was putting it on Ellie's forehead. "God, let her be okay. She *has* to okay!" he pleaded, seeing Ellie's eyes flutter open.

"I'm okay, Henry. Help me sit up," Ellie whispered. Gently, he did as she asked. Then, she noticed Comet. "Oh, no! Not this!" she wailed, as Henry helped her to the horse's side. "It's okay, boy. It's okay," Ellie said, trying to sooth the animal while checking for injuries. "Help me look, Henry. Do you see a broken leg?"

Just then, a noise was heard. Looking around, they saw no one. Then, an insidious laugh was heard from the path above. There was the same rider, this time standing beside his horse.

In that moment, Henry's furor erupted. Reaching for the rifle in Comet's saddle, he pulled it out and quickly cocked it. Raising it to his shoulder he aimed and fired. A cry of pain was heard as the rider grabbed his thigh and fell to the ground.

Throwing down the rifle, Henry raced up the embankment, his anger spurring him on toward the evil he hated; the evil that nearly robbed him of his sister whom he loved so dearly.

His lungs burned from exertion by the time he reached the path, but still his anger raged inside him. At his feet the rider lay, curled in a ball and whimpering in pain. "How does it feel?" Henry seethed, ripping the hat from his head. When doing so, a mane of blond hair fell from its confines.

———————

Below, Ellie knelt beside Comet as she softly comforted the horse she loved so much. Tears streamed from her eyes fearing the inevitable. In the grass the rifle lay. "Oh…I just can't do it!" Ellie wailed, realizing she'd never be able to shoot her beloved horse.

"Ellie, guess what? It's a woman, a dirty rotten one," Henry called out.

Suddenly, she knew. "I'm coming up," Ellie

called back. "It's okay, boy. I'll be back," she told Comet who now looked at her.

Although feeling distraught over her horse, Ellie started up the incline. Slow and steady, she crawled over bushes and through the weeds, all the while knowing she'd find Belle Johnson under Henry's control.

When she'd finally reached the top, Ellie felt light headed, and weak. Yet, she found strength to speak. "You're a sick woman, Belle. Sick and mean-spirited and for no reason," Ellie told her. "You've had it made your whole sorry life, and yet, you stoop to this? Trying to kill me because I'm married to Chad? Why?"

Not expecting an answer, Ellie was surprised when she received one. "You don't understand!" Belle blurted defiantly. "I loved Chad and I did more for him than you'd *ever* do."

"You don't know how to love," Ellie replied, taking hold of Henry's arm until the dizzy spell passed. "Love is giving, caring and sharing."

"I gave *everything* for Chad. I *killed* for him!" she shouted, shaking her fist at Ellie.

In that moment, Ellie could only stare down at the woman who once had everything life could offer. Yet, it had crumbled in ruin, leaving her lost and alone. Although wanting to say more to Belle, Ellie was too tired. "I need to lie down while you ride for help," she told Henry.

Just then, she heard a whiny from down the hill. Looking, Ellie could only stare when seeing Comet on his feet. "Thank you, Lord," she whispered as her eyes welled with tears of joy. Taking Henry's arm, Ellie headed for a grassy knoll. As she looked toward home, she noticed a rider coming.

"That looks like Chad," Henry told her. "I thought he was hunting."

Sure enough, Chad arrived a minute later and pulled his horse to an abrupt halt. "Max came home without a rider so we knew something had happened," he quickly explained, kneeling beside Ellie. Then he noticed Belle on the ground. "Tell me what happened here," he told Henry, wrapping his arms around Ellie.

When Chad had heard the whole story, he cradled Ellie even closer. "Oh, my darling, I'm so sorry," he whispered. "It seems my past nearly cost you your life."

With Belle's confession, the case of her father's murder was finally closed. She would be gone for a very long time.

For Ellie and Comet, everyone was overjoyed to learn the bushes and weeds had cushioned their fall, preventing any major injuries. Within yards in either direction, the jagged rocks would have meant certain death. A slight concussion for Ellie, and Comet apparently only had the wind knocked out of him, plus, receiving minor scrapes and bruises.

For everyone at Ryan's Roost, they were grateful that the hunters had bagged their bull elk the first day and were home when Max showed up.

For Henry, he knew he'd witnessed his second

miracle…the first was when he found his sister. The second was when her life had been spared on a hillside, overgrown with brush.

CHAPTER TWENTY-EIGHT

As summer ended, everyone looked forward to winter and the coming holidays. For Ellie and Henry, they rarely mentioned their years of abuse or the incident with Belle Johnson. Instead, they reveled in their overwhelming joy of finding each other.

Due to Lucy's ongoing relationship with the girls from Covenant House, it was decided a Christmas reunion would be fun, so plans proceeded to make it an event to remember. Marie was in her glory as she cooked and baked a full week in advance. Rose made Christmas stockings for everyone. They would appear Christmas morning, filled with an array of gifts from Matt and Lucy.

On December twenty-third, six former residents of Covenant House arrived to begin their four day visit. For the eight boys now living at Ryan's Roost, their excitement of going home to see their families suddenly lost its appeal when seeing the lovely young women.

"Sure glad *I'm* not leaving," Henry whispered as his eyes lingered on one pretty dark-haired girl.

"That's sweet Amy," Ellie whispered back. "I'll introduce you." Soon, the house was filled with merriment as the girls were greeted with open arms of welcome. True to her word, Ellie took special care to introduce her brother to Amy. From her smile, it was easy to see the now sixteen-year-old girl was thrilled to be singled out to meet such a handsome young man as Henry.

During those four days, fun and festivities reigned. There were sleigh rides, sledding and ice skating. At night, everyone gathered around a bonfire. Here is where feelings were shared and hearts were opened.

"Seeing all of you again has made this one of the best Christmas' ever," Lucy began as her eyes drifted across the faces around the fire. "Each one of you came into our lives hurting and scared. You came to us believing what we said and you worked hard to improve your lives. By God's mercy and love, you're no longer in that pit of hopelessness. You're productive young women, improving your education and working to support yourself. We're all so *very* proud of you and *thrilled* that you've come to join us."

"Bravo...bravo," Matt cheered, clapping his hand as others joined in.

"If I may, I'd like to say something, too," Alexandra spoke up a moment later. "When we came to Covenant House, some of us were very young. Our hearts were broken and we were crying out for some stability in our lives. We needed *and* wanted some rules to live by and you gave us those, Lucy. We tried your patience, I know, but when you enforced those boundaries, it made us feel loved and protected. We knew you wanted the best for us and I for one feel totally blessed to have lived at Covenant House," she concluded, as loud cheers erupted.

"Me too," Amy said then, standing to her feet. "Because of you, Lucy, one day I want to help girls find hope. In Los Angeles where I live, I see so many young women, daughters who are crying out for love and direction, just as we were. And, I want to be someone who'll point them to the truth. And, *thank you* for inviting us here to this beautiful place and for all you've done for us."

With that, everyone stood to their feet and seconds later, began singing. "Lucy's a jolly good woman...Lucy's a jolly good woman...Lucy's a jolly good woman...for she wiped every tear from our eyes." By the time the song had ended, Lucy's own tears were evident.

The fire was nearly out by the time everyone reluctantly said goodnight. Because of their early morning departure, the girls hugged Ellie and Chad goodbye.

Henry and Amy exchanged addresses and telephone numbers. It was apparent the two had formed an endearing friendship. Would it grow into something long lasting? For Ellie, she wanted nothing more for her brother than to find the kind of happiness she had found with Chad.

As they headed for their cottage, Ellie couldn't wait to tell Chad her good news. A visit to the doctor today confirmed her suspicions: a baby was on the way. *July fourth ... what a birthday that'll be!* Ellie thought smiling...

To contact the author please e-mail her at:
writedc1@juno.com